Village Secrets

William Wood

Circaidy Gregory Press

Copyright information

ISBN 978-1-910841-60-0

Printed in the UK
April 2024

Author contact
williamsvillagesecrets@gmail.com

Published by

Circaidy Gregory Press

In loving memory of Anna
who missed all this

Editor's Introduction

I first came across author William Wood's work when reading the shortlist for an Earlyworks Press writing competition, way back at the start of the current century. I was to come across him in the same context quite a few times. His stories invariably had the finely worked, rich nature that gets competition stories shortlisted and I was delighted, a few years later to have the task of producing his first collection, entitled *Stories for Sale*, which also happens to be the title of one of my favourites in that collection.

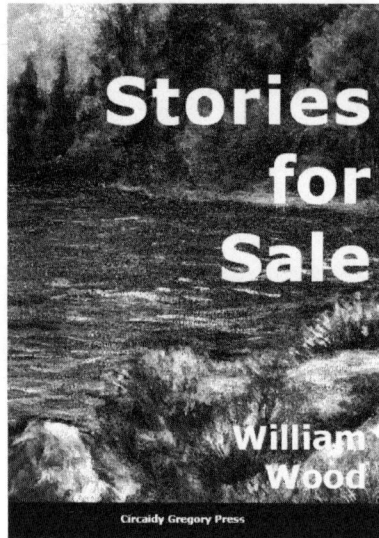

From when I first knew William, his stories and reportage have been enriched by his extensive travels during his working life but in latter years, William has settled into village life in Cumbria and as a result, this collection brings us a wonderfully evocative (and at times, wickedly tongue-in-cheek) portrayal of a life that is becoming a rarity as the world changes around us – not, William would suggest, for the better. If you love English village life, if you love Cumbria, or if you just love a well-crafted story, I think you'll enjoy *Village Secrets*.

-- KG spring 2024

Author's Preface

All the stories in this collection have been written either during or since the Covid pandemic, lockdown and subsequent liberation. I have composed them all in my house and garden in the prettiest village in England. The precise location of that village in the Eden Valley is one secret I shall not reveal, but what I hasten to make clear is that the village in the following stories is entirely fictional.

The houses, the farms and the geography are products of my imagination. This goes for the characters, too, who are also fictional. Any reader who strays into my real village will not find them here. The only common feature is my ocularium, a raised patio which, in my fictional village I have placed in a corner of David's garden, overlooking the river and the village green. When the weather is fine one can sit there and observe the heron fishing, the sheep crossing the footbridge, children playing in the water and the people walking their dogs. Strictly speaking an ocularium is the part of a daddy longlegs' body that houses its several eyes. Its lookout, if you will.

One of the writer's pleasures is to swap ideas with a trusted editor. I worked with Kay Green on several projects when I lived in East Sussex. It has been fun renewing our collaboration from Cumbria. Levelling up and down, you might say.

– WW spring, 2024

Contents

Village Secrets

A woman, not even wanted by her own MPs in parliament, let alone by the public, had been selected by aged party members to be the next prime minister. She had been to Balmoral to get the blessing of her monarch who was too ill to receive her in London. For some reason best known to itself the BBC covered her whole journey from Northolt Airport to Downing Street. They did so from the air while presenters felt that they had to keep up a running commentary of the mundane drive through London traffic.

A few days later the Queen died and there was nothing on the BBC but a rehash of her life and times that had already been narrated ad nauseam during the recent summer's jubilee. The country was in grief, at least that part of it where common people wanted to express their sorrow in front of microphones and TV cameras.

In Cumbria, far away from this concocted hysteria David sat on his ocularium, a raised patio in the corner of the garden that looked out over the village green. It was a warm September's day, the village was drenched and refreshed after welcome overnight rain. Everything sparkled, the river water tinkled over the stones, a heron stood on the footbridge and a dragonfly landed on David's knee.

He understood that people might be sad at the loss of a figure who had been there all their lives and most of his. He remembered her coming to the throne when he was ten years old himself, had shaken her hand once or twice at various ceremonies during his working life, but he was baffled that people could weep tears over someone they did not know, a remote figurehead at most. He conjectured that they were crying for themselves. Perhaps that's what such grief was. Loss and self pity. He smiled at something that he had heard the new King say when he had turned on the TV in the hope of getting news about some other events in the world. "Flights of angels" that would be conveying his "darling mama to rejoin his darling papa", or words to that effect.

David looked up. No angels in the blue sky here but the swallows were gathering on the power lines in preparation for their migration.

"Don't blame you," he said out loud. His voice startled the heron in the beck and it took off on slow beating wings.

Over the following days, other than deliberately avoiding the news that was devoting itself entirely to the death of the Queen he thought no more about what was going on in a grieving nation invented by the media. His own world remained unchanged, or so he thought. He was yet to uncover the 'secret' as he was briefly to think of the revelation on his doorstep.

True, when arranging to go into Penrith, his nearest large town, to collect a painting he was having framed, the picture framer had told him to come any day except Wednesday.

"Oh, do you close on Wednesday?"

"No, I am going down to London for the day. To the funeral," he explained and David was once more reminded of the national grief that was spreading like a virus. He could think of many good reasons to go to London for a day or two. To spend six hours on a crowded train to stand blindly blanketed amidst thousands of mourners was not one of them.

"Good luck with that," he said. "I'll drop in on the Tuesday, then."

The weather continued fine and David's routine was unchanged. His garden provided him with fruit and vegetables, the grass was still growing strongly and needed mowing once a week; it was time to pick apples. As every autumn, he was surprised at the number of people in and around the village who let their apples and plums ripen, rot and drop while in the shops other people paid a good price for imported fruit. At least the birds benefited in the winter from this neglect. They devoured the windfalls in the coldest months.

In the evenings David set out a teaspoonful of meat on a saucer for the hedgehog. The animal appeared soon after dark which at the moment was eight-ish, and ate the treat before patrolling the garden for slugs. This evening before bed however, when David went out to retrieve the saucer he found two slugs licking it clean, as were a pair of daddy longlegs. "Living dangerously," he smiled.

Most days David went for a walk. One of his favourites was past the old watermill that had been converted into a holiday home, along a wooded bridleway down to what had once been a quarry and was now almost a nature reserve in its own right. Tawny owls lived there, and sometimes deer gathered. The bridleway led him alongside the grounds of Quarry Manor, a large pink stone building that had stood empty for as long as David could remember. The stones were faded and the house quite dilapidated, as far as anyone could tell from the public path. The garden it was set in had become almost a jungle and too impenetrable for even the curious to explore. The footpath continued past this extensive and neglected property and rose up into the fells, but there was still a track that once was the driveway down to the house.

David was returning this way back from the fells a little later than usual. Dusk was falling and through the trees he could see the outline of the house where to his surprise a light was shining over what must have been the front porch. There was no other sign of life, no vehicle, no sound, just the porch light. He had not noticed a light before and he wondered if someone had moved in. He resolved to return the next day and make himself known to the new occupant, if there really was anyone there. For now he was set on getting home after his walk and preparing supper for himself.

Just then he heard children's voices. Probably kids from the village though he could not think who would be out this late. In his day children would already be having supper before being put to bed. When three tousled and blonde-haired children almost ran into him from the direction of Quarry Manor he was more perplexed than ever.

"Steady on. You nearly knocked me down."

"No we didn't," said the older child. "We are not here. You haven't seen us."

The child was a girl, he thought, though like the others she was dressed in ill-fitting clothes that might have been hastily snatched from a charity shop. All three wore shabby jeans and trainers. The girl had a long-sleeved T-shirt. One of the boys, as David imagined they were, wore a stained grey T-shirt, the other just a floppy cotton sweater that fell nearly to his knees. What really distinguished them however, even in the fading light was their identical shocks of blonde hair that seemed to have a life of its own, floating round their faces, unruly strands waving on the breeze. To David's eye the trio looked like trolls emerging from the undergrowth for a night out. For a child of about eight years old, the girl's words had also held surprising menace to which David replied, "But I have seen you. I can see you now," he said firmly. "Where are you off to at this time of the evening?"

"We are going on an adventure," volunteered the youngest.

"Where to? Where will you sleep?"

"Under the stars."

The second boy piped up, "We will probably find a baby."

This sounded sinister. "You think so?" probed David.

3

"Yes, Daddy is always having adventures and sometimes one of the mummies comes back with another brother or sister for us."

"Do you want to find a baby, then?"

"No way!" said the girl. "They are a pain. Augustus and Pinocchio are bad enough." She indicated the small boys.

"We are not babies," they protested. "Anyway the adventure was your idea." The children all started squabbling and it was clear to David that they did not really know what they wanted to do.

"Look," he said, "let me take you home. You are living in Quarry Manor, I take it?"

"We do for the moment," admitted the girl.

"Your Mummy must be worrying about you."

"We've got different mummies," said the little one.

"Same Daddy, though," affirmed the other boy. "We know. We have all got his hair."

"Is he home?"

"Oh no," said the girl, shocked. Daddy is a secret. So are we. Actually we are running away because they want to give us a haircut tomorrow. Make us even more secret, you see." She took David's hand and explained, "that's why I said you haven't seen us."

David was becoming intrigued. He persuaded the children to follow him back down the drive towards the house. More of a grassy path now, it was long and very overgrown. No vehicle could have approached from this side.

"So," said David, "just now your Daddy is not at home."

"No. He comes when he can get away."

"Sometimes," said the bigger boy in a spooky voice. "He's not really interested in us. Sometimes he just comes to see the mummies. He goes into their rooms in the dead of night, one after the other. Like Count Dracula."

"Last time he came in a helicopter and took us all for a ride though. He had other children with him, all our brothers and sisters."

"And a new mummy, too."

"Goodness," said David. "And who looks after you all?"

"Well, when he can borrow enough money, we have governesses."

"He has donors, you see," explained one of the boys.

His sister ignored the remark. "The governesses are always very pretty but not very bright," she opined, "but they worship Daddy. That's what my Mummy thinks, anyway."

"Otherwise our mummies do everything," said the small boy. "They all have their jobs. My Mummy teaches us, Augustus's Mummy does a lot of cooking, other mummies come and go."

"My Mummy is a dancer," said the girl.

"So you are not going to school in the village, then?"

"No, Daddy says they are all oiks. Besides, we are not here. We are his secrets."

"But," said the younger boy, "when we are bigger we are going to a school called Eton. He says there are enough of us boys alone to make up our own class."

"What about the girls?" David asked oldest child.

"By then I expect boys and girls will all go there. I don't care much. I don't need schools anyway." she replied.

David paused. "Let me get this straight. For the moment you are secret children. You are not here."

"Exactly.

"There are dozens of us. One day Daddy says, we will rule the world," boasted the middle one.

"Shsh," said his sister. Daddy is a secret, too. At least he is a secret here."

"Everyone would recognize him, you see. He once ruled the world."

"No, silly. He was Prime Minister of this country," corrected the girl.

"Then," giggled the youngest boy, "he got sacked for telling fibs. He says telling fibs is good, especially if you want to be King of the World. He is cross they sacked him."

"Are you all fibbing to me, then?" asked David.

Surely these children were too young for political satire. By now they were close to the house. The only light was still that over the porch. There were no signs within of concern for any children that might have wandered off, gone missing.

"We have nothing to fib about to you," the girl told him and, releasing her hand, said, "thank you for bringing us back." She seemed relieved that her short-lived adventure had come to an end. "Goodbye," she said.

"Goodbye. My name is David by the way. Uncle David Let me see you to the door."

"Better not," she said. "There might be trouble." The girl hesitated a moment looking troubled before deciding to tell David, "I am Pandora." In the darkness David discerned a slight smile, her first, before she before scurried off.

5

David questioned her no further but he did wait to watch them approach the gloomy mansion. Pandora, Augustus and Pinocchio. The trio did not go to the front door as he had expected, but pushed a way through the flower beds overgrown with shrubs and climbed in through a sash window, helping one another over the sill. No doubt this is how they had escaped and their absence had not been noticed yet. It was getting dark. Perhaps, David thought, the rear wing of the house had been renovated and was now habitable. That portion of the building was out of sight of passers-by and he had never felt curious or brave enough to struggle through the jungle to look for himself. He had noticed once, looking back from further along the bridle path, that there was a lake beside which an area of land the size of two tennis courts had been cleared and mown. It was difficult to make out from a distance, screened as the whole domain was by ancient trees. If the children had been telling him the truth, this would make a safe landing place for a helicopter, thought David.

With the children safely inside, David, still standing in the overgrown driveway, felt nervous. To all intents and purposes the building seemed quite abandoned, ruined in places. There was no sign of life this side at least. Not so much as a dog. He was relieved to regain the legitimate, public path. Emerging into the village he followed the river back to his house. As he did so he thought he heard the sound of a helicopter in the sky towards Quarry Manor.

Next morning was warm and sunny. The previous evening's walk and his encounter with the untidy children now seemed to David like a dream. He took his morning coffee out to his ocularium with its view over the village green. All was peaceful but after the first sip of coffee he felt a presence behind him. He turned to see two men in light, summer suits, white shirts and matching ties.

"Oh no, not Mormons," was his first reaction but they lacked those missionaries' inane, happy smiles and both wore very dark glasses.

"Is your name David?" demanded one of the men. Despite his dapper appearance he had the aggressive manner of a bouncer.

David stood up to face the men. "That's my secret," he replied, attempting a joke.

"It's not *your* secret that bothers us," said the man.

"It seems everyone has their secrets these days. Why don't you tell me yours and what you are doing in my garden. Sorry, that sounds rude of me. Would you like a coffee? Take a seat while I refill the pot."

"No thank you, sir," said the second man in a surprisingly cultured voice. David could not remember the last time anyone had called him sir.

"We hear a lot of stories. We just wanted to make sure that *you* were real."

"How do you do that?"

In reply the first man grasped David's arm. He felt a sharp pain and collapsed back onto the wooden garden seat. The men disappeared.

Between David's garden wall and the river a footpath followed the bank. He would often chat to passers-by so it was natural that Denis, one of his neighbours out walking his dog, should call out over the wall, "Hello, David. You all right?"

David did not reply. At first Denis smiled, thinking his friend had dozed off. But he was a first responder and he felt that there was something odd about the way David was lying. He called out again and still got no response. Calling his dog to heel he entered the garden by the riverside gate and crossed the lawn to the ocularium. To his relief David was beginning to stir.

"Do you feel all right?" David heard Denis asking.

"Yes, I must have dozed off. I feel very tired; a bit weak. Damn it, the coffee has gone stone cold."

"Stay there. I'll make you another."

When he returned David was fine but could not explain what had happened.

"I wonder whether you have had a TIA," said his medical friend.

"TIA?"

Transient Ischemic Attack. It's a kind of mini stroke. You will probably be fine again, but as a precaution I think you should see your doctor."

"You are scaring me, Denis."

"Oh, it's nothing to worry about. Glad I was passing. It's nice up here on your ocularium. Your watch tower. Seen anything of interest lately?"

"Not that I remember. Oh, a kingfisher flew upstream the other morning."

David did recover fully. He went to his GP the next morning, who found everything normal.

"You don't remember what happened?"

"No. Nothing. I just dozed off over my elevenses."

"Well, we are all getting on a bit."

Neither the doctor nor David noticed the gap in David's recall. Everything was indeed back to normal. The Queen had been buried and the government was once again looking for another Prime Minister.

The Woman in the Bed

Marcus stepped into the spare room looking for another pillow and found a body in the bed. A dead body.

Ten minutes later, deep in reverie he was pulling on his walking boots and anorak. He was more puzzled than shocked. What more could happen this year? It was only March and no sign yet of sunshine or spring. There had been three consecutive weekends of storms and flooding; there had been power cuts, interruption to his mains water supply and loss of communications.

Like so many others he had got used to coping with each emergency and carrying on. Living alone in a small village he found most people were friendly and supportive. They all kept an eye out for one another. If Marcus did not know everyone by name he knew their faces.

The woman in the bed was not one of them. At first he did not realise she was dead, nor indeed that the figure beneath the embroidered duvet was that of a woman. The human form on one side of the double bed was entirely covered up. He assumed that whoever it may be was asleep until something in the stillness and the silence seemed wrong.

On top of the bad weather had come the coronavirus and as one of the older residents Marcus was supposed to be in self-isolation as they called it. Nevertheless he made the occasional sortie for food shopping. Who was he supposed to inform about an intruder in his spare bedroom?

"Hello," he had called.

There was no response. He approached the bed and pulled back the cover to reveal the figure of a woman lying on her side, her face turned away from him. All he saw at first was short, grey hair, an ear with a diamond stud and a right arm bare from the elbow. She was wearing a white, short sleeved cotton nightdress buttoned at the neck.

As Marcus strode along beside the river that ran through the village he wondered again how the woman had got in. He was too old for girl friends and since the death of his wife two years previously had entertained few guests. Certainly no one else had a key.

More to the point: who was this woman? He went over his actions of less than half an hour ago in his mind: his reaching out to shake the shoulder gently in order to wake her up; his surprise at how cold and inert it was. Lifeless. He had recoiled. Although he had been present at the deaths of his wife and of his father he had never touched a cold body before. However he had done enough to unbalance this body so that it rolled back on to the pillow offering him full view of the face.

She was a middle-aged woman, unmade up and seemingly at peace. It was no one he knew. She wore a gold wedding band on the fourth finger and a diamond ring that had presumably been for her engagement. Otherwise she was unadorned, her finger nails carefully filed and clean but unpainted. She showed no signs of illness or struggle.

Marcus had always found walking to be a good way of dealing with any problems. Letting the mind coast would release ideas and sometimes solutions would float up.

No sign of violence, then. No sign either of her clothes. She might of course have got undressed in the en suite bathroom and left them there. He had not checked. When had she got into the bed? Marcus had been in his room all night and indoors all the previous day. There had been no caller.

It was good to get out now despite the unrelenting rain. He followed the river noting the tide line of straw, branches and detritus where it had flooded. Sheep grazed on the village green and lambs that had never seen the sun skipped happily about in the wet. He passed a woman walking her dogs.

"Can't isolate the dogs, can we Marcus?" she apologised.

"Certainly not Cynthia," he replied pushing the nose of an overfed Labrador away from his crotch.

Marcus had no pets. In better times he and his wife had liked to travel, to leave home from time to time. They had not wanted to be tied down. Untied now, he was still finding his feet again as a widower.

The woman in his spare bed had been married. Was her husband still alive? Did he know where she had gone? As Marcus climbed up and out of the village he began to construct a picture of her life, hardly noticing the terrain he marched over. Usually it was dry and rocky but after these three months of rain, though still rocky there were rivulets running down the fell and puddling areas of bog and mud. Had she been a walker, too? He had not looked at her legs or feet. Not that they would necessarily have told him anything. He would have to search for the clothes on his return. They would provide further clues.

Normally in mid-March he would have taken a rucksack with provisions: bread and cheese, some dried fruit and nuts and certainly a flask of coffee. But the uninviting weather persisted and this walk was

9

unplanned, spontaneous. He was empty handed and his mind was elsewhere.

Indeed for some time he had been elsewhere. Normally active, he had found the succession of storms had discouraged him from outdoor exertions. Not one for the artificiality of gyms he had become housebound, reading, day dreaming and dozing much of the time.

This present hike, though unplanned, was doing him good. It was shaking off the lethargy. He had been feeling under the weather in all senses for the last few days. He strode on, squelched on in places, and his thoughts returned to the woman. A decade or so younger than himself, he reckoned from the little he had glimpsed of her. She probably had grown up children. It was difficult to guess her character from a dead face but judging from the old-fashioned nightdress and the no nonsense haircut he decided she had been modest, intelligent and determined. How else could she have broken into his house and serenely gone to bed in his spare room.

He recalled a similar incident from many years ago when he had been a field director for volunteer teachers in India. He was expecting the arrival of a new young recruit. He had given her his address, inviting her to stay until she had arranged her own accommodation. He had informed her that he might be out until late but that his bearer, Moses, would show her to her room. She was to make herself at home.

When he got back she was not yet there. He waited a while and began on his supper at last. As he tucked in his Indian neighbour phoned to say that he had found Marcus' Goldilocks asleep in his bed.

"Silly girl!" remarked Marcus. "I am so sorry Krish. I told her number 17."

"Marcus, we are all number 17 in this road. Administrative error."

There was one big difference. That story had ended happily while furnishing an anecdote for dinner party talk. The girl had not died. That there was presently a dead woman lying in bed in Marcus's spare room was hardly an error, administrative or otherwise.

Marcus had now climbed higher on to the limestone scar above his village. It was further than he had intended to go, and he decided to return in a long, gradual loop back down to the village. He was feeling tired, but it would be a downhill trek most of the way.

He had not got far into solving his dilemma. He supposed he would have to do what he should have done straight away. Phone the police. But what would they make of the situation? What would they think of him?

By the time he reached home he was unusually fatigued. All he wanted to do was to lie down. He removed his wet boots and top clothes and went up to his bedroom without even peeping in at the spare room. He just wanted to sleep.

He woke briefly many hours later and wondered where he was. He was lying in the dark in damp clothes. He thought at first that he must have fallen down on the fells, but he soon recognised his bedroom. Relieved, he stumbled into the bathroom for a wash. He felt very shivery and instead of putting on fresh clothes he changed into his pyjamas and dressing gown and climbed back into bed, pulling the bedclothes properly over him this time.

He slept the rest of the night, some of it in a sweat soaked delirium. Next morning he felt weak but a little better. He took comfort in a long, hot shower and went down for breakfast. He still avoided the spare room. In the back of his mind he hoped the woman had gone.

As his thoughts cleared over a bowl of cereal and a mug of coffee he grew incredulous at his own behaviour the previous day. Of course he should have dialled 999. What if the woman had not been quite dead? Either way, the police still needed to know. Now he had a lot of explaining to do, not least his delay in reporting the strange affair.

When he took his mug and bowl to the sink he realised just how weak he was. Nevertheless there was no time like the present. He would take another look in the spare room just to check he had not imagined the whole incident. He hoped, half expected to find the bed empty.

Climbing the stairs made him breathless. He had to pause a little way up, dismayed at how unfit he had become. After a brief pause he went on. He paused again on the landing to catch his breath before entering the room.

When he felt strong enough he opened the spare room door. The woman was still there. To his astonishment she was sitting up in bed facing him. She smiled.

"Don't you recognize me, Marcus?"

He stared. "My darling, I ..." he began, but was too short of breath to say more.

Twitch

No harm was meant by it. Not at first. In those early weeks of the coronavirus lockdown some of the villagers, no longer able to visit one another or to congregate in the pub or village hall set up a WhatsApp group. They called it Isolation Birders.

The brain child of Frank Green, a naturalist as often seen on the television as in the village, popular and active on both fronts, the group was initially aimed at those who had an active interest in the abundant bird life in their Cumbrian surroundings. Daphne Mundy, a retired but still feisty head teacher, seconded the group. Despite her fondness for clay pigeon shooting and the ancient twelve bore shot gun she kept above her fireplace, she was a passionate and well-informed nature lover. Soon the group was joined by others keen to learn more and to escape the monotony of isolation. It was an initiative to bring people together, if not in person, at least in spirit. In the long term, however, it did more than this.

Remember, people were allowed out for exercise once a day, provided they kept their distance from anyone else. In the countryside the regulations were not policed as severely as in the towns and cities. Nevertheless if some people exceeded the one hour, most walks and cycle rides were solitary. Typical of early observations on WhatsApp were:

"Saw a gold crest and nuthatch in the churchyard."

"The nuthatches live in the nest box above the litter bin at the end of Water Lane."

"Several bullfinches in the village. Probably waiting to strip the buds."

"Think I saw a red kite on Mornington Fell. Such a distinctive silhouette."

From the birders' point of view it was fortunate that this activity began in April. The arrival of sand martins along the river by Parlour Bridge, the house martins that nested beneath the eaves of certain houses in the village and the swallows that swooped along the length of the river that ran through the village, all these were spotted and noted. The only non-arrival was the cuckoo.

Apart from Frank, who could not resist adding extra information, two or three serious birders came to the fore recording birds such as ring ouzels or wheatears that many of the villagers would not have recognized even if they had hiked up into the surrounding fells.

Daphne posted the following: "I saw a stock dove in the recreation field this morning. Smaller than a wood pigeon and with no white on neck or wings. More like a feral pigeon but with more blue-grey and a glossy green neck patch. I have never seen more than a pair in the village before."

Garth, a keen bird watcher and cyclist clearly roamed far and wide.

"If you are going beyond King's Mill there is a pond to the right of the junction where you will see shellduck and redshank."

The next day he reported from the opposite end of the village high up of Wolf Fell, "saw a meadow pipit near the Robert Bruce Oak."

No one minded too much that the enthusiasts went beyond the confines of the parish. The police were not going to check anyone's movements or how long they were out. Many appreciated further lessons from Frank. "Saw a dunnock on Hopper Hill. Known as a hedge sparrow to some, but really it's an accentor, not a sparrow at all."

In fact it was possible to trace the habits of others in the village from their postings.

"A flock of golden plovers on Wolf Fell, near the waterfalls," to which the expert commented, "great. We have been looking out for them. They arrive in flocks on their way to the coast in Spring. Glorious when they fly together in good light."

"Agreed," came Garth's reply, not wishing to be outshone.

And so it proceeded, experts and novices alike in wonder at the diversity of the local bird life. A green woodpecker was heard yaffling in Dripping Woods; a greater spotted woodpecker visited several bird feeders in the village. Every nest in every garden or wayside of blue tits, coal tits, blackbirds, nuthatches, wrens, robins and others were recorded. Those roaming further afield and higher up saw pipits and skylarks. In the lower fields lapwings and curlews did not escape notice. Willow warblers and wagtails and the odd kingfisher were noted in the river but oddly, no one mentioned the herons, probably because they were such a fixture that they were taken for granted. Indeed one house near the weir was called Heron View, and that had been there hundreds of years. Similarly pheasants, bred for killing and common as chickens, were ignored.

It all proceeded along these lines and when the lockdown was extended for another month more people joined the group. It was then that things started to go wrong.

No one minded novices such as Moira, a young single mother relating the comings and goings of her garden birds. Someone tried to warn her against putting peanuts in her bird feeder during the nesting season, but others said the danger of aflatoxin poisoning had been exaggerated. Besides, Moira was popular. Before this isolation she had always joined in all village activities bringing her smiley face and winsome figure to whatever event it was.

By the time the lockdown had proceeded to its second month, the Isolation Birders group had more than doubled. Now not everyone knew everyone else. Members still came only from the two villages that made up the parish and everyone knew of Frank Green from his television presentations or knew him personally from local contact. The following post of his caused quite a stir, "I have spotted a very rare bird. Before I reveal its location I would ask all of you to keep it to yourselves. Should the media hear of it, especially the social media, we will be besieged by birders with their tripods and cameras. Not even the coronavirus pandemic will keep them away. So I am trusting you for now to keep this to ourselves."

Frank should have known better. His post had the opposite effect to that intended. It aroused too much excitement despite many messages of support, anticipation and promises of secrecy. He alleviated the impatience a little by posting a few days later, "sorry to have kept you in suspense. I just wanted to be sure I was right. It is better than I hoped. The bird is actually nesting. Forgive me if I still do not disclose where. It must not be disturbed."

Almost immediately the following messages appeared.

"OK, Frank, but what is it?"

"Stop teasing us Frank. What have you seen?"

"You ARE pulling our legs, aren't you?"

To which Frank explained, "it is called a Lesser blue rudder in this country. About the size of a jackdaw, it has unremarkable brown plumage but it has bright blue legs, especially noticeable in flight when it holds them out behind itself like a rudder. It is a rare visitor to this country. One was blown here in the great storm and did not survive. The last live sighting was by the great Victorian ornithologist, Elijah Witherby. The blue rudders usually bred in Scandinavia and were thought to be extinct, even there, by the turn of the century."

14

This news elicited a variety of replies from those beseeching Frank to reveal the exotic bird's whereabouts to those demanding proof of the sighting. Amongst the postings was this from Daphne, "Frank, as you know I admire your television work very much and I am glad we have set up this group, but I think a person of your authority should refrain from cheap hoaxes of this nature. We all know there is no such bird as the blue rudder, greater or lesser. Let's, please, get back to serious bird spotting."

Someone else added, "I have no idea whether Daphne or Frank is correct, but surely a photograph would settle the matter."

To which Frank replied, "I am loath to get too near while the birds are nesting. I should have added that they are a pair. Blue rudders mate for life and are inseparable." After this Frank failed to respond at all and many still thought it was an elaborate joke. Outside of the WhatsApp exchanges, some people telephoned one another or even talked about it across the road if they met during their release from lockdown.

Moira posted, "you were joking really, Frank, weren't you, about the rudderless duck or whatever?"

This prompted Roly, a simple-minded but harmless man whose presence was tolerated in the village and in the group to react, "yeah, I saw an ostrich one night when I was walking home from the pub."

Now the Tarnished Crown had been closed for a month at least but it did not stop some wag from replying, "sure it was not a pink elephant, Roly, or a flamingo?"

The more serious contributors were concerned that their Isolation Birders group was losing its way and its purpose, degenerating into something akin to the awful Facebook. However, when Frank had still failed to respond himself, nor even to post any further observations, the following bombshell appeared from Garth whom everyone knew to be a serious and informed bird watcher.

"I can corroborate Frank's story. I have not seen the lesser blue rudder with my own eyes but I have heard it. Its call is unmistakeable, unique in the ornithological world: it emits sounds like muffled gunshots, usually at dawn."

When asked what he was doing at dawn Garth said he had slept out in Forge Woods so as to hear the full dawn chorus. He hastened to disabuse those who assumed that the lesser blue rudder was nesting in those woods.

"The blue rudder flew over above the tree canopy so I could not see it. I followed its call into the distance rather like one does with the cry of a cuckoo, another bird more often heard than seen."

Still Frank was silent. Since his first revelation no one had seen him about the village. He often did disappear to go to a TV studio and even in these days of lockdown when many media personalities were broadcasting from their rooms guests did sometimes appear in studios.

In the village reports reverted to normal. The mallards on the river produced ducklings and their every move was noted. One brood of nine was quickly reduced to five by the herons' appetite for small animals. A barn owl was seen circling in broad daylight and the roosts of the more familiar tawny owls discovered.

Around this time however, a curious, nay scandalous posting appeared.

"I was trying out my binoculars when I spotted a white flash. At first I thought it was a swan. But no, it was a White-Arsed Philanderer. Keep your lecherous hands off her or else. You know who you are."

Some took this to be a bad joke, an attempt to lampoon Frank Green's report, true or false of the blue rudder. But why the threat? More intriguing, who was Jack Stalker who had posted it? For unlike much of the social media, WhatsApp cannot normally be anonymous. The name of the writer appears at the top of their posting. And the only way to join a group is by invitation. No one knew a Jack Stalker.

Another member of the group, Krishnaswamy, who worked in a telephone shop in Penrith but lived in the village, explained that if someone had a second phone, called a burner phone, they could join under a false name. Even so, he agreed, they would have to be invited. Someone inside the group must therefore know who Jack Stalker was – a wife, a partner. It might, come to that, be the same person, a current member accepting his own alter ego.

This explanation spread by word of mouth. Someone was bold enough to ask Krishnaswamy why he never reported any sightings.

"I follow yours," he said. "I am interested in human behaviour rather than the habits of birds, though I am finding it educational on both fronts."

"Well, you've got plenty of behaviour to follow now," said his sponsor.

Indeed, lockdown did not mean that mouths, ears and eyes were closed. Those in the group were on the lookout for anyone carrying new binoculars.

Most of the speculation was centred on who the offending couple might be. Was it a man or a woman's behind and was it a man or a woman beneath?

16

"We must get to the bottom of this," posted Roly, unaware of his own humour.

For a few days there was a more serious distraction. Old Roger Hornby, another founder member, died of covid-19. He had not contributed much to the group because at his age he did not get out much. He was known more generally in the village at large as a friendly old man knowledgeable about fishing. He had tried to weather the illness at home but died a few days after his admission into intensive care.

This death of a familiar character brought home the seriousness of the situation and several of the birders thought twice about going out so much, albeit into a landscape devoid of human beings.

"All the more reason to report our sightings," advised Garth, as unsentimental as ever. "We were set up to relieve our isolation. By the way, I saw a merlin early this morning when I went up the fell."

Many had forgotten his endorsement of the blue rudder sightings. Some thought at the time that he was humouring Frank, others that he was mocking a man he saw as a rival in some ways. Few now considered the blue rudder sightings anything more than a joke.

"Yes," agreed Moira, "we need distractions more than ever. I've got chaffinches and coal tits on my bird feeder as I write this. Not exciting, but at least they seem cheerful to me."

Gradually momentum built up again even though Giles, one of the younger farmers and too busy to join the group succumbed to a milder dose of the virus. It was an anxious time for his wife and children who knew they would all have to remain in quarantine for two weeks after his recovery.

It was not long before Jack Stalker put up another post.

"The white-arsed philanderer is at it again. Or barn owl are you now? Yes, you were in the hay. Keep away from one another. This is a final warning."

This prompted another admonishment from Daphne Mundy in her best school ma'am tone.

"I remind you all that this group was set up to educate and inform one another while most of us were confined to our homes, allowed out only for brief periods on essential business or for recreational purposes. We founders of the group intended it to be an enjoyable but serious activity. We did not expect it to degenerate in this tasteless way. I am not without a sense of humour, but a practical joke like this is going too far. I appeal to all of you only to report bona fide sightings or pictures of our wonderful local bird life."

While Daphne's plea was heeded there were some who took this last threat even more seriously. They wondered if the police ought to be informed.

Frank remained uncharacteristically silent. He neither defended his sightings of the blue rudder nor did he endorse Daphne's appeal. Then his wife informed the group that he had caught covind-19 and was in bed, hoping to pull through on his own. She was tending to him and of course would have to completely self-isolate as well.

With fewer of the more active bird watchers reporting their sightings and those who remained within the village becoming predictable, use of the WhatsApp group waned. When several people heard the sound of muffled gunshots late one evening not one of the group reported, not even in jest, that they had at last heard the blue rudder. The truth of the matter was discovered a few days later when the bodies were found. Giles, still weak from his illness had gone out to inspect some stone walling that was on the point of collapse. In the corner of his field, in a glade of rowan trees, he found the bodies of a man and a woman. They had been disfigured by crows and foxes but he recognized the man as Frank Green. He could not tell who the eyeless woman was but did not think she was local.

The press had a field day. Headlines such as, "Famous naturalist shot in flagrante," and "Double Murder in Eden" shocked the village.

Daphne's decision to call the police was caused by her realisation that she was going down with the symptoms of covid-19 herself. She was a straightforward woman, still vigorous in mind and body and known to be handy with a gun. Above all she was honest. She invited Detective Inspector Blood to her house, warning him to put on PPE before entering. She had vital information to impart. She did not seem to be an attention seeker and the detective came round wearing a face guard. He was nevertheless taken by surprise when she confessed to the double murder. He found it odd that such an apparent pillar of the community should have committed this atrocity, let alone admit to it. She was not boasting, either, just reporting the misdeed as though she had lost a dog or suffered a minor burglary. She did however seem flushed and a trifle breathless. His first thought was that perhaps after all she was excited by what she had done.

"Why did you shoot him?" he asked. "Surely there was no sexual motive. No jealousy I mean. He was a married man with a devoted wife, so I hear."

"Of course I was not jealous, Inspector. I knew of course that he had always been what before 'me too' was known as a lady's man. It was even indulged in those days." Her explanation was interrupted by a series of coughs. The detective instinctively stepped back, glad now he had donned his protective visor. Daphne continued, "as you may know, he occasionally went too far. He lost his slot on the weekly Country Tales programme on the BBC as a result."

"I think I recall some scandal now you mention it," said the inspector, wondering how ill this woman really was, or how mad.

"So you did not kill him," he humoured her, "on account of, what shall we call them, his peccadilloes?"

"No. I was as proud of Frank Green as if he had been my son. He had been a star pupil of mine. I like to think I kindled his love of nature, of the life sciences. I was happy to join him in the Isolation Birding group." Again she had a coughing fit, but controlled it and carried rapidly on as though her time were short. "I was disappointed when he invented that blue rudder sighting. It was not like him at all. He was a stickler for accuracy and truth. As am I." She seemed to be overcome by emotion but the inspector realised she was struggling for breath. "I did check. I have all the volumes of Witherby's bird books. There was no mention of a blue rudder in any of them. It was that mischievous tart that must have put him up to it. As you know, she was a girl who liked to have a bit of fun. In more ways than one. So I shot them both."

"All right, Miss Mundy, Take it easy. There is no hurry. Can you tell me why his wife covered up for you?"

Daphne looked uncomfortable, flushed perhaps with the urgency of her narrative. "Another of my pupils. A meek little thing. She put up with her husband's womanising for a quiet life and a nice home. I would take morning coffee with her and chat and we became close."

"So close she covered your murder? She did not report her husband missing. Was she complicit in the killing?"

"Not at all. She was terrified only that the blame would be pinned on her. She was the obvious suspect."

"Justifiably so."

"I am sorry, inspector. I know this is unorthodox, but could I trouble you to fetch me a glass of water. Have one yourself if you like. Glasses above the kitchen sink."

When he returned and handed her the glass of water she was almost reclining on the sofa and perspiring. She raised herself enough to take a few sips and continued, "no, inspector. She telephoned me a week or so before the blue rudder sightings. Said she thought Frank was seeing someone again. Despite the lockdown. This time she thought it was serious. She suspected he had gone back to the young researcher who had caused him to lose his place on the country programme. At the time she had accused him of harassment and more. It was hushed up but he had lost his job all the same. I cannot think what brought them together again after all this time. Perhaps he had originally promised to leave his wife for her and gone back on it, but that is speculation. I told Sarah, his wife, I would investigate."

"So the so-called white-arsed philanderer did exist?"

"Yes. It was her bottom. She was on top. I got a glimpse of his face beneath, eyes closed in lust."

"Why did you post it?"

Daphne was struggling. She did not seem to hear the question but after a few laboured breaths she continued, "Sarah's idea. A warning. Unfortunately it did not deter him. Neither did the second threat. The rest you know. There is no need to involve Sarah in this."

"I am afraid that even if she is not complicit in the crime itself she did withhold evidence from the police."

Daphne's breathing had got markedly worse. Detective Inspector Blood wondered whether it was wise to arrest her.

"Miss Mundy, I think you ought to go to bed. Rest a little. I do not expect you will try to escape, will you?"

By now Daphne was gasping for air. "I think, Inspector, my days are numbered. I suspected as much before I acted so rashly." She could say no more and the detective called an ambulance, remaining with her until it arrived. By then Daphne had dozed off.

It was late evening when they bore her out to the ambulance on a stretcher. She woke and muttered, "If only he had not invented that ridiculous bird."

"Don't try to speak, love," said one of the ambulance men. As they crossed the garden there was a sound of muffled gunshots. The ambulance man, one of the two bearers, ducked and almost tipped Daphne from the stretcher. At the same time two birds flew overhead. In the flashing lights of the ambulance it looked as though their outstretched legs were blue.

Knocked Down

Passing too close from behind, the Range Rover clipped the rear wheel of Bob's bicycle. He felt his helmet clunk on contact with metal before he was flung to the tarmac, his bike on top of him. He skidded along grazing his exposed right arm and shoulder and tearing his thigh.

He lay still in the quiet country lane for a few seconds. The Range Rover had pulled up on the verge just ahead. He sat up smarting in anger and in pain. Nothing broken but his shoulder was bleeding and his thigh was very sore.

He heard a voice.

"Are you all right?" A woman's bare legs stood in front of him. His neck was too stiff to look up at the rest of her.

"I think so," he muttered.

"We had better get you out of the road. Can you stand?"

"Give me a bloody chance!"

"Let me help." She put an arm beneath his clean, left arm and he saw the face of a conventionally pretty woman with shoulder length, straw blonde hair. Her blue eyes showed concern.

"Wait. First help me get this helmet off." He gingerly raised his head while she unclasped the chin strap.

"I should not be doing this," she said. "Social distancing."

"If you observed that," he remarked, "you would not be driving around the countryside killing cyclists. You should be in lockdown. Locked up, even."

She made no apology, simply laughed. "There's nothing much wrong with you. Now move over to the verge."

He allowed her to help him. She was careful to keep her summer frock clear of his injured side as she did so, but he sensed the warmth of her body as she eased him to his feet. He stood, moved his neck from left to right, tried his arms and legs.

"You're right," he said. "You have failed. I am alive." All the same he felt very weak. "I just need to sit down a minute." He lowered himself slowly to the grassy bank, squashing some cowslips. The woman wheeled the bike over.

"Bike's a bit bent."

"Shit!"

Why hadn't he heard her coming up behind him? He had not been pedalling, having just crested a steep hill up from a small village and was coasting down the long and gentle slope towards the River Eden. He had not been expecting traffic during this coronavirus enforced period of self-isolation. Even at the best of times in this part of Cumbria there was little traffic. Along these country lanes you were more likely to meet tractors and quad bikes than cars or vans. Nevertheless he had kept to the side of the road and he had not swerved around any pothole or other obstacle. He had simply been sailing slowly down the hill, the wind in his face. He may, though, have been a bit distracted, thinking over recent events.

The woman sat down beside him clasping her arms around her knees, her hem slipping down to reveal her sun-tanned thighs. She was looking at him closely.

"You need to get cleaned up."

"Yes." He took off his singlet and started to sponge and stem the blood with it. She noticed him wince, but continued, fascinated to watch this rugged man. He had strong hands and fingers, she noted. A man who made his living from manual work. She still held the cycle helmet she had removed to reveal an unshaven face, strong too in its way but rather too pale at the moment beneath his generous head of thick hair.

"What are you staring...?" He stopped in mid-sentence as their eyes met and some unacknowledged pulse passed between them. He looked quickly away. He did not want sympathy, empathy. He wanted an apology. Then he remembered something. Just a flash. "You were on your phone, weren't you?"

The woman's confident manner briefly deserted her. "What do you mean?"

Bob put his hand on her knee as if he could squeeze the truth out of it.

"You were on your phone. You did not see me. Did you?" He squeezed harder for a reaction, but the response he got was unexpected. She removed the arms still encircling her calves, put them behind her, leant back and slightly parting her legs challenged, "And if I was, what do you intend doing about it?"

For a moment he was tempted to respond to this provocation, accept her invitation, if such was intended, to run his hand up her thigh.

"What do you suggest? I am not threatening you, if that's what you think. Or blackmailing you."

"You don't have to."

The sun went behind a cloud and a shiver all of a sudden shook Bob's body. "I don't suppose you've got a coat in your car?"

She stood up and smoothed down her frock back and front.

"I've got a horse blanket. Look, I have wrecked your bike. Allow me to take you home."

"Your place or mine?"

"Whichever is nearer, judging by the state of you."

"Which is?"

Bob had cycled about fifteen miles from his village while the woman was on her way back to her house down by the river.

"I think we had better get you to mine first," she said. "You can have a shower and I dare say I can rustle up some suitable clothing. Then after a cup of tea I'll take you home. Unless you prefer otherwise."

"You seem to have got it all worked out," he said, wondering whether he might not be walking into a trap. But so what? "A cup of tea sounds grand."

Together they lifted his bicycle into the back of the Range Rover. He climbed into the front seat and she put a scratchy blanket around his shoulders. He felt too bruised and battered to fasten the seat belt.

"Don't worry. It's not far."

"Watch out for cyclists," he said. "And I'll try not to soil your seat."

After five minutes she turned down a stony track that led to a converted barn on the banks of the River Eden.

"We shouldn't be doing this," he said as she drew up on the gravel outside an imposing front door.

"Going into one another's homes during lockdown you mean?"

"That too."

During this period people were allowed out for essential purposes only, such as shopping or for one hour of exercise. Here in the countryside no one took any notice of how long you walked or cycled. Bob had been out all afternoon, partly to digest the news he had received from his absent wife. No one had been into his house and he had not visited anyone else since lockdown and as a carpenter this had rather inhibited his work. But in the circumstances he was not worried about entering this bossy woman's house. Already both of them had infringed the social distancing code. He remained suspicious of her motives, but persuaded himself that perhaps she was acting only out of guilt and self-preservation.

"Beautiful oak door," he remarked.

"Isn't it? Though I expect you could have done as well."

"How do you know?"

"Tell you later. Let's get you cleaned up first."

She led him to a large wet room with a shower and handed him a huge, fluffy towel. She also gave him a pair of loose, grey jogging pants and a pale blue linen shirt but told him not to put them on until she had rubbed some antiseptic into his grazes. Seeing his dubious expression she said she knew what she was doing. She had when younger trained to be a St John's Ambulance volunteer attending horse events, country fairs and even the odd concert. She asked if he needed any help with showering. He declined.

A little later, wearing only the towel around his waist, Bob did allow her to dab him down with Savlon and to apply a few plasters here and there.

"You know," he said, "we are not applying the two metre rule here either."

"Naughty us," she teased, raising the towel to begin treating his thigh.

"I can manage that," he said, but he was feeling faint from the hot shower and had to sit down on a stool.

"If you are sure you are all right I'll go and put the kettle on, then."

When he emerged in the borrowed clothes he found her sitting in a large window seat with a teapot, two cups and saucers and a plate of scones on a low table in front of her. She indicated a comfortable rocking chair on his side of the table.

"Hello. Feeling better? Take a seat."

He was in fact feeling unusually weary but answered, "I'll be fine after a strong cuppa or two."

"Milk no sugar?"

"Normally, but I think two spoonfuls of sugar might help just now." He really was feeling very dizzy.

As she poured the tea the woman said, "It is time I introduced myself. I am Marianne."

"Pleased to meet you."

"Are you?"

He ignored this taunt, this plea. "I'm Bob."

"Yes, that's right."

"Of course it is. I might have taken a knock on the head but I know who I am."

"No, I mean we have met before. I thought I recognized you when you were admiring my front door. You are Bob Martin, the carpenter."

He could not remember her but she said she had probably been wearing her gardening clothes and had different hair then. Besides, she had only spoken to him face to face very briefly. It had been a few years back when she and her husband owned The Green Halt Garden Centre. Bob had been engaged to erect an orangerie. She had subsequently watched him at work from her upstairs office on the site where she was first and foremost a garden designer and still building up a clientele.

Over a second cup of tea and Bob's third scone she told him that when she and Max had split up they had sold the garden centre and taken half each of the income. She had kept some of her clients and continued her own landscape business, working from home now.

"Only with this corona epidemic everything is very much on hold and I am alone in the barn."

"Not a bad place to be alone in."

She supposed it was much the same for him business-wise.

"Well, I have my own workshop so I can still carry out commissions, but no one wants me to do any work for them indoors."

"And your wife is away?"

"Why would you think that?"

"Otherwise you would have called her, asked her to come and fetch you perhaps."

He explained that his wife and children were stuck in Spain. They had gone out to visit his parents-in-law who had retired to Andalusia. With this virus they had all been confined to the house. Lockdown conditions in Spain were even stricter than in the UK.

"Not that Vera is in any hurry to come back," he said, and since our schools are all closed there is no reason to, even if travel were possible."

"Doesn't she miss you?"

He did not tell her that that very morning his wife had indicated to him she did not want to return at all. "I doubt it. Too busy," was all he said.

Marianne did not ask Bob whether he missed his wife. Lulled by the tea and conversation he felt more and more drowsy.

"I'm sorry, Marianne. I feel rather peculiar. I wonder whether I should go to A&E. Get checked over."

Marianne suppressed a look of alarm. "What, and catch covid-19? I would avoid hospitals if I were you. You are about to suffer a reaction. You just need more rest."

Before she had started to clear away the tea things Bob fell asleep in the big rocking chair. He was vaguely aware of her at some point bending over him and suggesting, "Bob, I think you had better have a proper lie down before I drive you home."

He remembered her leading him by the hand to a bedroom where she showed him to a double bed. She raised the duvet and he sank gratefully into a soft mattress and slept.

It was night and quite dark when he sensed her slipping into the bed beside him. He found he was wearing no clothes and Marianne's arm lay across his chest.

"Bob, I have an awful confession to make."

Half asleep Bob grunted and turned his head away.

"Bob, listen to me. I was not talking on my phone. I was trying to film you. I deliberately knocked into your bike but I did not want to hurt you."

"What?"

He tried to raise himself but she held him down saying, "I've been stalking you for weeks. Since I first watched you working on the orangerie I was attracted to you. I wanted to come down and bring you tea, to chat, but things were difficult with Max. He was easily provoked to jealousy."

Bob was more awake now. "What on earth is the time? I must go home."

"Just listen." She put her leg across his. It was too dark to make out her expression but her voice was husky with emotion. "I put you out of my mind during a long divorce and the sale of the centre. Then a few weeks ago I saw you again in Morrison's on your own. I wondered why and I followed you home. I learned your routine."

"I don't believe I would not have noticed you watching me."

In reply she eased her body on top of his and kissed him on the mouth. He was too weak, too tired either to resist or to respond. He could not move. She must have put something in his tea. As he drifted off to sleep again he imagined she was trying to enslave him and he could not work out if that was a good or a bad thing.

When he woke he was in the same bed wearing the jogging pants again and shirt he had worn since taking a shower. It was daylight now and he could smell coffee. He got out of bed and found his way to a large and sunny kitchen. Marianne was busying herself with the percolator and warming some milk. She was wearing a light cashmere cardigan over a different, floatier summer frock. She had sandals on her bare feet.

"Good morning. You slept well. For a while I thought I really would have to call the doctor."

"I'm fine, but I seem to have outstayed my welcome. I must go home."

"I'll drive you back after breakfast. Do you like croissants?"

"If that's all you've got."

A little later, much fortified on bacon and eggs though still stiff and sore, Bob climbed into the Range Rover beside Marianne, who had swapped her sandals for a pair of trainers. The bicycle was still in the back. She offered to take it to bicycle shop in Penrith but Bob said he could do that.

"Send me the bill, won't you?" She made no mention of her nocturnal confession and when they drove into Mary's Beck where Bob lived, she slowed down and asked, "Where to now?"

Bob had assumed she knew his house but he said, "Turn left over the bridge and it's a little way up the hill." When they approached a detached stone house with a slate roof he said, "This is it. You can drive straight in."

She did so and got out of the vehicle to help him lift his bicycle out. She pulled the rear door down and turned to face him. He was still holding the bike and the helmet unsure whether to thank or to blame her.

"Look," he said, "I'll wash these clothes and bring them back later."

"Don't bother about that. I have no use for them." She paused before getting back into her car. "No ill-feeling, then?"

"No," he decided. "And thanks for looking after me so well."

"Least I could do. Let me know if there is anything else."

"You too."

As she drove off she blew him a kiss and said, "I will."

Load of Bullocks

A dozen bullocks broke out of the farmyard opposite, galloped across the road in the lunging way that cattle do, and came across the green. They stalled briefly at the riverside beneath David's study window. Here some kicked up their hind legs and ran in circles; others tore greedily at the thick, green grass at the water's edge. The herd emotion was of exhilaration and of excitement.

David would not normally have taken a second look. Farmer Harry Richardson was past the age most people retire and if some said he was careless with his animals it was true that had no one else to help him. His unkempt and often lame sheep were permitted to roam the village green; his other livestock was meant to be kept on the farm.

David turned to concentrate on the work on his desk. As he picked up his pen the phone beside it burped, announcing a WhatsApp message. He opened it to find a photograph of the very scene he had just witnessed. It had been posted by his neighbour Audrey, a retired teacher who lived a hundred yards upstream. She had posted the picture on the Parish Tree Group site to which the volunteers all belonged. She had subtitled the image, *On the green now.*

David wondered why she was concerned, looked out of his window again and noticed one of the more vigorous black bullocks biting off the top of one of the young oaks they had planted last winter during gales and sleet. All the trees, for the group had worked their way along the river bank, were protected from sheep with metal cages secured around them by two sturdy posts. Now in summer some of them poked their branches above the tube, too high for sheep but a treat for an attentive cow.

David immediately posted the following comment on the Group's WhatsApp himself, *Yes, I am watching a black bullock nibbling one of our trees over the top of its cage. I will pop out and discourage it.*

What followed this brief exchange was astonishing. The country was still in lock-down to some extent but what he was to learn over the next twenty minutes was that, just like the established trees on the green, large maples and oaks and horse chestnuts, that all speak to one another through their root systems, so the village community were all in instant communication with one another through the ether; they were all, it seemed, on permanent watch.

Another neighbour also with a view over the riverside posted, *This is quite a regular occurrence but I did not think we had to provide cattle-proof cages on the green.*

Outside the village where there was livestock the volunteers planted the trees in so-called crates, a wooden square, fencing in three or four trees. They also defended the saplings against deer. The village green, a broad expanse on both sides of the river hosted only sheep. Moreover, at either end of the village there were cattle grids to keep the sheep in and anything else out. Not that this prevented unfortunate break-outs from the farm that lay within the village.

Quite distracted from his work by now David wrote back, *I feel concerned about the old ladies walking their dogs. The cattle are skittish.*

Within minutes, Joseph, a rather surly and officious Parish councillor from the other end of the village, was taking it all very seriously: *The grazing licence is for the sheep. To the best of my knowledge the bullocks should not be there. I will check with the parish clerk.*

By now everyone was chipping in with their scraps of knowledge and hearsay. An older volunteer, no less pedantic, wrote, *Cows have historically been driven across the green for milking but right of way does not amount to a right to graze (even if you cannot stop them taking a mouthful of different grass along the way.)*

Another person immediately added, *From the photo they do not look like milkers to me.*

By now David had given up any idea of trying to work. A conversation was on the go and he replied, *No, they are bullocks all right. They often get out. Usually they are rounded up by the sheepdogs with a little human help.*

Debbie, another of the volunteers who did bed and breakfast had also been following the exchanges and commented, *I didn't know cattle wasn't supposed to be in the green. I took a pic last Spring. Can't find it at the moment.*

Before David had read this the Parish clerk confirmed that the cows should not be there, something everyone knew, and Nigel, one of the pro-active volunteers posted photos of other trees grazed by the bullocks. David had quite forgotten his intention of shooing the beasts away and then a spelling mistake or perhaps WhatsApp's predictive spelling caused a more humorous exchange. An apologist for the farmer wrote, *The cows do a skype occasionally despite Harry's best efforts to keep them in.*

To which David's schoolteacher neighbour said by subtle way of correction, *Well, given that they are smart enough to skype perhaps we should think of electronic cages.*

Not to be outdone her husband now joined in equally illogically, *Maybe electronic tags.*

So he was not working either. This was developing into quite a party and David added his bit, referring to a field of goats just beyond the bridge that were always getting out.

Good thing, he wrote, *that the wall-climbing goats have so far not reduced the village green to the Sahara Desert.*

This was answered almost immediately, *I'm surprised we've not had hundreds of goats in the village given their numbers and their Houdini capabilities. Maybe they have not sussed the cattle grids yet.*

To which David went on to explain that even the sheep had worked out that they could walk along the raised concrete edges of the grids until someone had cleverly blocked these with car tyres. Someone else immediately intervened to say that in Wales sheep had learned to lie down and roll across the cattle grids.

Then David's neighbour returned to his point with this: *I have always wondered why we had fenders on our cattle grids. I assumed it was something to do with the Village Navy who so proudly boast a boat sentinel at each edge of the village.*

She was referring to a large cabin cruiser on a trailer in a garden one end and a more dilapidated sailing yacht in a farmyard at the other end. David had never seen either used, not even Noah-like in the floods.

By now the bullocks had moved out of sight. Messages became serious again with opinions about the state of the damaged trees. Then the cavalry arrived. Not on horseback but in a battered Mercedes car. It was their popular and charismatic leader, Jake, who lived in the next village. He screeched to a halt and David saw him walking up the river bank to investigate. His work, too, must have been punctuated by this inane WhatsApp "conversation".

Within ten minutes of his arrival the neighbour informed everyone, *Jake has worked his charms and the cattle are all safely home.*

One of his many admirers posted, *Jake has? Is he a cattle whisperer?*

More like a peace-maker, as well as all the other wonderful things he does, added a second admirer.

The next message that appeared on the site was typical of Jake. *Just let me adjust my halo.*

He had somehow herded the cattle back to the farm, spoken with the farmer who usually resented criticism and in his own words added, *Joking apart, the deal with Harry is we'll plant him some hedges if he tries harder to keep his cattle away from the trees.*

At this point the posting on WhatsApp petered out. David was still at his desk looking out of his window when he saw Jake's Mercedes drive off and over the road Helen, one of the experts whose main task was the after-care of the trees, thumbing a last message into her phone, *No need for panic, the trees will survive, although we should try to limit cattle damage.*

It was only eleven o'clock. David should have got on with his work but he saw no harm in first going down to his kitchen. After this flurry of excitement he felt he needed a morning coffee.

Citizen's Arrest

The Prime Minister had been married four months and was bored. His wife was now running the country though not much better than her husband had done, and in the evening she was bathing and feeding the baby; she did not always have time for Daddy now. To escape he decided he would self-isolate to Chequers where he would persuade that young filly from the Treasury to isolate with him.

The country at large was in confusion at the government's messages about who could do what and when, particularly when it came to wearing a mask. Some people who objected to the government's diktats were even more angry and confused when certain shops tried to enforce the wearing of masks.

The incident that David witnessed in Sainsbury's that day in Penrith was not untypical. He had just walked past a woman stacking shelves and had noticed that she bore the same name as his late wife. This made him give her an involuntary smile but the middle-aged woman's attention was distracted by another man. Most of the customers continued to wear masks but this man, covered as much in tattoos as clothes, dressed only in shorts and a stained singlet stretched over his beer belly was bare faced. The woman rose to her feet as he approached the wrong way down the aisle and politely challenged him.

"Excuse me, sir," she said, "would you mind wearing a mask."

"Yes, I would."

"And," she continued unabashed, "please would you follow the arrows and keep your distance."

The man was outraged. "Who are you to tell me what to do?"

"I am asking you, sir, that's all."

"Well fuck you," he said and spat in her face.

She was a feisty woman despite her fatigue and slapped him hard in his face. He grabbed her arm and forced her back against the cans of pasta bake sauce. Suddenly there was no one else in the aisle. No one except David and he was a timid man. He had never had a fight in his life.

Nevertheless there were still traces of gallantry in his slow pulsing old veins. He put an arm on the man's bare shoulder.

"Stop that, mate." He had never called anyone mate before either.

"Wotcha say?"

"I said let go of her."

The man shrugged off David's hand and presence as a mere annoyance and continued to shake the woman.

"Right," said David, more loudly than he usually spoke. "I am arresting you." He gripped the man's shoulder more tightly.

In the short term this stopped the man, allowing the woman to struggle free.

"You the police?" mocked the bully.

"No. I am David. And I am making a citizen's arrest."

"You're joking."

"Far from it."

The man looked bewildered at this turn of phrase. Amused even. David handed his basket of purchases to the woman and said, "I'll be back for it." To the man he ordered, "Follow me."

"Where are we going?"

"To the police station."

"Oh yes? You even know where it is?"

"A fifteen minute walk I would say. But I can drive us there if you will put on a mask."

"Aint got no bleeding mask, mate."

"I've got a spare one in the car. Which is it to be? Walk or car?"

"Or I could scarper, couldn't I? You couldn't stop me." He seemed intrigued at the possibility.

"Not by force, perhaps, but you realise what the consequences would be?"

"Consequences?"

"You'd be resisting arrest."

"You are out of your mind."

David thought the man might be right but he continued, "You think so, too? I advise you to follow me."

"Where's the car, then?"

"In the store's car park."

"Go on. Mind, I'm only doing this for a laugh."

"What's your name?"

"What's it to you?"

"Nothing. What else have we got to say to each other?

"You're taking a bloody liberty, you know that."

"In a sense I suppose I am." He laughed, they both relaxed and the man said,

"Sam."

"Can't think why you followed me, Sam."

"Well, I thought, this old git's got a nerve. I like that."

"You're still under arrest."

"Sure."

"Do you live here in Penrith?"

"You questioning me now?"

"It's called small talk. Same as when I asked your name."

"Two can play at that," he said and tried to put on a posh accent. "You come here often?"

"Not often, no."

"Where do you live, then?"

"A village. You wouldn't know it. Mary's Beck."

"Yea, I know Mary's Beck don't I. Bloke there into cock-fighting. Lost a few bob in Mary's Beck, I have an' all."

"Cock-fighting is illegal."

"Many things are. But it's done secretly isn't it?"

"I wouldn't know."

"No," said Sam, giving David a shrewd look. "I don't suppose you would." They pulled up outside the police station. "What now?"

"I'm taking you in."

"This'll be a laugh, mate." said Sam, following David into the station. The officer at the desk recognised Sam and nodded to him.

"Ah, sergeant. I have arrested this man, said David.

He says his name is Sam."

"And what am I to do about it, sir?"

David explained that he had made a citizen's arrest and that he was handing Sam over for causing a disturbance and for threatening behaviour if not assault on a woman.

"Is this true?" the policeman asked the trouble maker.

"Well, it's true that he arrested me. Don't know what evidence he's got."

David gave his account of the incident and said he felt sure that Mandy, the shop assistant would corroborate his story. The sergeant looked doubtful and asked whether David had used force or coercion to get Mr Walker to accompany him to the station.

"Mr Walker. So you know him?"

"We are old friends," said Sam. "We go back a long time."

"I did not use force. Mr. Walker has been most cooperative," interrupted David.

Soon the three of them were discussing the incident quite amicably. Sam admitted he had lost his rag.

"I was out of order. It's me mental 'ealth, isn't it?"

The policeman suggested it would be best for everybody's mental health if Sam returned to Sainsbury's to apologise to Mandy and no more would be said. He asked whether David agreed and the old man thought it might be a good way out of the predicament.

"Good idea," he said with some relief. "I'll drive him back there now."

When they reached the supermarket Mandy was off duty. The manager listened to this unlikely couple's story. Mandy had not reported the incident though she had left a basket of groceries for an elderly customer to reclaim. Staff, the manager explained, were subject to harassment and abuse several times a week. Mandy was pretty tough, but he would pass on the apology. It might make her day, who knew.

"Give her these flowers, would you," said Sam. "From Sam."

On the way out David asked Sam where he had got the flowers from.

"From the store. They were on display at the entrance so I took a bunch."

"Did you pay for them?"

"No one asked." There was a pause. "No mate. Not again. You're not going to arrest me again."

"No. Let me buy you a drink."

"Why?"

"Tell me about yourself. I'd like to write your story."

"Only if you will let me take you cock-fighting."

"I do not want to watch cruelty to animals."

"Blimey!" said Sam. "You couldn't make it up."

But David did.

One Jab

The secret Cumbrian laboratory would never have been revealed but for their remarkable success, or as the unimaginative saw it, their spectacular failure.

Until the covid pandemic of 2020, Avian Labs had been researching bird flu. As it happened one of their scientists came from Wuhan Province in China. When Covind-19 came to Cumbria he went to his boss revealing that he had inside information about the origins of this new plague, and suggested that perhaps Avian Labs might develop their own vaccine against it. Dr Stabbem agreed and they set to work secretly at first. No one knew that the research was funded by Hahawi.

The initial selling point for the vaccine was as its name. One Jab implied that only one inoculation was required, thus saving the government a lot of money.

At first all went normally. Vaccination for anyone over 60 was arranged at Sharpby Medical Centre. An orderly queue formed in the car park and pensioners walked through the centre where teams of blue clad nurses in space helmets injected them as they passed by. In a field adjacent to the centre was a spacious marquee where the patients were advised to rest ten minutes in case of side effects. To entice them in volunteers offered tea and mince pies. Many would have preferred sherry but Dr Furrowbrow of the Centre had vetoed this. As it turned out, alcohol was to be the least of his problems.

There was the usual rabble of anti-vaxxers standing outside with banners and jeering at the elderly patients.

"It will turn you all into chimpanzees," yelled Thickie Planck, their leader.

Apple cheeked Granny Smith turned to him and retorted, "Better that than become a gorilla like you."

The first sign of trouble, if you can call it that, happened in the marquee. Grandpa Lightfoot began to feel rather dizzy.

"Have another mince pie," said his wife.

"I'm all right. It's just that my bones feels a bit…"

"A bit what?"

"A bit light."

The next thing they knew, both of them had floated up into the air.

"Don't worry love. It's probably a side effect of the vaccine. I am sure it will wear off."

It didn't. The effect grew stronger and once the old couple had got over their initial alarm they found they could move around above the heads of the others. They could fly. As their confidence grew they swooped down through the opening of the marquee and up into the grey, Cumbrian sky.

"I am going to piss on the anti-vaxxers," laughed Grandpa Lightfoot.

"Don't you dare," said his wife. "You are not a pigeon."

Soon others felt the same lightness of body and they floated up into the sky too. After a while scores of elderly people were circling and whooping above the medical centre. Dr Furrowbrow was called out. He frowned at his patients and said, "it's probably just mass hysteria. Give them half an hour and they will come back down to earth."

He went back inside to continue his vaccination programme. Nurse Skittle, however, quite bowled over by events, jabbed herself and ran out to join the bodies in the sky.

Not everyone suffered these side effects. One disgruntled old spinster complained to the niece who had brought her in, "I told you it wouldn't work."

"Well Auntie, you never were a flighty woman."

"What's that supposed to mean?"

Now among the anti-vaxxers in the car park were some who opposed vaccination on religious grounds. One of these, Enid Feargod shouted, "It's not right. If the Lord had wanted us to fly he would have given us wings."

Jeff Armstrong, former blacksmith and still possessing a muscular body, thought, "that would explain the itching." He ripped off his jacket and shirt in front of the protesters. Enid almost fainted in disgust,

"Mr Armstrong, that is tantamount to exposure."

Indeed it was. A revelation, too, for from Mr Armstrong's magnificent shoulders sprouted a pair of colourful wings. He was as surprised as anyone. He flapped his wings, felt them gaining strength and bulk. Within a few minutes he rose into the sky.

Enid Feargod fell to her knees in prayer. "Thank you, thank you Lord. You have sent me an angel."

Meanwhile Benjie Easypenny had been fishing nearby. Hearing the commotion he strolled over to the centre and the phrase 'quick buck' flashed through his mind. He hurried into the woods and later that afternoon returned with a dozen besom brooms. He stood at the entrance to the marquee where he offered them at £25 a piece. They were soon sold out. The pensioners were as gleeful as children with a new bike, as they swooped and soared over the little town of Sharpby.

By nightfall the side effects wore off. Thankfully their weakening was gradual. Only Madame Hoity, who owned a bespoke fashion shop, suffered an accident. She was circling quite high displaying an expensive gown when her power of flight suddenly failed her and she plummeted headfirst into a duck pond. She was rescued, spluttering, "Look what it's done to my hair. I shall sue the medical centre, I shall sue the NHS."

You might have thought pictures of the phenomenon would have filled the airwaves and social media. Strangely, those who tried to film the flying oldies on their phones got only a blank screen. Only those with Hahawi phones felt they might have captured something but could not retrieve the images. By the time the TV reporters arrived the flying had finished. The only reporter who had seen it all for herself was from the local paper. She was delighted to have some real news to report at last but her sceptical editor rather played down her report. There was just a small piece on page five in the next edition of the Herald headed, "Pensioner falls into pond."

Although the side effects had disappeared by dark, those affected could talk of nothing else. Those who had not witnessed the event tended to agree with Dr Furrowbrow's diagnosis: it was nothing more than mass hysteria.

This did not prevent hundreds more queuing for the vaccine next morning. Some even came back for more and had to be weeded out as a second inoculation so soon did contain a risk and was unnecessary. Sadly for the second group of vaccinees nothing dramatic happened. It is too soon to say how effective the vaccination was. The only deaths so far have had other causes, too much excitement for example, rather than covid-19.

One odd thing did happen though. The government, to distract from its own blunders and incompetence reprimanded China for imprisoning opposition activists in Hong Kong. The Chinese media was furious.

"How dare this country of witches tell us how to behave," they fulminated and posted film of old women flying around and above Sharpby on broomsticks.

It was a puzzle how they had concocted these images.

Antivaxxers

Gibril was driving a white, refrigerated van along a country road in Cumbria. It contained a precious cargo destined for a distribution centre in Appleby. A hundred yards ahead of him a police outrider led the way on an unmarked motor cycle. He wore ordinary bikers' leathers. No one wished to draw attention to this important delivery but, due to antivaxxers' hysteria in the larger cities, whipped up by the still legal social media, itself worse than any virus, Gibril was given this limited protection as a precaution.

He drove slowly but knew that the vaccines in his van had to reach colder freezers within the next two hours. There could be no delays. He was not particularly worried. Nothing much happened hereabouts and traffic was light.

All of a sudden a tractor drove out of a farmyard, knocking the policeman off his motorcycle and with its long trailer straddled the road. Gibril came to a halt thinking he had merely witnessed an unfortunate accident. He was concerned for the policeman, but relieved to see him sitting up in the road and reaching for his phone. However the tractor driver was upon him and snatched the phone away. At least that was what Gibril glimpsed before a herd of bullocks stampeded out of the farmyard and blocked his view. At the same time two men in balaclavas and armed with sub machine guns approached his van. One of them came up to the driver's door and with his gun signalled to Gibril to get out. Gibril wound down his window.

"Good afternoon," he said. "I am glad to see you are wearing your masks."

The armed man was not amused and shouted, "Get out!"

Gibril had no choice. He realised he was in the hands of vigilantes. How they had got wind of his vaccine delivery he did not know. Or perhaps they were just modern day highwaymen taking advantage of the quieter roads. They took him to the rear of the van and ordered him to open the doors. In the cold interior were several long containers. They were all beige except, closest to the door a smaller one which was of a primrose colour. Gibril remembered a plain clothes man who had sidled up to him at the collection point with the words, "I don't suppose you will run into any trouble, but should anything happen, open the yellow container."

The man had disappeared before Gibril could ask any questions. Besides he had to move off. Other vans were queuing. The distribution effort was vast and countrywide. He drove off without thinking further of this curious incident.

"What's in the containers?" asked the man with the gun.

"Hospital supplies," answered Gibril.

"Oh yeah!" jeered the man. "Like vaccines?"

"No. Gloves. Masks. Protective equipment."

"So why does it need refrigeration?

"To prevent contamination."

"Open them up."

Gibril pulled the yellow box towards him apprehensively, raised the clasps and hesitated.

"Lift the lid."

When he did so the incredible happened. A score of small insects swarmed out. They looked like scorpions but on their bodies between head and rising tail they wore what appeared to be a woolly coat with bobbles all over, not red like the virus but yellow. Their stings swung like segmented hypodermic needles. Almost at once they began to grow, swelling to the size of small dogs. Gibril was as terrified as the armed men, now four in number. Another was approaching on a quad bike. The restless bullocks were also uncomfortably close.

The Scorpions ignored Gibril and leapt upon the men. One of them fired his gun in panic. The shots went wide, hitting a bullock, enraging it and making it charge blindly into the group. Gibril jumped into the back of his van. The Scorpions paralysed the men with their stings, then like sheep dogs they rounded up the cattle and while some of them drove the beasts back into the farmyard the others gathered around the villains.

Cowering inside his van Gibril could not believe it when he heard the lead scorpion say to him in an East London accent, "It's all right, mate. We won't hurt you. You can come out now." He watched as they lined the vigilantes up, wondering aloud which one to eat first. During this discussion the policeman limped over. To his amazement Gibril recognised him as the same man, presumably an intelligence officer, who had advised him at the depot about the yellow box.

40

"Well done, lads," he said to the Scorpions. There's better food laid on in Appleby. Don't eat these men. Just inject them with the shame and truth serum. It might just change them into rational human beings."

"Of which there are far too few," remarked one of the Scorpions.

Gibril watched as the Scorpions climbed onto the chests of the vigilantes, raised their swinging tails above their own heads and those of their victims and inserted their sting in the ears and into the brains of the terrified, paralysed men.

"Right," said the policeman, "you okay now, Gibril?" Gibril was shaking and could not find the words to reply. The policeman continued, "You don't really want to remember this, do you, Gibril?"

"I don't know."

The policeman winked at the head scorpion, "Okay Skip, make it quick and painless."

The creature did as it was bidden. It grabbed Gibril in its pincers and darted its tail into his thigh."

Less than an hour later Gibril drove into the industrial park outside Appleby where huge freezers had been set up.

"Ah, here comes our Angel Gabriel. Good journey?" asked his mate, helping him with the containers.

"Yes, much as usual. Quieter if anything," replied Gibril, wondering how that jumper had got into the back of his van, a woolly blue one with yellow bobbles.

The Beast of Shap Fell

Isabelle's first reaction was a gasp, then a step back. There it was at her feet. She had been striding up the fell, head down, the peak of her cap protecting her face from the squalls of rain. It also limited her vision. In the blustery conditions she could see only the tussocky grass immediately before her. Then this.

Isabelle's initial shock turned into curiosity. Was it a real hand she had so nearly stepped upon? It looked clean, fresh even, but there were no traces of blood around it and none flowed from the severed wrist. The finger nails were thick, clean and unbroken. No sign of a struggle.

Isabelle, or Belle as the thirty-one-year-old probation officer was better known, was no stranger to bodies, dead or alive. Wiping her rain-soaked face she stooped to examine the hand more closely, suspecting it might be the discarded part of a shop window mannequin. On closer inspection, however, she ascertained it was real enough, a large hand with prominent knuckles, hairy at the fingers' stems. The nails were definitely male, she decided, as was the strong, thick wrist.

She wondered what to do. She was well wrapped against the blustery weather but was carrying no rucksack. Her pockets were hardly large enough for the hand apart from which she did not want to soil them. For surely there must be some blood, clotted perhaps, around the wound.

A sudden compulsion made her want to touch the hand, to pick it up. She was unprepared for what happened when she did. She felt a surge run up her own arm. It was the same thrill she remembered when as a young girl she had for the first time reached for a boyfriend's hand in the back of her parents' car when they were being driven home from a party and he had shyly squeezed hers back. An almost electric charge. Here on the fell she screamed and dropped the hand back down on to the wet grass. How could this have happened? The hand was cold. Just dead flesh and bone.

Having quickly regained her composure, she knew what she should do. She should call the police, leave the hand where it was and try not to disturb the evidence any more than she had done. However she knew that in the unlikely event of there being a phone signal it was far too cold to hang about possibly for hours until the police arrived. On a warmer day she would not have minded. She was at the highest point of a perimeter fence that encircled Shap Fell Quarry. She knew there was a good view from this now abandoned and water filled excavation across to the Nine Standards Rigg on Hartley Fell and to her right in the distance, the Howgills. Today with the low cloud and gusts of rain-filled wind she could not see down even as far as the reservoir.

There was another reason she did not want to call the police just yet. She had deliberately disappeared- for a week, walking out on an abusive partner in the urban squalor of Barrow where they both worked. She had come for some peace and quiet and some 'me-time' to the peaceful village of Mary's Beck where she had rented a former brew house, now converted into a small holiday cottage. She had even changed her phone so as not to be tracked down. She intended spending her time reading, hiking and taking stock. To ease her conscience she had brought along notes for a complex case study she had to write up. Belle was a fit young woman who could look after herself and that is what she intended to do.

For the moment she decided simply to leave the hand where it was and to alert the police later. It occurred to her that they might not believe her or that someone else might try to move the hand. She therefore took a photo of it with her phone before continuing on her way. She walked back down through Oddendale farmyard, emerging eventually behind the Butcher's Arms pub in Crosby Ravensworth. From there it was a half hour walk along a footpath following the River Lyvennet back to her cottage in Mary's Beck.

When she had showered, changed her clothes and was warm and dry again she felt it was time to phone the police. Then she remembered that there was no phone signal in the village. She felt no inclination to get dressed again and climb the road called Meaburn Edge to a higher point where she might get a signal. It would have to wait until the morning.

She flipped over to her phone app to see how her picture, taken in a squall of rain, had come out. She got a second shock. She had seen a hand, had indeed picked it up and experienced that strange pulse. The photo on her phone showed more. The hand had not been amputated at the wrist. It was part of a full-length arm. Still unclothed it revealed a swarthy and muscular limb with the tattoo of a briar rose on the outside of the shoulder. Like the hand she thought she had seen, the arm, too, seemed clean and bloodless. She could make no sense of this. Even though visibility had been poor in the rain she was convinced she had seen only a hand. Her phone told a different story.

She had a troubled night dreaming of the hand in the grass and of how she had touched it. In the dream she was overcome with a sense that she was being watched; that a murderer had perhaps all the time been sheltering in the dripping copse that grew on the cliffs above the quarry. Perhaps there was a mutilated body there under the trees.

In the morning she was too distracted to make a start on the report she had taken time out to write. The weather was drier now though still overcast. She resolved to return to the spot where she had seen the hand and to settle her doubts. Before involving the police she had to get her story straight. With luck someone else might have stumbled upon the hand or the arm, whatever it was, and done something about it. Directly on a footpath, the place could hardly be described as remote. On a quiet day a hiker could hear the sound of traffic from the M6 motorway. Indeed, a road at the far end of the quarry led down to the southbound carriageway. Anyone with any knowledge of the area could have driven in and walked up in half an hour to deposit a hand, an arm, a whole body. Why they should want to lug it to somewhere so exposed was another matter. Although just off the footpath it was hardly a hiding place. No one had even tried to conceal the limb. For now she was beginning to think it must have been a whole arm if that's what the camera showed.

Belle filled a thermos with hot coffee which together with a pair of gloves she put in a small backpack. She pulled on her walking boots, still damp from yesterday's tramp in the rain and set off, determined to sort out this mystery once and for all.

Little over an hour and a half later, as she approached the summit, she felt drawn to the spot by more than curiosity. It was as though the hand was beckoning to her if not physically in some more subtle way. She had passed no other hiker on the way up and, breathless, she pushed through startled sheep, traced her way among the occasional exposed slabs of limestone pavement towards the grassy knoll where she knew she had left the hand.

When nearly there she was seized by disappointment. Someone seemed to have beaten her to it. They seemed to be reclining, perhaps picnicking on the very spot – but the figure she saw was lying very still. Belle continued cautiously, fearing a trap. What she found was worse. There where she had found a hand, photographed an arm, the shoulder was now connected to a torso, or half at least – a very hairy man's chest. No head, no lower limbs, no clothes. This time Belle took no picture but turned in horror and ran back down to the bottom of the hill level with the lower lip of the water filled quarry. She didn't stop there, either, but made for the farmyard, sheltered as it was by a stand of fir trees.

Beneath one of them she removed her backpack and shakily poured herself a coffee from the flask. Had there been anyone in the yard or in any of the barns she would have run to them for help. But it was deserted except for a dog on a long leash that she had spoken to on the way up. A small herd of highland cattle grazed on the moor behind.

The coffee restored her. She convinced herself she had been imagining things, that all she had seen had been some rocks catching the light that filtered fitfully through the low cloud cover. She knew that she was overwrought, that she had come here in the first place for a break and to escape her jealous, overbearing partner; she also wanted time off from her stressful work, using the writing up of her case work as a pretext for a short absence. She had prescribed herself peace and quiet punctuated by exhilarating walks. The walks were turning out rather more than exhilarating. She admitted to herself she needed to get more rest, give herself more time to reflect. She had big decisions to make. She didn't need this extra hassle.

When she stood up again to return home she felt a strong pull to go up again, to take one more look at whatever it was she imagined she had seen; and to take a picture of it. She resisted the urge, intending to go back down to the village, perhaps drive into Shap for fish and chips and then buckle down to some serious work.

The late afternoon saw the clouds clear away and Belle went to write at the picnic table outside her cottage on the village green. Behind her children were playing on the swings, their mothers sunning themselves as they chatted by the weir. A collie came up to Belle and deposited a tennis ball in her lap. She knew that if she threw it the dog would bring it back for more. She saw its owner coming so she stood to throw the ball just once and the dog returned it to its owner. Belle felt relaxed, more at peace, trying to get the images of the limbs out of her mind. She hoped, too, that by now if there was indeed half a corpse on Shap Fell, someone else might have reported it.

Nevertheless she had another troubled night. She got up to a cloudless sky and by the time she had eaten breakfast the sun was shining again. Instead of spending the morning completing her case notes she needed once more to climb up to the top of Shap Fell Quarry and see once and for all what she had stared at in the murk of rain or the murk of her imagination. She felt an irresistible compulsion not only to understand but to return to the presence of these human remains. If there was indeed still a body or part of a body there she would take more photos and drive straight into Penrith to show this evidence to the police.

The attraction, both intellectual and visceral, to return to the spot was countered by the dread of what she was getting into. Wrestling with indecision she eventually came down on the side of caution and procrastination. She could get most of her report done with a steady morning's work. This would allow more time for some other walker to discover the remains.

She settled down with her notes and her computer and concentrated on the task in hand. It focused her mind, taking it off darker thoughts. Mid morning she took a break to walk round the village, following the banks of the river that glittered cleanly through the Green. A heron was perched on the footbridge, a pair of immaculate goosanders swam in the relatively still water above the weir and sheep sat contentedly on the lush grass with their eyes closed, chewing and enjoying the warmth. All was peaceful.

But Belle's mind was not quiet. She felt she should not be here. Someone up on the fell needed her, was calling to her. She had to return if only to dispel these thoughts. She had come away not only to work on her report without distraction but to lay a ghost. She wanted to escape the unreasonable demands of her troubled and troubling partner. She had come to get a bit of perspective.

After a bite of lunch therefore she buried herself for the final time in her work. If she could finish it today she would still have a full week for leisure and more exercise, especially if this weather held. When she broke for tea she could not help picking up her phone. She thumbed through searching again for that photo of the arm. She almost dropped the phone when the image appeared. The body had grown. Her phone seemed to be burning her own hand. She flung the device away from her across the room. Had she really just seen a complete, though still headless body? Naked as though sun bathing? She started shaking, told herself to calm down. It had been a trick of the sunlight. A screen is difficult to read with a bright shaft of light falling on it. She retrieved the phone from the corner of the room. She touched it gently fearing a shock but the phone was neither warm nor electrically charged in that sense. She took two deep breaths, waited until she was breathing normally and searched for the photos again. There was nothing there. Not only had the full length photo disappeared but her original picture of the hand had also been deleted.

Belle concluded that she had damaged the phone. She took some photos of her room, of her desk and of the Green outside. They all came up on the screen as normal. She scrolled back through earlier photos. They were all there, all except for those of the hand and the arm. The full body image had also been wiped. She felt a despairing sense of loss. Also a sense of relief. She must have imagined the whole thing. She had needed this break. She was getting back to normal.

In a mood of celebration she walked into Crosby Ravensworth a little later for an evening meal at the Butcher's Arms. The irony of the pub's name was not lost on her, though she was unaware that the butcher in question was not a tradesman but a notorious general. She found a small table for one just inside the door. The pub was already quite busy and a group of people in their sixties and seventies who stood at the bar were talking about the trees they been planting. One of them mentioned the restoration being carried out in Shap Fell Quarry. Belle strained her ears but no one spoke of any missing person or gruesome discovery.

She rounded off her meal with an espresso, paid at the bar and stepped outside. It was later than she had thought and getting dark, but the moon was rising, the sky was clear and her eyes would adjust to the twilight. It was no problem to walk back along the river the way she had come.

Only she did not do this. As though propelled by some other force she turned down beside the pub, crossed a small footbridge and followed the lane that led up towards Oddendale. Enough light reflected off the tarmac lane to give her adequate visibility. By the time she reached the grassy track and field edge towards the farm the moon had risen higher and her eyes were accustomed to the dark.

Passing through the farmyard itself she roused neither dog nor man. The old stone buildings formed a tight ghost settlement of their own. There was no light on in the farmhouse. Only the sweet, warm smell of cattle in the cowshed signalled signs of life. When she emerged on to the open hillside that surrounded the former quarry she paused to catch her breath and to question what on earth she was doing. It was still half an hour's climb to the spot where only a few days ago she had almost trodden on the severed hand.

The moon seemed huge now. It illuminated the sheep dotted around the moorland and was reflected in the steely surface of the water in the quarry below. Whether it was bright enough to reveal the arm was another matter but if she could locate the right area again Belle had her phone with which to shine a light on it.

Belle knew that what she was doing was idiotic if not dangerous. She should turn back, go down to Crosby, past the pub which would be closing, walk along the river and cuddle up under the duvet in her cosy cottage. But there was nothing rational in her behaviour now. She was no longer in control. She was being drawn to that cursed patch of tussocky grass and limestone whether she liked it or not.

She began the last climb, really little more than a steep slope upwards. Apart from avoiding rocks and loose stones she hardly had to slow down or even pause for breath. She was filled with an exhilaration that she could not explain, other than the pleasure of walking in the night away from human sound and light.

That excitement turned first to anxiety then to terror when a figure rose up before her. At least that was how she experienced it. She had not noticed anyone there until the tall form loomed suddenly in her path. Motionless. Now she wanted to turn and run but her body was attracted like an iron filing to a magnet towards this creature. She was sure that he was the embodiment of the limbs she had seen, that it was the same person, the completed jigsaw of his remains.

The man was fully clothed. Over what appeared to be heavy boots and thick twill trousers he wore a long great coat buttoned to the neck. She assumed that both arms were inside the wide sleeves of this coat. He wore no hat but had such a mane of black hair falling to his shoulders that no other covering was necessary. His face was in shadow but she sensed he was unshaven and saw the glint of his colourless eyes. Still motionless the apparition stared at the young woman frozen in her tracks. Her body might have been paralysed but her mind was racing. Was she dreaming this? Was this some kind of grotesque scarecrow? Worse, was it a real being?

Then he spoke. The voice was deep, less threatening than pleading,

"I have been waiting for you."

"I know," she said and this admission relieved her, gave her confidence. She knew she was right to have confronted the monster.

"You know what you have to do to complete the task," asserted the figure now with a hint of menace.

"Task?" she stammered.

"Through your presence you have put me back together. Now you must complete the task," he repeated, and came forward, too close, too close. Belle stepped back. "To give me my life back," the wretch growled.

"How?" whispered Belle.

"Kiss me, Beauty." He was close. His breath stank of death. Belle looked at him. She was quite calm at last.

"You wish!" she exclaimed and turned her back on the Beast for good.

48

Presence

As soon as he stepped inside from the storm, Edward noticed the cottage was warm. This was not what he had expected. He was braced to riddle out the cold ash and clinker from the kitchen range, light a new fire and wait until its warmth heated the water and radiated through the house.

From the car to the front porch was only a matter of yards but in taking his bags from the boot then searching in his deep pockets for the house keys he had become soaked by the sluicing rain. He now stood dripping on to the wooden floor and puzzling why it was warm inside. He switched on the light and looked around. Yes, the house had stood empty for over six months but it definitely felt warm. He breathed slowly in. The air was not even damp or clammy with cold and mildew as he had dreaded. It was scented with the faint trace of coal smoke.

He should have been pleased and in a way, after the long and difficult drive, he was pleased to feel comfortable, at home even. But not relaxed. Not only did the house feel warm, it smelled and felt lived in and this alarmed him.

He dropped his bags on the porch mat and opened the door into the kitchen. He went straight over to the range but he had no need to touch it to find out if it was burning. On top the big, smoke blackened kettle, in his mind and memory very much part of the range itself, was quietly singing. A tea pot and one cup and saucer had been set on the bare, wooden table with a tea caddy, a spoon and the little brown jug filled with milk beside it.

Edward looked round the rest of the small room; cast his eye over the dresser and the open cupboards. All the other cups and plates were undisturbed; a bird book lay where he remembered leaving it on the window sill. There was no other sign of occupation. He dismissed the idea of squatters moving in.

He also remembered filling the coal scuttle before he left at what now seemed half a life time ago, but he knew he had not laid the fire. He could not have done for it had still been burning when he left.

The scuttle, curiously, was still full or it had been refilled, for someone had lit the fire. He opened the cast iron door using the oven glove that always hung on the hand rail. The coal, mixed ovoids he recalled, glowed slowly and steadily. Clearly it had been alight some time. He turned the tap on over the big, stone sink. After a while the water ran hot.

If not a squatter, then who? It did not for a moment occur to him that the house had been heated, the tea things set out for him. Besides, no one knew he was coming. None of his friends had asked to borrow the house; few of them knew about it anyway, and he would certainly not have let it to strangers. He went back to the porch and peeked into the sitting room on the other side of the cottage. Nothing seemed to have been disturbed, nothing removed, nothing added. Except, he realised, for a small pile of mail that had been stacked neatly on the coffee table. Someone had gathered them up; otherwise he would have trodden on them when he came in the front door. He shuffled through them. There were one of two personal letters and cards that were several months old. All these were from people who by now knew what had happened or at least knew that he was no longer there, some of them he had even seen since. There was the usual junk mail, one official letter about electoral registration and a mail order catalogue from a firm from whom he had once or twice bought shirts. But one letter, an invitation, to a fund-raising event in a nearby village, was dated only yesterday. Someone had been here since.

For a moment he thought he was in one of those horrid situations like a surprise birthday party. He would open a door and everyone he knew would break out into "happy birthday to you." Only it wasn't his birthday and he was convinced he had not let slip his plans about coming down here in the first place. Even if he had, no one else owned a key. Not any more.

Outside the storm raged on. He had brought provisions with him but since the kettle was hot and the tea at hand, he would make do with a cuppa before unloading the car. First, though, seeing the house was warm, he would take the bed clothes out of the trunk upstairs and give them an airing before making the bed. He had actually brought a sleeping bag for the first night, thinking he would have to wait at least one night for the damp chill to leave the mattress and the sheets.

He removed his coat, still dripping, hung it on the peg inside the porch, and climbed the stairs. He was still suspicious. Whoever had lit the fire and set out the tea things might be hiding, waiting upstairs. He thought for some reason of Goldilocks and the Three Bears. Though he was unsure which character he would be in the fairy story.

His bedroom door was ajar. There was no Goldilocks, no Sleeping Beauty in his bed, but what he encountered surprised him almost as much.

The bed had been freshly made up, an edge of the duvet turned back and a bowl of late flowering roses arranged in a vase on the bedside table.

When he had left so suddenly all that time ago he may not have made the bed, but those sheets would not have been so crisp and sweet. That is why he had intended to take clean ones from the trunk. But it was not necessary. He took the pillow up from the bed and buried his face in it. The pillow was freshly laundered. He pulled back the duvet and sniffed the sheets. As far as he could tell, no one had slept in them. And yet, and yet, what was this? Carefully pulling the duvet right back, there was the impression of a body, as though someone had at least been resting there. He flung the duvet back over, thinking what nonsense! He was just tired; and it was an old mattress full of bumps and lumps and depressions.

The only other oddity upstairs was that a clean towel had been hung on the towel rail. Everything was in order. Much less dust than he had expected, but otherwise the cottage had stood up remarkably well to his absence.

He made a thorough search of the house just to ascertain no one was hiding away and that no cameras had been installed for some reality TV show or other. He found nothing else.

He did not feel watched; he no longer felt threatened. His mind was numbed by the long journey during which he had had to will himself to return to the cottage, to the place if not the scene of the tragedy. It was time to clear everything out, to find an estate agent and to put the cottage on the market. No point in leaving the building and its few contents to moulder slowly and to fall into disrepair. He was ready to draw a line. It was for the best.

He could not explain the excellent state of the cottage, its warmth, the tea and the made-up bed but it was nothing to be afraid of. It was a benign influence. So much so that he went downstairs, brewed tea and dozed in the warmth of the kitchen range. It was like old times. It was as if nothing had happened. Except that now he was on his own. At least, he supposed he was.

He was so weary that he did not bother to fetch his provisions from the car. He was not hungry. He was so very tired that he automatically stoked up the range, drew the curtains and went up to bed. The only precaution he took was to bolt the door on the inside. It would all make sense in the morning.

Before he had run through in his mind the various tasks he intended to do for the rest of the week, or indeed, as long as it would take to rid himself of this cottage where he had, until last year, been so happy, he fell into a deep and undisturbed sleep.

It was already light when Edward woke up. The storm had abated though water still ran in the gutters. For a moment he wondered where on earth he was. He became aware of a pleasant, burning smell. Suddenly realising what it was he stumbled out of bed and hurried downstairs in his pyjamas. This time he would catch the intruder. The door, he noticed, was still bolted shut. The kitchen was empty, though the curtains had been drawn to let the sunlight in and there on the table lay a plate of bacon, eggs and fried bread with tomatoes and mushrooms on the side.

Hungry though he was, he was too alarmed to touch this ready breakfast.

"No, no," he cried and ran back upstairs, hurried to the bathroom though he did not pause to shave or shower. He dressed and repacked his bags. This took only minutes but he fumbled and stumbled, his eyes blinded by grief. "No, no, my darling," he cried. "You can't do this. There is no way back now."

At the foot of the stairs he struggled with the front door bolt and opened the door. Light and fresh air burst in. He turned round and called back into the house,

"Don't you see, my love, we shall not ever be together again. Not properly. I am going now for good."

He shut the door firmly and got into his car. Tears were streaming down his face. But he had made his decision. He would not change his mind now. The past was the past. He would leave the cottage for her to haunt if that was what she was doing, but he would no longer be part of it. He would never return.

The Curse of the Silver Spade

Once there was a man who in his spare time planted trees. When he heard about a group of volunteers that had begun an organised project on the farms and fells around his village he asked if he might join in.

"You are more than welcome, Eddie," said Danny, their leader, who told him that next weekend the gang would be planting oaks on High Fell Farm. "Just bring a claw hammer and a spade."

When Saturday came Eddie put on his old cord trousers and worn wax jacket and pulled on a pair of sturdy boots. He had decided to walk up to the farm, even though few in the village dared use the footpath that passed through Wych Elm Forest, a dark place even now in winter when the trees were bare. The path followed the river at first. Over centuries the water had carved a steep gorge with precipitous banks. In places Eddie had to cling perilously to the rocky walls for fear of falling into the rushing river below. He had put the hammer in his pocket but he was encumbered by the spade that he carried over his shoulder like a gun. It was too late to change his mind and turn back now if he was to reach the farm on time.

He came to a level point where the narrow path passed in front of a black cave before winding ever higher above the tumbling stream. At the mouth of this cave he paused for breath.

Suddenly a ragged creature darted out of the cave. It so startled Eddie that he let go of the spade he was leaning on and it clattered down into the water below. He saw now that the creature was an unkempt old woman. She challenged him in a fierce cackle, "Who are you and what are you doing here?"

"I might ask the same of you," he replied, almost choked by her fetid stench. "You quite surprised me and now I have lost my spade."

"Why did you bring a spade? It is forbidden to dig up orchids and truffles."

Eddie turned his head for a moment to breathe some fresher air then faced her again. "There are no truffles here and I have no intention of stealing wild plants of any kind. I am walking up to plant trees on High Fell Farm. Or I was, when I had a spade."

On hearing this the old hag smiled a smile that contorted her wart covered face into a hideous grimace exposing her blackened teeth.

"I like it. Tree planting. That is good, young man. Wait there." She turned round and hobbled back into the cave. It was some years since Eddie had been called a young man but when the woman returned she had lost sixty years herself and stood before him, a green eyed beauty with long black hair. She was barefoot and clad in a loose, hemp frock. A delicate fragrance, like an orchard in spring replaced the lingering fumes from the old woman.

"Thou mayst well look surprised," said this apparition in a lilting but old-fashioned Cumbrian accent. "Thou wouldst be more surprised if thou didst but know that I have been waiting for thee. Forget thy old spade. Take this one. It will serve thee well."

With a warm smile she handed him a beautiful spade. A work of art. The blade and shaft were made of silver, topped with a wooden handle. Eddie recognised it as ash, a wood traditionally believed to have magical properties. The beauty of this tool made him take his eyes momentarily off the astonishing young woman. When he looked up she was gone.

Eddie could hardly comprehend what had happened. Had he suffered some kind of a stroke? Had he really seen an old witch and a young witch or the same witch? It could not have been a dream for he still held the spade: the silver spade. The young woman's sweet scent still lingered on the shaft. He shrugged, shouldered it and carried on up to the farm, lost in deep thought.

Emerging from the forest he followed the river, now little more than a stream, for another half hour that could have been a life time. When he arrived at the farm some of the volunteers were already at work.

"Welcome, Eddie," said Danny. "Glad to see you have come prepared."

"Yes."

"Don't get that lovely spade dirty," joked one of the other volunteers as its silver blade glinted in the sunlight.

Eddie was given a bunch of saplings and shown where to plant them. The site had been marked out with posts, and guards lay ready to put around the trees for protection against deer and sheep. He worked solidly for a couple of hours. The other men and women were impressed by the ease with which he sliced into the soil, rocky in places, and by his work rate. After a while they all gathered for a break in the yard. Lisbeth, the farmer's wife handed round mugs of cocoa and the man who had mocked

Eddie came up to him and said, "That's a grand spade you have there. Where did you get it?"

Eddie still had not come to terms with what had happened and replied simply, "It was a gift," and changed the subject. "Fine views from up here, aren't they?"

"Yes, you can see right over Wych Elm Forest."

Eddie shuddered at the thought of walking back down through the forest, but for now he set to work again. He was in a group set the task of planting a hedgerow at the bottom of the farmer's garden where it ran into the field.

They worked on steadily until Eddie struck something. He thought it must be a big stone and pushed hard on his spade. It was not a stone but bones of some kind. He had no time to examine them for up from the hole leapt a large black Newfoundland dog, knocking him over and bounding across the lawn towards the house.

"Where did that great bear come from?"

Indeed the dog was called Bear, for the men heard shrill laughter from the house and Lizbeth's cry, "Bear, it's never you. It is. How..."

The woman and the dog walked down to the volunteers. She was in tears, but tears of delight. "I should have warned you."

As the incredulous men listened, between her gasps of joy and incomprehension she explained that her husband had buried their dog at the bottom of the garden some years back. Eddie must have disturbed the bones.

"I'm so sorry. I didn't know."

"Nothing to be sorry about. You have brought her back to life. This," she said pointing at the dog at her side, "this is Bear."

It didn't make sense. They looked in the hole to humour the woman but found no bones.

"Well, there wouldn't be now, would there?" reasoned Eddie. He for one knew he had seen bones.

They went back to work with no further surprises. When they had finished Eddie said, "I'd best make haste before it gets dark. That path through the forest is a bit hazardous."

"Oh," said one of the men, "I'm driving back down to the village. I'll give you a lift."

Eddie gratefully accepted. The last thing they heard as they drove away was the dotty Lizbeth calling for the dog. It seemed to have disappeared again.

A few weekends later Eddie joined the group of volunteers once more. This time they were in the valley where the river was wider and flowed with a slower purpose. Most of them were planting fruit trees along the bank but Eddie and Danny were some way away digging in mature trees where there had been a landslip.

"These should stabilize it."

"Yes, in about fifty years' time perhaps," agreed Eddie. He thrust his spade into the ground and to his surprise found an obstruction. "Not more bones," he muttered hopefully, but the earth quaked.

"Watch it!" shouted Danny. "Eddie, run back. The ground is moving again."

Eddie joined Danny, scrambling onto firm ground. Neither could believe what happened next. From the landslip emerged a huge, horned head followed by its heavy body. It had the massive shoulders and stance of a bison but wider horns and smoother hair. It was still shaggier than a domestic bull, and taller. The beast eyed the men, snorted and slowly strolled off, sniffing at the grass.

"What's that?" asked Eddie

"If you ask me we have unearthed an aurochs. A live one!"

"Aurochs are extinct."

"Not this one, evidently."

"I should have taken a picture of it," said Danny, fumbling for his phone. "Where's it gone?"

"Look," said Eddie, "I don't think we should mention this to anyone. No one will believe us." He was beginning to connect this resurrection with his silver spade.

"They would if I get a picture of it." But the aurochs was nowhere to be seen and over the next few days there were no reports of escaped rare breed cattle or the like.

Eddie wanted to test his suspicion that in contact with the bones of a dead animal his spade somehow brought them to life. He knew a place where during the foot and mouth outbreak a few decades earlier, many cattle had been buried in a pit, a mass grave. The ground was thought to be contaminated and access was restricted. He waited for the next full moon, so he wouldn't need torchlight, and sneaked into the forbidden paddock carrying his silver spade. It gleamed chilly in the pale light. Eddie began to dig. He had to go some way down but eventually he felt the implement strike something solid. He leapt out of the hole he had dug just before a Friesian cow rose from the ground. As the cow wandered off into the darkness he refilled the hole and went back to bed. Presumably it would disappear soon, or some farmer would claim it. He hoped it was not still infectious.

His mind went back to the aurochs and he wondered about older animals such as woolly mammoths, dinosaurs, sabre tooth tigers. Would his spade work on bones in a museum? What a stir it would make if he could revive a tyrannosaurus rex. Or even a mammoth come to that.

Now Eddie was a simple man who liked the simple life. He did not much enjoy travelling and had no ambition for fame or fortune. There was nowt wrong with Cumbria, his garden and the fells. But even nearer home there were possibilities, and one big idea began to trouble his racing mind, a much bigger dilemma tortured him as he lay sleepless in bed. If his spade could bring animals back to life, what about human beings? He had lost both his parents. They had been cremated, their ashes scattered. But many people were buried in graves. He thought about going to the churchyard and digging up a corpse. But the same questions repeated themselves. Who? And Why? And how old would they be? For a wild second he imagined what a fortune he would make by bringing back people's loved ones. But how cruel it would be to reunite them just for a few hours. He dismissed the idea. It was sick and sickening. Besides, who was he to play God? Or the Devil for that matter? The silver spade, he decided, was a curse. The notion even crossed his mind that the witches had set him some kind of a test. Whether he had passed it or not he could not guess, but he knew what he had to do.

The very next morning Eddie marched up to Wych Elm Wood. He was carrying his spade. When he got to the cave the girl with green eyes was waiting for him, still barefoot despite the chill, but she had thrown a fleece around her shoulders.

"Thanks for the loan," he said to her, handing her back the spade.

"It was a gift," she replied in her quaint dialect, "but I knew thou wouldst bring it back."

"It is cursed," he said.

She leant towards him over the silver spade and Eddie felt her apple blossom scent sweep over him with dizzying effect.

"What dost thou wish me to do about that?" she beseeched.

"Marry me," he heard himself say and he grasped her hand. He thought he heard her whisper despairingly, "I can't," before the soft voice turned into a cackle of laughter, the scent of apple blossom was overwhelmed by a horrible stench and an eighty-year-old woman in filthy rags stood before him. In his hand he felt the witch's claw tighten its grip.

Witch Cottage

"Do you know who the parents of those two girls are?" asked David. He was drinking morning coffee in the garden of his neighbours Alice and Marcus.

The couple exchanged a puzzled look. The old man had been acting strangely recently.

"Which girls do you mean?" said Alice.

"They must be sisters or close friends. They seem to be staying in Witch Cottage. They sometimes play in the river opposite."

"Surely, David, they can't be staying in Witch Cottage. It's been empty for years. Since long before we moved here. More coffee?"

"Thanks."

Alice rose to fill his cup and David remembered that his friends had been away for the past fortnight visiting their grandchild. Witch Cottage lay along the same riverside lane as their own houses. As Marcus had pointed out it had been deserted and the garden overgrown for so long that on his daily walks around the village David, as often as not lost in his own thoughts, passed by the almost hidden cottage without a second glance.

It hadn't remained empty because of the witch who had reputedly lived there centuries ago, but because of the murders that had taken place in it more recently. It had caused a sensation at the time and no one in the know had wanted to buy the cottage. David was not even sure if it had even been put up for sale. Abandoned, it had gradually fallen into neglect.

David sipped his coffee, replaced it in the saucer and said, "Have you not been down the lane since your return from your daughter's?"

"Not yet. We only got home yesterday."

"Well," continued David, "I was passing by on my daily round the other day and there were two children, young girls, sitting just inside the front gate. They had set up a table in front of it and were selling things."

"You sure?" asked Alice.

"Yes, and what's more the path behind them to the front door had been cleared. The door was ajar, and I noticed an upstairs window was open."

"If someone has moved in," said Alice, "we should pop round and welcome them to the village."

Marcus was more sceptical. "How old were these girls?" he asked David.

"About eight or nine I should guess."

"School age, then. It's not half term yet, is it?"

"That didn't occur to me. I was curious to see what they were selling. There were paintings obviously done by themselves, some sweets, biscuits, bunches of wild flowers they must have picked from the garden or the roadside. Also some flapjacks."

"Did you buy anything?"

"Yes, to humour them. I bought a couple of flapjacks. I asked if they had made them themselves and they said yes and that would be one pound. 50p each."

"What were they like, the flapjacks," asked Alice, herself a keen baker.

"Very good," replied David. "If they are there again I will buy some more."

What he did not tell them, because he knew they thought he could be a bit of a dreamer, was the remarkable effect of those flapjacks. David had all the aches and pains of old age, though he tried to be active. That afternoon his body had been feeling heavy. At tea time he had taken his flapjacks out on to the patio that overlooked the river. He almost stumbled as he carried the tray up the stone steps, but the moment he sunk his teeth into the first of the flapjacks he relaxed. Not only did his body feel lighter but after a few more mouthfuls his anxieties, too, floated away. He felt so relaxed that he must have dozed off. When he woke the teapot was cold.

When Alice and Marcus went to check out David's story the girls were no longer there, the cottage looked as overgrown as ever. The path up to the front door was hardly discernable beneath the overhanging shrubbery. As far as they could see the door and all the windows were closed.

"Poor old David," sighed Alice, "he is losing touch with reality."

"Well," agreed her husband, "he does have an imagination. He used to write stories."

"I wonder whether he knew that two of the murder victims were young girls," mused Alice.

"Wasn't there some story that it was the girls who had killed their parents?"

"There were all kinds of rumours."

"I don't know if David ever heard them. I think he is more likely to have imagined this latest episode."

"Clearly. There is no recent sign of life in the cottage."

"What shall we say to him, then?"

"Just say the girls have gone away, I suppose. If it crops up. He might have forgotten the whole thing by now."

Almost disappointed, the couple returned to their own immaculate home and garden.

But David hadn't imagined it. Walking back from the bus shelter where he collected his Saturday newspapers he saw them again: the two girls, sitting on wooden chairs behind the table at the front gate. It was a warm, late spring day and they wore cotton frocks and straw hats like two little old ladies at a village fête. Behind them the normally sinister cottage smiled in the sunshine. It was a house much as a child might draw, with a front door dead centre and a window on either side, two upstairs windows above them and a chimney pot. To David it seemed to have been smartened up.

"Hello again," he greeted the children, examining the goods spread on the table top. This time there were shop-bought liquorice allsorts, toffees and Penguin chocolate bars. The candles, cakes and flapjacks looked homemade. "Ah, you have baked some more flapjacks," he remarked. "The ones I bought the other day were delicious."

The girls smiled and looked at one another as though daring one of them to speak.

"Would you like some even more special ones?" asked the older girl.

"Yes," added the younger child. "Ones we have kept wrapped up." From beneath the table she brought out rectangles folded in white paper napkins. They are the same price. 50p each."

"What makes them so special?"

"They are for special customers."

"And I am a special customer?"

"If you want to be."

"I am flattered. I will take a couple." He wanted to ask their names, inquire about their parents but he did not want be too familiar. These days people could be suspicious, spread nasty rumours about any adult that approached children, especially young girls. He did think that even in this friendly village there should be some parental supervision though. He handed over a pound coin. "What are you going to do with your takings?" he asked.

"We are saving up to buy back the house."

"Buy back? What do you mean?"

"This," explained the bigger girl, turning to indicate the uncurtained and apparently still empty cottage, "used to be our granny's house."

"Great granny," the other girl corrected her.

"I see," said David, though he didn't. "That would have been even before my time."

"Ours too," they piped.

"Thank you for the flapjacks. I will keep them for my tea." The girls were paying no further attention for they were re-arranging their table top. David moved off.

Between Witch Cottage and his own house he would have to pass by Marcus and Alice's home. He resolved to knock on their door and tell them the girls were back. If they went now his friends could see the girls for themselves and maybe buy something. Perhaps Alice could extract their names and get information about their parents. Only their blue electric car was not in the drive. Alice and Marcus, as was their wont, had gone out for the day.

The weather was still fine and once again David took his tea and flapjacks into the garden. The village was still and very quiet apart from the birdsong, the bleating of lambs and the tinkling of the river over the stones. He poured himself a cuppa, unwrapped and bit into the first of the flapjacks. As before, after a few mouthfuls his body felt very light. He was so relaxed he did not know whether he was floating or sinking. Then he noticed that he was more than floating. He had risen above his garden. He was flying, still clutching the flapjack. If I was in Alice in Wonderland, he thought, a bite of the other flapjack might make me descend again. But the other flapjack lay on the garden table below him. Instead he ate the rest of the one he was holding and soared higher and higher. All his worries left him and he closed his eyes.

Later that evening when Marcus and Alice returned from their outing Alice said, "I'll just look in on David. He seemed a bit odd the other day." A few minutes later she hurried back across the road to fetch her husband. "I think you had better come," she told him.

They found David lying on the ground beside the garden table on which was a half empty tea cup, a torn paper serviette and the crumbs from some kind of cake that the birds must have tucked into.

"We had better not move him," said Marcus, feeling for a pulse.

"Is he all right?"

"Let's hope he's only dreaming," replied her husband.

Voices in the Wall

Is anyone there? Can you hear me? Why does no one hear me? Get me out. Please get me out of here.

Two boys, almost young men, rucksacks on their backs, entered the abandoned farmyard from the disused track that led up to Blisterdale. They had trekked for two hours in blustery, wet weather from the main road. They needed a break.

"This looks like a good spot," said Luke, stopping alongside a derelict stone cottage past which ran the footpath. There were several other deserted buildings now tumbled down and sprouting vegetation like lost temples in a Cambodian jungle.

"It's a bit gloomy," said his companion, Marty.

"Yes, but we'll be sheltered up against the wall of that house or barn or whatever it is." In that moment the sun came out. Luke smiled and added, "It's a sun trap, too."

Marty was still doubtful. "How do we get to it through all these nettles?"

"They won't sting us through our trousers, particularly not these waterproof ones." He trampled through the green, thigh high stinging nettles, removed his backpack and sat down in the dry and sheltered porch to the cottage. Any wooden door had long since disappeared. Only the open frame remained. Marty joined him and soon the pair was sharing a flask of hot coffee and relishing the nuts and dates they had brought with them as an energy boost. Their backpacks contained food and equipment for their planned overnight stay in a bothy much further up on Nun's Peak.

"I needed that," said Luke, throwing his head back to bask in the sudden sunshine. Marty was more cautious.

"It feels eerie here," he said looking around at the ruined stone buildings, but he gradually relaxed as they soaked up the gentle warmth of the spring sunlight.

Where have you all gone? Why don't you answer me? Why don't you help?

Luke was looking at his map. "We're not doing badly," he said. "We are well into Blisterdale now. This must be the remains of Abbot's Farm. It's the last settlement before the high fells.

"And this is probably the farmhouse; all those nettles have taken over the front garden," said Marty.

"Not much of it left now," said Luke.

"Still some fruit trees. Look, there's a cherry and those I think are apple trees." Indeed the cherry tree was just coming into blossom.

"We should come this way again in the summer," suggested Luke rising to his feet to peer through the open doorway behind them. The walls were still standing and a large stone acted as a lintel above where the door would have been. Above it the second floor's stones were much looser, and crumbling. The roof had fallen in and grass and moss now covered the ground inside. Like the doors the rafters had either perished or been taken out for firewood or for use elsewhere. Another empty doorframe across the room opposite the entrance led into a wilderness of docks, tall grasses and trees.

"I don't think this can have been the main house," said Luke. "It's too small."

"Nothing much else though," said Marty, "apart from that ruined barn and those, what, sheep pens? It was probably just a small farm."

"Good position though. Sheltered, beck running through for their water supply, wonderful old trees. Just look at that enormous beech further up the track."

"Probably grown a lot since anybody lived here."

"I wonder how long ago that was."

What have I done? Let me out. Please let me out. Please. I am so cold.

For a moment the boys fell silent, caught up in the brooding atmosphere of this forsaken place. Luke noticed Marty had gone tense.

"What's up?"

"Listen. Can you hear something?"

"No."

"I thought I heard a voice, a whisper, a kind of scratching sound. As if someone is calling."

"Probably the wind in the branches. It knocks them together. Makes all kinds of odd sounds."

"Like the voice of an old woman?"

63

"Maybe."

"But I don't think it is the trees. I think the sound is coming from the inside this house."

"Don't be daft. It's empty. Not even a rabbit or a squirrel."

"You're right. Anyway rabbits don't make human noises."

"They can scream," said Luke. This was unhelpful. He had never seen his friend looking so spooked. "Come on," he added, "let's have a search, then."

"No, don't go in. Something might fall on us."

"Anything that was going to fall has already collapsed."

"The walls are still standing. And the chimney stack over the hearth."

"I will keep clear," said Luke, stepping carefully inside. Marty followed, leaving his rucksack beside Luke's on the step.

"Not many rooms, unless there was an upstairs."

The boys faced the hearth. There was an open fireplace beneath the still standing chimney. It was scarcely wide enough to have been an inglenook. On one side was a pile of fallen masonry.

"Odd," said Luke. "My great grandpa lived in a cottage a bit like this but they had a kitchen range."

"Yeah, there must have been a main house somewhere else with a proper kitchen. I think this here was just an open fire with a bread oven on the side where that heap of stone is now."

Why is no one listening? Why can't you hear me? Anyone. Someone. Get me out of here. I am so cold. It is so deathly cold.

Marty froze, "There it is again."

"I can't hear anything."

"Like a whisper in the wall."

"The walls are pretty thick, I grant you, but not thick enough to conceal a person. Only large houses had a priest hole."

"Let's get out of here."

As Marty spoke, a few stones tumbled down from the looser, top wall, dislodged by a raven that had come to investigate. It crronked thrice as it flew away. Luke was not as startled as his friend. He was thinking of treasure.

"I wonder whether anyone has ever been here with a metal detector. I bet they would find something."

"What! These people would not have been wealthy. I doubt they had any possessions other than essentials."

"There is probably an earlier history though. People might have lived on this spot for centuries before these farm buildings were erected."

Marty shrugged. "I dunno. Anyway, let's get going before we stiffen up. We've got a long climb ahead."

Luke lingered for a last look. "What's that?" he said. He pointed at something near the hearth. "Looks like a bone."

"Leave it," said Marty. "Probably some animal died in here."

Luke heaved some stones aside.

"Careful," said his friend, eyeing the chimney, still buffeted by the occasional gust of wind.

"It's a hand," exclaimed Luke.

"Nonsense," said Marty. "It's just a claw. Come on Luke, let's get out of here."

"No, look," insisted Luke, "it's tiny. It's a child's hand." He shifted more slabs.

Whether it was another strong gust of wind or Luke's disturbing the rubble at its base, first a few stones tumbled from the chimney piece and then the whole stack began to collapse.

"Get back," cried Marty pulling his friend, still absorbed in his find, away from danger.

It seemed to the boys that the following few minutes passed in slow motion. Their legs were paralysed with fear as they watched the whole edifice fall down with a dull rumble. But slow or not they just had time to leap clear, ending huddled at the other side of the room clouded in dust. The fireplace and the pile of stones beside it were now completely buried beneath this new rock fall.

"That was lucky," said Luke.

"You call that luck! We might have been buried alive!" They were both trembling with shock. "This place is cursed. I want to get right away." Marty was almost in tears.

For once his friend agreed. "So do I." They staggered out of the cottage into the clearer air. Luke mused, "I wonder how long it would have been before we were found, if we had been buried alive under all that stone. No one would have thought of looking for us there."

"Someone would have found these," said Marty, hastily shouldering his backpack. "It would have been a clue."

"Otherwise it might have been years before anyone discovered our bodies."

"Skeletons by then," laughed Marty, beginning to feel some relief at last. "Come on. Let's hope Nun's Peak is a more cheerful place."

With that the boys strode out through the stinging nettles and marched on up the path to the fells. Behind them, buried beneath the debris they did not hear a child's voice sobbing,

Daddy. I'm sorry, Daddy, let me out. I am hungry. I'm cold. Daddy. Please Daddy, let me out.

Hide and Seek

One figure stood out, remote from the group chatting in the evening sunlight on the lawn. They were relaxed after their meal and talking happily. An old man, more tired than his guests understood, detached himself from the group and walked up to the isolated figure. He put an arm around her shoulders, turned her to face him and hugged her. As he did so he felt the weight of exhaustion for a moment lift, his fear recede. He held her even tighter as though it were a matter of life or death. Tears spilled from his eyes. She was gone. Melted away like candy floss in the mouth.

"Grandpa, why are you crying?" he heard his little granddaughter asking.

"I'm not crying, love," he said, stifling a deep yawn. "I'm tired. Just very tired."

On cue her mother called from the house to the children who had been allowed to stay up and mingle with the guests.

"Time for bed Jake, Belinda. Come in now."

David walked slowly across the lawn avoiding the stragglers. He went past the fish pond and up the steps to his ocularium with its view over the river and the village green beyond. In warm weather he often sat here to drink a coffee, eat a meal or simply to contemplate. It was a quiet village. Tonight, although the sun had set the western sky had the delicate pink of the inside of certain shells.

Behind him the last of his guests were dispersing, car doors slammed, engines started and vehicles drove off. He had said his goodbyes earlier and was glad no one came to thank him again. It had anyway been mostly a family gathering and a very pleasant one, too.

He did not know how long he was lost in thought, but he was brought back again by the voice of his granddaughter. She had run out in her pyjamas with her brother to say good night.

"Good night, Belinda. Did you enjoy the party?"

"That was a party?"

"A garden party."

"Not much of a party. We didn't play any games."

"Not even hide and seek," piped up her brother.

Grandpa smiled, kissed them good night and told them to run along now. He watched them skip back indoors pausing on their way to look for frogs in the lily pond.

"I am not so sure," he thought to himself, "that some of us didn't play hide and seek."

The Witch's Grandchild

Ted had not wanted to kill anyone. Teach them a lesson, perhaps, but not kill them, especially not Mrs Quinlan, one of the few adults in the village who had exchanged kind words with him. His only consolation was that no one knew yet that he was the cause.

Ted was eight years old and lived with his grandmother, known as Old Lil, in an overgrown cottage on the edge of the village.

Old Lil had lived there for as long as most people remembered. On the few occasions she emerged she was a recognisable figure on account of her gait. She was a small but upright figure who always leaned slightly forward, holding her arms straight down in front of her as though she were pushing a wheelbarrow. Or as some whispered as though riding a broomstick. She generally wore a long, black dress over which in winter she would draw a hooded cloak. Summer and winter she wore the same stout black shoes. She kept herself to herself, not participating in the various coffee mornings and other gatherings in the village hall nor in the sewing, reading or choral groups that took place in private houses. No one knew Old Lil well, though from time to time she had shared her remedies with those who believed in herbal medicines. It was rumoured that she had once been a shepherdess but whether she was now a spinster or a widow no one could say.

It was a revelation and no little surprise when a grandson, Ted, came to live with her. If anyone knew about the boy's parents no one said anything. At least his presence forced Old Lil out into the community once more, if only to ensure that Ted got to school and back and was provided with the necessary food and clothing.

The other children in the small village school were not hostile to the newcomer but when they asked about his mum and dad he clammed up. After a while he became a loner; he was never invited to birthday parties or play dates.

One of the teachers, Miss Pink, noticed the boy was becoming withdrawn and after a while managed to win his trust. Ted walked home by himself after school. It was not far and the traffic was light. One day

Miss Pink said she was going the same way and would he mind if they walked together? Ted shrugged but his smile said yes.

The couple fell into step and their walk took them past the bus shelter. There were no longer any buses but the shelter was the social hub of the village life. It was where those who still read newspapers collected their copies, where second hand books were left and exchanged; where notices about meetings and events were pinned up or flyers for them laid out on the table. Excess produce, strawberries, plums, apples lettuces, potatoes, beans, according to the season were often left with an honesty jar for donations. Sometimes there were even extravagant gifts: on Mother's Day one generous villager left slices of fruit cake for any mother to help herself to; at Easter she baked simnel cake for the taking and at Christmas individual puddings. Even Old Lil had been known to sell her hen's eggs there when they laid more than she needed.

"Let's see what's in the bus shelter today," said Miss Pink to Ted as they passed by. There was nothing except for a pile of Parish magazines. "No goodies today, alas,"

"Sometimes there are sweets," said Ted.

"Perhaps you could leave something," suggested Miss Pink.

"How?"

"Make some cards. Bring something from your garden. Does your Gran like gardening?"

Ted did not answer this but he was thinking, "I could make some cookies and collect money for the animal sanctuary."

"Can you cook?"

"You know I can. We did cookery at school. Anyway Granny can help me."

This is how it all started, with the most innocent of intent.

The idea of raising money reminded Miss Pink of something else and she asked Ted, "Will you be coming on the sponsored walk next week?"

"I can't."

"Can't! Why not?"

"I've got no one to sponsor me. I don't know any grown-ups except for old Mrs Quinlan and she is not rich."

"That doesn't matter, Ted. It's the walking that counts. Doing something for a good cause. No one knows how much each individual collects."

"Unless they boast about it," said Ted. The pair walked on in silence. Ted's thoughts returned to good causes. Before he and Miss Pink parted ways he said, "I think I will make some brownies for the bus shelter."

70

"Save one for me," smiled Miss Pink. She was pleased to see that Ted had more of a spring in his step after their chat.

After tea Ted asked his grandmother how you make chocolate brownies.

"It's quite easy, love. I'll show you."

"But I need to make them myself."

"So you shall," she said, stroking Blackie the cat that was sitting on her lap, "but first you must learn how. I didn't know you were so keen on brownies."

"They are for the bus shelter," he explained.

Next day on his return from school he found on the kitchen table eggs from the hens in the jungle that was their garden, butter made from their own goat's milk, sugar, flour and cocoa powder.

"What's all this for?" he asked.

"Brownies," answered his Gran.

The project was a success. Ted had not wanted to be seen leaving the brownies in the shelter. Only Miss Pink would know he was the baker. He slipped in early on his way to school to set his wares out on a tray with a sign saying, "For the animal sanktry."

On his way home after school he saw that all the brownies had gone and the jar was full of coins. Some pedant had even corrected his spelling. He gave the money to his Gran.

"Well, we can't afford to do that too often, but well done. You can do another batch next week perhaps."

Before Ted got round to baking his second batch the school walk took place. Ted had no particular friend to walk with and he lagged behind, lost in his own world. Billy, a big fat boy and a bully in the playground, was also finding it hard to keep up on a proper walk on account of his bulk. He was tiring and sweaty and this made him bad-tempered. He took his discomfort out on Ted.

"What are you doing, witch's boy? Can't keep up?"

"Don't call me that, Fatso. Of course I could keep up if I wanted to. I am not fat and lazy like you."

Noticing that the main group was indeed a long way ahead he tried to hurry on, but Billy blocked his path. Ted pushed him aside, the bully lost his balance and toppled into the ditch. He tried to save himself by grabbing the barbed wire fence and gashed his arm badly as he fell. His shrieks had the teachers running back. Miss Pink was shocked to see one of her pupils lying in the mud all covered in blood."

"What happened?"

"The witch's boy pushed me," cried the fat boy who was twice Ted's size.

Ted was furious. "I said don't call me that," and he kicked Billy who was still on the ground. Ted felt Mr Mallow, the other teacher, take him by the elbow and firmly pull him away.

"Enough of that, Ted. Leave him be."

"He said… he said," but Ted could not get the words out. Before either of the teachers could stop him he was running back the way he had come. A law unto himself.

Billy's parents made a fuss but they had had to face issues before over their son's behaviour and they were persuaded to let the matter drop when the head warned them that any further hurtful language by their son would not be tolerated. He also said he would speak to Ted's grandmother and ask her to buy Billy a new shirt if he would apologize to Ted for the way he had spoken to him. Billy's parents doubted they could make their son apologize. They said the torn shirt did not matter.

By the time of the parent teacher evening the incident on the walk would have been forgotten. True, when Old Lil arrived dressed in black and pushing her invisible wheelbarrow some of the children, led on by Billy, tittered.

"Look," whispered the fat boy loudly enough to be heard. "It's the old witch."

Lil turned and walked right up to the rude boy. He froze, as did his gang. But the old woman said nothing, she just gave the bully a piercing look that made his blood run cold. After a few long seconds she turned and walked on into the classroom to meet up with her grandson.

"She gave you the evil eye," gasped one of Billy's acolytes. Billy remained speechless.

The teachers told Ted's Gran that they were pleased with Ted's work and that his attitude was improving too. No mention was made of the incident on the charity walk.

"Ted doesn't tell me his troubles," said Old Lil, "but I know certain children make fun of him. You should teach them some manners." Whereupon she got up, smoothed down her long skirt and said, "Come on, Ted, let's get along home."

Ted made another successful batch of brownies, and then some weeks later Miss Pink took her class out on a nature walk. She asked Ted to stay near her for fear of another fight because Billy and some of his friends were unwilling participants in the same group. The children followed a footpath across the meadow behind the school and down into the woods. Miss Pink asked the children to collect leaves and to identify the trees they came from. Ted thought this was too easy.

"Why can't we look for something interesting?" he asked her.

"Such as?"

"Hedgehogs, red squirrels, dormice."

Miss Pink agreed this was a good idea but today they were to concentrate on trees and plants. Suddenly she noticed something and cried out in alarm,

"Jenny! Stop!" The girl had plucked a shiny black berry from a plant with bright purple flowers and popped it in her mouth. "Spit it out. Quick!" Jenny did as she was told but the teachers panic frightened her and she started to cry.

"She's right, Jenny," said Ted, trying to comfort the girl. "Miss Pink has just saved your life."

The teacher recovered quickly and reassured the girl she had done nothing wrong.

"Except," said Ted with surprising authority as the others gathered round, "that is belladonna, or deadly nightshade. One berry could kill you."

"Cool," said the fat boy, taking an interest at last.

"Thank you, Ted," said Miss Pink "no need to scare Jenny any more." And to the girl, "You'll be fine, Jenny. Just rinse out your mouth with this." She passed her a bottle of water to swig.

Since she now had the full attention of her group Miss Pink said, "Children, I think we can learn from this. Deadly nightshade is not the only dangerous plant. Can you think of any others?"
This was better than identifying leaves.

"Stinging nettles," said one boy.

"They don't kill you though," said Ted. "Foxgloves are poisonous."

"Indeed," agreed Miss Pink. "I'm sure you all know what foxgloves look like. They are pretty but should not be handled."

There was a brief discussion about foxgloves, where they could be found and how they might harm you. Ted resisted the temptation to tell them about the potions that could be made from them. Someone brought up toadstools and Miss Pink said that perhaps they should have a lesson in the Autumn to learn what were edible mushrooms and which other fungi were poisonous.

"What's fungi."

"Toadstools," said Ted "Mushrooms, too."

"They are all fungi," said Miss Pink. "Now anything else we might find at this time of the year?"

Ted put his hand up.

"Yes, Ted?"

"Wolfsbane is deadly, too."

"Can you describe it?"

"It's quite tall," said Ted holding his hand about chest level. "The flowers are blue. You can use the sap to poison arrow heads," he added.

Miss Pink was astonished. "How do you know that?"

"My Granny told me. She showed me how to extract it. She calls the plant the Devil's Helmet."

"Is that," piped up Fat Billy, "because she's a witch."

"Puts it in her brew with frogs and newts," laughed his friend, displaying surprising Shakespearean knowledge for his age.

Ted flew at both boys. Miss Pink fought to separate them. Jenny began to cry again.

Before the children went home that afternoon the head teacher called an assembly and addressed them all. He gave them a stern talking to about bullying and name calling and how they should all respect one another. All the children were there except for Ted who had run off home straight from the woods.

"It was not Ted's fault," Miss Pink had explained. The Head kept Billy in and telephoned his mother to pick him up. He told her he had given her son several warning previously, as she knew, and that now he had no choice but to exclude him from school for a week.

There was another plant that sharp-eyed Ted had noticed when he ran away from the nature walk. Growing in marshy land by the weir he recognised hemlock masquerading as cow parsley. His Grandma had warned him about that, too, and described its uses. She had told him the story of an ancient Greek philosopher called Socrates who was sentenced to death by drinking a solution containing hemlock.

"But you don't need to make a drink of it," she told her grandson. "The seeds are poisonous enough."

74

Ted remembered this when he returned home distraught. Old Lil sensed something was wrong.

"What's up, love? Have they been picking on you again?"

"I'm fine."

"Something happened."

"Miss Pink saved Jenny Roberts' life." He told her about the plants but made no mention of the fight.

"Well, good for Miss Pink. Children should be taught these things." Just then the telephone rang and Old Lil hobbled over to answer it.

"Yes, he's back. No he's fine. Thank you." To Ted she said, "The school just wanted to know if you got home. Someone cares for you, Ted." She asked no further questions.

Billy's words still rankled with Ted, who wondered how he might get his revenge on the fat boy. He knew that Billy's mother was one of the customers for his brownies and guessed they might eat them with their tea after school. All he had to do was to poison them slightly. That a few other customers might also fall sick did not really register in Ted's mind. His main concern was that no one should trace the poison back to the bus shelter. He decided only to make a small batch of brownies and not to set them out until he was on his way home from school. He was sure he could get to the shelter before Billy's mum came to collect him in her car. He wondered what they would think if they knew who had actually cooked the brownies.

A few days later, instead of going straight home, Ted slipped down to the marsh and gathered some hemlock seed in a paper bag. When he came to bake the brownies he ground the seeds in the pepper mill and sprinkled them in with the flour and cocoa powder, adding a little brown sugar to conceal the taste.

When several children, including Fat Billy did not come to school in the morning Ted guessed his plan had worked. What he had not witnessed, however, was the effect his brownies had had on Mrs Quinlan, the old widow who always greeted him kindly and let him pet her dog on his way to or from school. She was asthmatic and breathed heavily at the best of times. The previous evening after her supper she finished with a brownie swilled down with hot chocolate. Almost at once she felt queasy. Unaccountably she began to dribble and her eyes became wide and staring as though she had seen a ghost. She tried to rise from her chair to call for help but she could not move. She managed to pull her telephone from her pocket but struggled to punch in 999. By the time she managed it her speech was so slurred that the operator could not understand her. With a supreme effort the widow repeated her name and address. When the ambulance arrived they found her on the floor still clutching the phone in a rigid fist.

Ted was asleep at home and did not see the blue lights flashing past his house. It was assumed that Mrs Quinlan died from respiratory failure and no post mortem was thought necessary. The poisoning therefore remained undetected. The few sick children and other victims were on their feet again in a couple of days. The received wisdom was that they had suffered some mild viral infection. No one connected it to the offerings in the bus shelter because no investigation was made.

Whether or not Old Lil had heard about the sickness and indeed of the death of Mrs Quinlan, she made no mention of it to her grandson. She did notice that his mood was a mixture of elation and concern.

She was not surprised when he asked her, "Granny, can you cast spells?"

Instead of being cross or indeed, of feeling insulted by the insinuation that she might be a witch after all, she simply gave Ted a piercing look.

"No more or less than you," she replied and Ted knew that she knew what he had done.

"And are all spells bad?" he asked.

"Look, Ted. The word spell supposes magic and that is nonsense. Knowledge is more powerful than magic. After all, it scared God. He did not want Eve to pluck the fruit of knowledge, did he?"

"Who is Eve?"

"Goodness, boy, don't they teach you anything in that Church of England School? She was Adam's second wife, created for him after Lilith left him."

"Why did she leave him?"

"She was stubborn. She did not want to be told what to do by God or by a man."

"Like you, Grandma. You are Lilith, too."

"That's as maybe. The point is that knowledge can be used for good or for evil. That's where your parents went wrong, lad and they paid the price. I have always tried to be a healer. I don't know if you have inherited the gift but if you have you should use it wisely."

"Granny," he said aghast, "Granny, do you think I have messed up?"

"We all make mistakes. Sometimes they are found out, sometimes not. Let's hope you will be given a second chance."

Topless

He was a giant of a man. Since the English did not correctly pronounce his name, Bjørn to rhyme with burn, but called him Bjørn rhyming with born, he translated his name to Bear, which is what it means. Ironically the Norwegian could not himself pronounce Bear correctly in English: it came out as beer. It was not long before his confused friends in the village gave him instead the nickname of Ogre, on account of his size.

Every morning he walked his dog Snowdrop along the river bank through the village from where he lived in a static caravan just outside. The dog was a tiny, white creature that he could and sometimes did hold in the palm of his hand. He never let it off the lead because it seemed not to heed his commands, but the lead was a very long one that could be wound in.

David, who often observed the pair from his ocularium, the raised garden patio overlooking the river, always thought Ogre was like a fly fishermen casting off his dog and every so often reeling it back in. One day as he returned along the river bank with the newspaper he had collected from the bus shelter, David caught up with Ogre and fell into step with him. The dog took no notice of either of them but ran rings around their legs, causing them to stop and extricate themselves from the lead.

Neither commented on the experience since it had become commonplace. More unusual was the question Ogre put to David as they walked on,

"Have you heard these stories about the topless woman?" he inquired.

"No. Not likely to find anyone topless this weather, man or woman."

"No, I do not mean topless, bare breasted" (He pronounced it beer breasted which made David smile to himself) "I mean really topless."

"I don't get you," replied David, wondering if Ogre was referring to mastectomy.

"Topless. No top."

"What? Was she carrying her head under her arm or something."

"Worse than that, from what I have heard."

"Ogre, what on earth are you talking about? Have you seen this woman?"

"Not personally, but everyone is talking about it." He wound the lead in and picked up the little dog. It did not seem to mind, now that it had done its sniffing and shitting.

The two men walked on, David clutching his newspaper to his chest, Ogre with the dog in his fist.

"It's not like you, Ogre, to make jokes like this."

"I am not joking. I am just telling you what I heard in the pub last night. Several people have seen a woman walking about the village but she has no body from the waist up. Just the waist down and walking."

"How do they know it's a woman?"

"In all the sightings she is wearing a long, black robe."

"Could be a priest or a monk."

"That would be even more unusual, to see a curé or a monk in this village. It's not the South of France."

"Well," suggested David, perhaps an LGBTQ plus."

"I say, you are very woke. I think we would know who the cross dressers are and 'they', note the pronoun, would not go about topless."

"Me, woke? You have been eating too much tofu," laughed his friend.

"I don't even know what tofu looks like."

The pair had reached the footbridge where they parted ways, David to cross over to his riverside cottage, Ogre to return to his caravan. As a parting shot David asked, "What's the explanation then?"

"Come down to my place for coffee later and I will tell you my theory."

Back in his own house David gave no further thought to this conversation. He went into his study and browsed through his newspaper for half an hour or so. Then, as he was clearing the breakfast things from the sink he remembered Ogre's invitation to morning coffee and his apparent need to continue his mad story about the topless woman, as he had described her.

David was more puzzled as to why his friend was so taken up with the rumours than any suggestion that a topless woman prowled the village. Perhaps Ogre was cracking up, his large frame cooped up too long in the single room of a caravan with a dog the size of a bumble bee. David strode off to have his morning coffee with the odd couple.

Inside the caravan the smell of freshly ground, roasted coffee created a pleasant miasma even before it began percolating.

"Take a seat, David," said Ogre. "Snowdrop does not like to be disturbed," he added, although the dog seemed to occupy the only comfortable seat. David perched on a camping chair at the table. As the two men warmed their hands on the bowls and sipped the hot coffee in contentment, Ogre broke the amicable silence.

"Did you know that in the old days a mill race had sluiced through your end of the village? It turned a large water wheel at the site of Mill House."

"Yes," said David. "The wheel has gone and the house is just another holiday let."

"Did you know about the accident there?"

"Can't say I have heard about it, no. What, some drunken tourist fell down the stairs?"

"No, this was a hundred years ago when the mill was working. One morning while the mill race was running high and fast after a night of heavy rain the miller stepped out to raise the wheel believing the flood water might damage it. Before he could do so a young woman who had slipped into the race further upstream was swept past him and crashed into the wheel. The wheel was still turning and it sliced the woman in half."

David said he had never heard that story and did not believe it either. A wooden wheel would not sever anyone like that. He reckoned someone had made up the story to justify the so-called hauntings by the topless woman, if haunting they thought it was.

Ogre looked embarrassed. "Sorry, just a theory of mine. Actually I made up that story myself in order to try and explain all the sightings."

The coffee had cooled down. David tilted his bowl and took a big gulp, almost emptying it. He looked across the table at the big Norwegian.

"So this whole topless thing was just a ruse to get me over to enjoy your coffee? It's very good coffee by the way," he said, offering his bowl for a refill.

Ogre poured out more, protesting, "No, I did not make the topless woman up. Only the mill story. People really think they have seen her. That is what is so extraordinary. I was trying to imagine why."

"Not very rational if you re-invent her as a ghost, though," mused David.

"Better than thinking half the village has succumbed to a loss of reason."

"Well, they voted Brexit," laughed David, though the national suicide had itself been no laughing matter.

David returned home and thought no more about Ogre's concerns for a day or two. Then other people kept talking about the topless girl as she had now become known.

Again, returning with his newspaper, he met Gladys, a little octogenarian. "What do you make of it, David?" she asked, clinging on like a water skier behind her two dogs that together were double her own weight.

"Make of what?"

"The topless girl. Haven't you heard?" she said, bringing her enthusiastic dogs to a stop.

"Oh yes. Several people have mentioned it," he said nonchalantly. "I shall be more convinced when I meet someone who has actually seen this woman for themselves. It is always someone who knows someone who has seen her."

"Yes, I know, but so many different people tell the same story. It's spooky," she added before her dogs dragged her off again.

The rumours continued to spread like a pandemic. A topless WhatsApp group was set up but its members were hunters, not eye-witnesses. As far as David could ascertain no one had actually seen the phenomenon at first hand. He was surprised that so many people really believed the apparition existed. The next time he met up with the Big Norwegian, Ogre had a new theory. If not an epidemic it was some kind of hysteria. He likened it to those cases that sometimes occur in girls' schools, for example, when whole classes all start fainting, or the historical case of the Salem witch trials in the late 1600s when scores of women were accused of being witches by a gullible or hysterical public.

"No one in this village, though," objected David, "is accusing anyone else of roaming around topless."

"It won't be long," said Ogre.

Despite his scepticism even David took to sitting on his ocularium in the evening to look out over the river and the Green, scrutinising the shadows. He never saw anything stranger than sheep, or if he sat out long enough, bats and owls.

Call it some kind of psychological epidemic, mass hysteria or the wishful thinking of the ungodly, it came to an end in a shocking manner. A shot of reality in the arm dispelled the wishy washy speculation that probably no one had believed deeply.

Two steep roads led down to the southern side of the village nestling at the bottom. Both were twisty and one of them, Snake Slope Lane, was not only very narrow but contained no fewer than three entrances to different farmyards along its two mile stretch. Although this lane was the most direct route out to the great beyond most car drivers in the know would use the longer, wider route to avoid herds of cattle, flocks of sheep, tractors and other traffic. Only tourists, strangers and white delivery vans using their satnavs were sent this way and cyclists, thinking it quieter, chose it of their own accord.

One fateful day about three weeks into the topless mania a young couple who were on a cycling holiday passed this way. The hill was steep but as experienced cyclists they did not need to dismount. They merely put their bikes in the lowest gears and ascended the hill with just enough momentum to stop them toppling.

A young agricultural student at High Farm had been asked to take an empty trailer down to Marsh Wood at the bottom of the lane and fetch some logs that had been sawn ready for collection. He had told the farmer he knew how to drive, the farmer had hitched on the long, heavy trailer and said, "I'll be down with the loader in ten minutes."

The older man had second thoughts when he saw how clumsily the lad drove out of the farmyard, not even pausing when he turned into the road, almost taking the gate post with him. He tried to call him back but the lad did not hear him. He was learning that driving a tractor, was very different from driving a car, particularly in the matter of stopping. He had not learned how to use the engine to slow down rather than just braking as you might do in a car.

He lost control and careered recklessly round the steep corners of Snake Slope Lane, trying to find how best to reduce speed. The tractor and trailer took up the whole width of the road but, having swung round two bends the student thought he was getting the hang of it. A second after rounding another blind bend, there in front of him were two cyclists struggling up the hill. They were going too slowly to be able to swerve clear. The tractor driver slammed on the brakes as hard as he could and turned into the hedge on his left. The shock threw him from his cab, the trailer jackknifed and overturned. The male cyclist dived into the ditch but his companion was not so lucky. The metal trailer came down on top of her, one sharp edge slicing her in two.

"There was an awful lot of blood," Ogre told David when he recounted hearing the crash and hurrying up to the scene. "Snowdrop's paws were quite red." Of course Ogre did what he could but because there was no mobile phone signal he had to hurry up to the farm with its own telephone to call for help.

Although the cyclists were not known to anyone locally the whole village fell into shock after this gruesome accident. Not only was the girl killed horribly but two other young lives were changed forever. It should never have happened and there followed many recriminations. There was only one positive outcome: unsurprisingly, after this horrendous experience felt by all, no one made mention of the topless woman again; neither were there any more sightings of her reported.

Get Thee

David was walking back from the bus shelter from which he had picked up his newspaper when he noticed a woman of about his age walking away along the river bank. Two things were unusual: she was not from the village, but then many hikers passed through; the striking thing was her gait. She prowled almost. In her seventies, he guessed and with a slight stoop, yet there was something feline about the way she put her feet down; something he had not seen for fifty years but which brought back to him, here in his retirement in Cumbria, those few distant but intense days... Unless of course he was mistaken.

He hurried to catch up with the woman, who was wearing light walking boots, black waterproof trousers, a pale blue quilted anorak and grey gloves. On her head she wore a matching blue bobble hat. Although it was spring a cold wind chilled the air. The beck was running fast. Over the sound of the water he called out, "Dr Brown?"

On hearing her name the woman paused and turned, "Professor Brown, actually," she said with a smile.

"Anita!"

"Yes," she said, puzzled by this old man clutching The Guardian, and equally well wrapped against the elements.

"You probably don't remember me. We taught together once, on a seminar in India."

Wiping the wind-blown tears from her eyes she scrutinised him and for a moment David thought she was going to faint. He reached to take her arm but she gasped, "No, I'm all right. David! You quite took me by surprise."

"Yes."

What she said next also took David by surprise. Not so much the sentiment as the mixture of passion and regret in her voice. "How could I ever forget you?"

"Well, it's been a long time. A life time."

Under the grey sky they walked on side by side. Professor Brown, now retired, was staying a few days in an airbnb in the neighbouring village and had set out for an early morning walk. David pointed out his riverside cottage just across the footbridge and invited his once, albeit short time colleague in for a coffee.

"Too cold to sit out," he said as they passed through his garden. They removed their hats, coats and shoes in his porch and he led her into the warmth of his kitchen.

"I'm surprised you recognized me," she said, settling down at the oak table while David measured out the coffee. "Especially from behind, and so wrapped up."

"And between us both, a hundred years older," he agreed. "It is the way you walk, Anita. You still have a lightness of step. It's the way you moved that first attracted me to you."

"So you did find me attractive," she breathed, almost to herself.

They had both been visiting lecturers on a course for teachers in a rural college in Kerala, South India. David could not remember how they had got there but he could still picture the lush green surroundings and, surprisingly for bustling India a quietness, pierced only by birdsong. He did remember that they had arrived together and most clearly her first lecture. She had not been to India before and had been nervous about how to pitch her delivery. She had asked David to sit in, partly as back-up if needed, but also for his feedback afterwards.

That lecture made an unforgettable impression on David. Not what she was saying, something about linguistics he thought, but her manner. Wearing a simple, white cotton frock and sandals she prowled about the rostrum in front of her enthralled audience, most of whom had never seen such an unblemished, pale skin, either. Restless, electric, she was a caged white panther. David was as mesmerized as the class she was addressing.

Afterwards she asked him, "How do you think it went?"

"You were excellent," he replied, still dazed and under the spell of this energetic creature.

"Do you think they understood?"

"I don't know."

"You're not much use, then, are you?" she mocked.

"I am star struck," he confessed. He did not invite her to sit in on his own pedestrian lectures. He felt inadequate.

What stuck in his memory even more than this vivid picture was the one night, or was it more, in their accommodation.

Sitting drinking coffee in David's kitchen on another continent in another age the couple did not immediately reminisce on old times. David told

Anita how he had spent decades at his peripatetic career in many countries before retiring to the North of England. He spoke of his family. In reply, Anita told him she had returned from India to her university where she continued an academic career with a spell in the United States. She had now retired to Oxford and did no further research or teaching. She had no family.

As they spoke, cradling their mugs of coffee, David looked into her face and wondered whether he would have recognized her now, had they been sitting opposite one another on a train for example. Her once black hair was now a natural grey, she wore no make-up then or now, and her face had become quite lined. But those inquisitive, green eyes were just the same, lively and intelligent. Perhaps due to her walk in the cold air her cheeks were rosy. The old woman at the table still bore the palimpsest of the young, prowling panther.

"Do you think," he asked, interrupting her account of some academic intrigue, "that you would have recognized me had we simply passed one another on the river bank just now?"

"Almost certainly not," she admitted. "But sitting down here together the intervening years have rolled away. You seem quite familiar."

"Sometimes it is a shock to meet an old school or university friend you have not seen for a long time," he said. "Men in particular lose their hair and run to fat."

"Neither of us has done that," she observed. "But it was a shock when you called my name just now."

"I'm sorry."

"David, I have never stopped thinking of you. Well, that's not quite true, but I do often think of India. Of what might have been."

This heartfelt remark silenced David for a moment. After a pause for reflection he asked, taking her hand, "Did it mean so much?"

"If you have to ask that," she replied, gently withdrawing her hand, "then clearly it did not mean as much to you."

She was referring to the evening of their first full day, the evening after that first lecture, when Anita had fled to him from her accommodation. On arrival the previous day David had been delighted with their rooms. Visiting lecturers had been put up, each in their own single cabin. To call it a chalet would be too much, but each rest house was set in a shady garden of sorts. The cabins contained a bed with a mosquito net over it, a desk, a lamp and a single chair and there were toilet facilities en suite. He could not remember whether there had been a shower, more likely a copper bowl with which to fling cold water over oneself to cool off. There was also a ceiling fan, essential in that climate. For David, used to travel in India, it was more than sufficient.

In the morning, as they walked over to the college together, David asked Dr Brown how she had slept.

"Not a wink," was her reply. "I was scared stiff and suffocating from the heat. I thought I heard things moving around my bed, too."

"Did you not switch on your fan?"

"No. I did not realise…"

"That would have blocked out any other sound. I find it soothing as well as cooling."

"Be that as it may, I got up and found that rats or something had eaten my soap. It had tooth-marks on it."

"I'm sorry to hear that."

Their conversation was cut short as they were greeted by the college principal and handed their agenda for the week.

Back in the present David asked, "Do you still have nightmares about those rooms?"

"Where they expected us to sleep?" She nodded with a shudder.

"I liked them. I liked the privacy, the stillness. But you were very nervous, weren't you?"

Anita studied David incredulously, not believing he did not remember. "I came to you that second night."

"I know, I know," he quickly reassured her. "How could I forget? I often think about it even now."

"Even though nothing happened?"

"You were gorgeous, Anita. Excuse the cliché. And I would not say nothing happened."

That second night indeed, as David was preparing for bed there had been a knock, or rather a timid scratching on his door. Half expectant, certainly curious, he opened it to find Dr Brown standing in the night, barefoot and wearing silk pyjamas. Her face was framed in the black hair that hung down to her shoulders.

"May I come in?" she whispered, not waiting for an answer. Catlike she slunk across the floor and sat in the only chair, turning to face him with big, frightened eyes.

"Goodness, what a vision!" he said. At least this made her laugh.

"David, I'm scared."

86

"Really, there's nothing to worry about. Did you switch on your fan this time? Good. So get under your mosquito net and you could not be more comfortable for the night." He did not say that he thought she would be a lot cooler if she took off her pyjamas.

"It's not just the mosquitoes. It's not just the rats and the humidity."

"What is it then?" He would have offered her a drink but there was nothing alcoholic, only the kettle and leaf tea that every lodge contained. "I don't know how I can help you," he lied.

"Don't you?" she implored, fixing him again with those eyes.

"I understand that you are frightened. I am scared too about where this may lead. I don't even know whether you are Dr Miss Brown or Dr Mrs Brown."

"Just now I am Anita," she replied.

"Come here, then." She stood to accept his embrace. He kissed her on the forehead and released her. "Is that better?"

"Better than nothing." She pulled herself together. "I am sorry I have disturbed you."

Indeed, David felt very disturbed. Aroused would be a better word for it. He did not know what to do. He looked around the room seeking inspiration. Anita was struck by a sudden realisation.

"Are you expecting someone? Someone else?"

"Of course not."

"Anyway," she hesitated. "I am sorry."

"Let me walk you home."

She laughed, "It's only ten paces. I expect you could hear me scream from here."

"Let's hope you will have nothing to scream about." He took her by the hand and she meekly followed him to her door which she had left ajar in her haste to escape. He went in with her to check there were no intruders. Finishing his inspection he said, "It is quite safe. Shall I tuck you in?"

"No thanks, but you may give me a goodnight kiss."

Extracting himself from that kiss, a proper grown-up kiss, was the most difficult thing David had ever forced himself to do.

"Good night. Sleep well, Anita."

Back in his own bed in his own room he asked himself why he had not stayed if only to comfort her. But that was precisely not the kind of comfort he had wanted to give, much as though she would have welcomed it. Yes, it was the 1960s when everyone is supposed to have slept with everyone. Perhaps they would sleep together eventually. He hoped so. But not under these circumstances when she was vulnerable, disturbed. What would she have thought of him weeks later? That he had taken advantage, used her? It was not until fifty years later that he learned that his scruples had been unnecessary.

Refusing another cup of coffee but feeling relaxed in David's cosy kitchen, Anita yawned, stretched and said, "David?"

"Yes."

"Do you remember when I came to your room that night and you sent me back to my own bed?"

"I wouldn't put it quite like that."

"You were expecting someone else, weren't you? One of those Indian girls. I overheard you earlier talking to the night watchman about their availability."

"Yes, he was offering me girls. Or boys, as I preferred. He did that with all his male guests. Females, too, for all I know."

"And what did you tell him?"

"Look, Anita," he said angrily, "there are plenty of very poor but attractive girls offering their services. There is nearly always a doorman or a receptionist prepared to pimp for them. But if it was female flesh I had wanted to sink into I would have chosen yours. A far healthier proposition."

"Oh, thanks a bundle!"

"I do not wish to sound brutal, but sleeping with one of those poor girls would have been risking one's own sexual health."

"And you were also married."

"No. Not then. I married later and lost my wife later still."

"So why did you reject me so cruelly? Was I so unattractive?"

David explained that he had not wanted to take advantage of a damsel in distress. He added that he had hoped to make a move later if she had still been interested. "Only the next night you did not return to your room. You had disappeared."

"Yes. Remember Sister Catherine? She was on the staff. She came from a teaching order and wore ordinary Western clothes, but she lived with a community of nuns. She took pity on me and said I could move in with them for the duration."

"Oh yes, I remember Sister Catherine. She had been in India for twenty-five years but still spoke with a Lancastrian accent. Quite severe with her students."

"She was a kind woman."

"Except that she stole you from me." There was another short silence as the pair of them reflected on the seminar. "Thou gottest thyself to a nunnery, sadly."

"Yes, and then events rather took over. We had little time to ourselves once the programme was under way and in the evenings I had to return and dine with the nuns."

"So you were not deliberately avoiding me?"

"Far from it. I was desperate for an evening with you outside the teaching schedule."

"And here's me thinking you had taken offence. I don't know what I thought actually. It was such a long time ago. You know, Anita, I don't quite remember how it all ended."

Anita gave him another of her searching looks. She was not going to remind him of the hasty goodbyes, the scramble for the airport. Instead she asked, "Has it ended?"

"Us you mean? I hope not."

Anita smiled and stood up. "I must not outstay my welcome, though." She walked towards the door followed by David.

"The porch is this way."

As she was pulling on her boots she said, "You should come and visit me in Oxford."

"I'd love to," he said, and helped her on with her jacket. Before he opened the back door to a break in the clouds he added, "Meanwhile, what are you doing tonight, Professor?"

"Whatever you like, sir," she purred.

Water Dog

Why was Katie's car hidden under the wild maple at the far end of the village? Had he not recognised her Mini Cooper David should have thought it stolen and abandoned. His curiosity getting the better of him, he retraced his steps back along the river that ran through the Cumbrian village. He crossed the footbridge opposite his garden, passed his own house and paused a hundred yards downstream outside Katie and Craig's riverside cottage. Craig's rescue Land Rover was not there, either. All the windows in the house were closed and when David knocked on the door there was no reply, no dog barked.

Odd, he thought. If they had gone away it could not have been in Katie's car. Besides he knew she was practising for a concert. Because of the coronavirus, indoor events were few but the Appleby brass band was scheduled to play on the village green, a summer concert for all to enjoy in the open air. Katie would not be one to miss that.

David often chatted with Katie or Craig when they walked their dog past his garden gate that opened on to the river. Rosa was a brown Portuguese water dog, a large, web-footed bitch with a tail like a rudder. She loved the river and would retrieve anything thrown in it. On the last occasion David had spoken to Katie she had told him Rosa was expecting puppies.

"She will certainly earn her keep," she said as the dog shook itself, its long, curly hair spraying them with water. "People will pay a great deal for puppies these days."

"I suppose they get lonely during lockdown."

"Yes, but I will make sure the puppies only go to good homes."

That had been some weeks ago, since when he had seen no Rosa and no Katie nor Craig. Not that he was looking out for them. A lot went on in this village, but he was soon to find out how much more than he suspected.

David returned home still wondering where Katie and Craig had gone and made himself a pot of tea. This he carried out to his ocularium, a raised patio that looked down over the river and the footpath alongside it.

He noticed a figure hurrying by, head covered in a light cagoule. He recognised her by her gait.

"Katie?" he called over the stone wall. This startled her but she paused and smiled a hello. "I wondered where you were. The cars…"

"Not here," she said. "I'll come round the back."

Surprised at her cloak and dagger response David met her at his rear gate.

"I've just made a pot of tea."

"I'd love a cup, but can it be somewhere less public?"

Soon they were installed beneath the apple trees well out of sight of callers or passers-by.

"How long were you sitting out there?" she asked. "Have you seen Craig?"

He told her he had only just brought the tea out and went indoors for another cup and some biscuits. While they drank and nibbled she told him her story.

Rosa had given birth to seven healthy puppies. After a few days Katie had found them so adorable she could not resist posting pictures of the litter on Facebook.

"But you had homes for them already," David remembered.

Katie thought she had posted only to friends and family but it was after that that her trouble started. A day or two later there had been a knock on her door. A rough looking man with a Scots accent said he had come for the puppies. Said he would take the lot. Taken aback Katie told him they were not even weaned from their mother yet. The man tried to push past her.

"What are you doing?"

"I want to see them."

"No," she told him. "This is not a good time."

When he persisted, she screamed and tried to block his way. At that moment Craig drove up, back early from his mountain rescue duties. He wondered why a white van was parked outside his house and, as he got out of his Land Rover, he heard the scuffle. He rushed to the door and grabbed the intruder.

Faced with someone his own size and in rather better shape, the thug backed down. He made no apology for his behaviour but slunk back to his van. As he drove off he shouted, "I'll be back for them when they are ready."

"Get his number, Craig."

Craig thumbed the registration number into his phone and hurried back inside to his shocked wife.

"What was that all about? Did he hurt you?"

She told Craig what had happened and admitted it was silly to have put the pictures up on Facebook.

"Ah well, we've probably seen the back of him. Nasty piece of work."

Nevertheless, as a precaution Craig reported the incident to the police. Being a member of the mountain rescue team he knew many of them personally. He was surprised, however, when Beth phoned back, asked if he and Katie would be home for a while and said she would be with them shortly

"Meanwhile, do not leave the house," she advised.

"Why…?"

"I'll explain."

Beth was the modern version of the local bobby, in that she drove round villages on her patch, attended coffee mornings, fund raising events and other gatherings to get to know as many people as possible. She also knew Craig through his work.

"This is not like Beth," he remarked. "She's normally so down to earth."

When she turned up half an hour later, the policewoman got straight to the point. They had identified the vehicle and from Craig's description; probably the driver, too.

"Good thing you were home, Craig. Not that I am saying you can't look after yourself Katie, but you were facing a violent man. In fact we have a situation."

"A situation?"

"Are the puppies still here?"

"Of course. Do you want to see them?" smiled Katie, regaining her usual happy self.

The policewoman shook her head, remaining in her official role. She told the couple to pack up what they needed for a few days, bring everything they needed for the dogs and not to tell anyone where they were going.

"Where *are* we going? What's this all about?"

Beth said she was taking them to a safe house where they were to lie low for a few days. It would only be a few days.

"What about my concert?" said Katie. "I need to attend rehearsals."

Beth told her she could probably resume in a week or so. Until then she must not be seen.

"They will track you back, you see."

"I don't see anything."

Gradually it became clear to the couple that they had fallen victim to a criminal gang that ran a ring of puppy farms. With so many people being in lockdown, the demand for a dog as companion was rocketing. Dogs and especially bitches were being stolen on both sides of the border. In remote, rural areas the criminals were becoming more and more reckless, thinking they could get away with threats and intimidation. The police had begun an operation to round up the gang leaders.

That remained the situation when David spoke to Katie in his garden. She had returned, she thought incognito, just to walk past her house and check that nothing was damaged. No broken-down doors or opened windows, for example. She also told him that Beth patrolled at least once a day, but it was best to make sure.

David couldn't say he had noticed Beth around. He offered to do anything he could to help. Katie asked if he could look after her car. She did not like leaving it out under those trees for too long. David said if he moved the tractor out of the barn she could hide her car inside under a tarpaulin, though the whole scenario seemed a bit far-fetched to him still. She was delighted. She told him Craig had left the Land Rover at his depot, where it aroused no suspicion.

More than a few days passed, and fellow villagers stopped asking where Katie and Craig had gone. Then one day David's doorbell rang and he opened it to a figure clad in cycling gear. When the man removed his helmet he saw with relief that it was Craig.

"Have you seen Katie?" he asked without preamble.

"Not recently. Come in."

"She's missing."

Craig calmed down a bit indoors and told David that Katie had set out to retrieve a book from her car.

"Well that's easy to verify. The car is in my barn. Let's pop up there and see if she has taken it. What was it?"

"A cookbook."

They went out the back way, Craig careful to disguise himself again in his crash helmet. The car was still under tarpaulin. Nothing had been disturbed.

"Doesn't look as though she made it this far, then," said David.

"I think they might have got her. Kidnap. Exchange for the puppies."

"Would it be worth their while?"

"God yes, each puppy is worth well over £3000."

"If Katie's not at home, where are the puppies?"

"They are being well looked after. And Rosa. She has taken quite a shine to the protection officer."

David had not realised quite how seriously this threat was being taken. Safe house, police protection. It was perhaps unwise of him to insist, "so you really think Katie might have been taken hostage?"

"That's what is worrying me, yes. This situation makes one unusually paranoid."

As they returned to the house they saw Katie at the front door. They both ran down to greet her. She was as surprised at seeing Craig there as he was pleased to see her. She had come to collect a book from the car, she said. "We know," they told her.

Katie had been delayed by a loquacious old villager who as a result of self-isolation was feeling very lonely and cut off. She had been in her front garden and had invited Katie in for coffee, not indoors of course, but in her back garden. Katie could hardly refuse.

When the couple had relaxed a little David offered to give them a lift but Craig pointed out that that might defeat the object. Someone might be watching and in any case David must not know where they were staying.

"Depends where I dropped you off."

"We're fine. Thanks anyway."

They did not seem so fine a few days later. Both of them came to David's back door asking to take shelter.

"Is it raining?"

"No, to hide. We need to lie low." Katie was trembling.

David showed them into his 'snug', a study cum library. They apologised profusely for involving him in their drama but said the whole thing should be over in a few hours. He was in no danger himself.

David left them with plenty of reading matter, maps and all of Wainwright for Craig, fiction and cook books for Katie. As he closed the door Craig whispered, "act as though you are on your own. Don't give our presence away."

"Not even for a cup of coffee?"

"Well, if you make it discreetly."

David thought Craig was being over dramatic, paranoid even, but before he had even got round to making coffee at 11am. the village filled with flashing blue lights and a helicopter hovered overhead. Police were going door to door. One of them, a stranger, rang the doorbell and showed his badge and a photo.

"Have you seen these people?"

"Yes," David replied. "They are friends of mine." Surely, he thought to himself, Craig and Katie are not the criminals in this story.

"What have they done?" he asked weakly.

"They are missing persons, sir. When did you last see them?"

The door to the snug, just off the front hallway, opened, and out stepped Craig. He addressed the police constable.

"Hello Ryan. I wondered when the cavalry would show up."

Ryan spoke into his mobile and said to Craig, "okay mate, just wait here until I say," and left.

"How about that coffee, then?" he suggested to David.

Over coffee, the much-relieved couple told David that they had been aware of an imminent police raid but that their cover had been blown. Afraid of jeopardising the police action and worried about their own safety, they had hurried over to him. They added that the police nationwide was involved in a coordinated operation aimed at this large and widespread trafficking of dogs, some of which was carried out by apparently legitimate boarding kennels and breeders. Behind a respectable façade existed several cruel puppy farms. By the time they had finished their coffee and chatter Ryan returned and informed them that it was all over. To Craig he said,

"You're safe to go back to your own house now, mate. Catch up later, yeah?" He apologised to David for the inconvenience and left again.

"I'll go and collect Rosa, then," said Craig and to David, he said, "about that lift you were mentioning."

"It's all right, darling" put in Katie, I have a car in the barn, remember? We can go together."

It did not take long for things to return to normal. Not only was Katie able to rejoin her rehearsals but on the day of the concert, she opened it with a solo fanfare from Copland. Villagers stood or sat in a socially distanced semi-circle on the green while the band played. Afterwards many players and some of the audience strolled up to the pub. Still aware of covid-19 David declined, relieving Craig and Katie of their dog that Craig had brought out to listen.

He took Rosa back to his house, measured out a Pernod and water and took the dog and his drink up to his ocularium to enjoy the late summer's evening. The large, curly haired bitch sat beside him gazing intently at the river. He wondered whether she still missed her puppies, now all in good homes. As for David, he stared across the river at the green, the farm beyond and the houses along the road. You never knew what was going to happen in this village and he did not want to miss any of it.

The Collector

The fine, wrought iron gates were evidently electrically operated. Bob noticed the keypad to one side and an intercom. He got out of his van, pressed the button and heard the crackle of static.

"Yes?" queried a woman's voice.

"Oh, hello. I've come to see Mr Denton."

"Mr Denton is not in. Have you got an appointment?"

"He knows about me."

"What time is your appointment, sir?"

"I am afraid I did not make an appointment as such. I just wanted to..."

"Well, you need one," she interrupted.

"And how do I do that?" was Bob's rather stupid reaction. He was staring through the gate towards the courtyard. It was free of any farmyard mess or muddle: no discarded fertiliser bags, no old machinery or piles of manure; no cats, no chickens. The impressive Georgian farmhouse, flanked by long stone barns, could have been an exclusive country hotel. He began to wonder whether he had come to the wrong place.

"This is Fowler's Farm?"

"You will no doubt have noticed the sign, sir."

"And Mr Denton is the owner?"

"Of course, but he is away. Who shall I tell him called?"

Bob gave his name and she relaxed to the extent of making an appointment for the following week. He thanked her and set off home.

Bob had no trouble with gates or with his reception the following week. As he parked his shabby van next to a very clean Range Rover in the immaculate yard, the man himself stepped out through his studded oak door to greet him.

"Mr Green?"

"Yes. Bob."

"And I'm Jack. Pleased to meet you, Bob. Sorry you had a wasted trip last time."

"I should have made a firm appointment."

Jack Denton was an energetic man of sturdy build whom Bob took to be in his fifties. He had thick, curly brown hair and a rugged, smiling face. He could well have been a farmer except that his hands showed no sign of manual work. He was wearing Rohan hiking trousers, well used leather boots and a Barbour jacket, all of which were explained by his suggestion, "I thought I would walk you around the property while you told me about your project. Have you got boots with you?"

Bob changed his footwear at the back of his van and Jack led him through a gate into the farm proper. Bob explained his tree planting project. The volunteers normally began with a survey of existing trees and hedgerows then planned with the landowners how many and what trees were acceptable. If agreement was reached they returned to do the planting.

"Who funds you?" he asked.

"Well, we volunteers are not paid. The trees and materials come from The Woodland Trust, National Trust, various lotteries, even the Co-Op. Where ever we can get it really."

"You sound well organised."

"It's the only way."

Jack seemed receptive to the idea and he told Bob of his own interest in re-wilding. This explained the unkempt appearance of the farm. He had ambitions to introduce fell ponies on the higher reaches and longhorn cattle in the wooded areas. He was negotiating the purchase of surrounding farmland as well.

"We will need robust tree guards if you go in for cattle and pigs," Bob pointed out.

"Who said anything about pigs?"

"Tamworths?"

"Anything but bloody sheep," he laughed. He was a man after Bob's own heart. He said he would love to join in with the volunteers but that at the moment he was rather tied up.

"You run a business from the farm?" Bob hazarded.

"Yes, I have two passions: nature and art. Let's go back. I expect you could do with a coffee."

Back in the courtyard Bob changed into his shoes and followed Jack into the main building. It was very much like an office lobby immediately inside. Private quarters took up most of the rest of the house. At the reception desk Jack introduced Bob to Deirdre, the woman whose voice he recognized from his conversations over the intercom. Jack then led him into his study.

"How do you like your coffee?"

"Latte, no sugar – or if that is too much to ask anything will do."

"No it won't. Latte it shall be. I'll have one myself."

Jack went out of the room Bob presumed to ask someone to prepare the coffee, but since he was gone several minutes it was clear he must be making it himself. Bob looked round the study. It was lined with books, mostly about art and antiques, but one wall was stacked with books about nature, trees, wildlife. If Jack had read these works by Jepson, Tree, Macdonald, Monbiot and other proponents of wilding he was obviously well versed in conservation issues. He returned with two large mugs as Bob was perusing this bookshelf.

"Ah, you have noticed the evangelists," he said, "so you will not be surprised that I am fully behind your project and your survey."

They both sat down in comfortable leather chairs and were silent a moment while they enjoyed the first sips of the coffee. Then Jack said he would welcome his visitor back any time but on one condition.

"I would rather you came on your own. Discreetly."

"I can manage that for the survey, certainly, but when we start planting..."

"How many of you will there be?

"Could be eight or more. They are mostly volunteers so you never know exactly."

He frowned. "I would appreciate it if you could keep the numbers down. Perhaps a maximum of two pairs at a time. You work in pairs?"

"Often," Bob nodded.

"And when the time comes to plant I wonder if you would allow it if I came to help."

"Great. We need all the help we can get."

"Fine. Then that's agreed."

Bob grew used to driving out to Fowler's Farm, sometimes on his own, later with one or two colleagues. Once or twice large vans drove into the courtyard and there were other visitors in expensive cars. He learned that Jack dealt in upmarket antiques and that some of his clients valued their privacy. Bob and his mates always kept a respectful distance on these occasions. To the dealers and others they probably looked like farm workers. Bob did notice that only when Jack himself was at home were the barn doors opened. Often he was away for days at a time and the big barn doors were firmly locked and watched over by CCTV cameras.

However Jack was as good as his word. One weekend when Bob was on his own planting dogwood and rowan along a bleak, stone wall Jack joined him and helped finish the job. He only paused once to admire a bird.

"Did you see that, Bob?"

"A hen harrier."

"Isn't she beautiful!"

"Have you seen her before?"

"There was a pair here last year. I was beginning to worry."

Their conversation turned to the sightings of various other birds Jack and his colleagues had noticed during their work. Bob could see Jack making a mental inventory. He clearly knew his birds.

During this time the pair fetched and carried plants, posts and mesh and chatted amiably while they dug and planted. Jack expanded on his dreams of wilding. He was even thinking of re-introducing beavers in the lower wood; he regretted that he did not have enough space, he reckoned for wolves. Not just yet anyway, unless some strayed down from Scotland. Suddenly he changed the subject,

"Are you interested in antiquities? Art?"

"Art mainly, but I am no expert. I go to galleries and exhibitions when I can get away. I do not buy or collect art, I'm afraid."

"I'll show you my collection if you are interested. Many of the wealthy people who buy art are more interested in the value than the worth. I am not saying you are a pauper. I simply feel you might appreciate art for itself."

"Well, I like looking at it, that's for sure."

It transpired that there were two sides both figuratively and literally to his antique business. In one barn he kept large artefacts and objects and pieces of architectural interest. The barn opposite housed his fine art collection and smaller bronzes. Bob was not to see that yet. Jack wanted first to show him what he called boys' stuff.

Both barns were large and on the outside mirrored one another. The first one was of traditional construction inside. It would originally have stored bales of hay, tractors and machinery perhaps. Now it was full of astonishing things: just inside the door was a Rolls Royce Silver Dawn from around 1950 and now very rare. Beside it was a much older Rolls armoured car from the First World War.

100

"I'd take you for a spin," said Jack, but the Silver Dawn has been sold and the armoured vehicle needs work."

More surprising than the vehicles was a 36-foot yacht with its mast up, comfortably berthed beneath the spacious beamed roof of the barn. It was the Roma Butterfly, the first sailing boat to have been navigated single-handedly and non-stop around the world. It certainly looked as though it had been at sea a long time.

"No real value," said Jack, "but of historic interest to some. Now," he said, pointing at a pair of cannons, "What do you make of them?"

"Sorry. No idea. A matching pair. Quite old, I guess."

"They are the Twin Sisters. They were used in Texas in various wars. They are of historical significance more than anything. Mysteriously, they disappeared in the 19th century and no one knew what happened to them. No one knows this is where they are now. I'll tell you the story another time." All he did say as he showed Bob round his exhibits was that much of his work involved collaboration with Art Loss International to search for stolen or missing art. "Mainly paintings, but sometimes I like to solve a mystery."

"Like that of the Twin Sisters. It must be exciting."

"There's a lot of routine. When you work at the top end of the market you get offered a lot of pieces of dubious provenance. War loot, too. We know who some of the art smugglers are and, indeed, we know the criminal gangs. We have to keep our own hands clean which is not as easy as it sounds. Criminals like to bargain. As I say my real interest is in fine art but we'll keep that treat for another time."

"Will you return the cannons to Texas?"

"Yes, all in good time. I like to hang on to my finds for a bit. Enjoy them. Counting my treasure, if you like, old miser that I am."

"I don't believe that. I should say your money is well spent."

"The thing is, Bob, there is an element of danger in my work so I try to keep it quiet. So this is just between you and me."

"I'm flattered."

"I'll flatter you with one real treasure before we go."

He walked across the barn to an area of furniture. Bob recognized a set of Chippendale chairs but little else. Jack approached a large bookcase cum desk.

"This piece is quite rare. It's called a Wooton secretary cabinet or bureau bookcase for obvious reasons. I already have a buyer lined up. But that is not what I wanted to show you." He pulled open the desk drawer and passed Bob something oval and solid wrapped in soft satin. "Open it carefully. Don't drop it."

Bob did so and gasped, "A Fabergé Egg!"

"Well done, but not any old egg. It's a commemorative piece made for Alexander III. It was lost during the Russian Revolution. You are the first person to have set eyes on it since. The first outside my team, that is."

"What are you going to do with it? Why show it to me?" Bob wondered whether Jack was pulling his leg.

Jack took the egg carefully back from Bob, re-wrapped it and replaced it in its hiding place. He asked bob to sit down. "I suppose I am a collector at heart," he said. "But I also get pleasure from sharing my art with someone I can trust."

"You hardly know me. I might be infiltrating your set-up through my tree planting wheeze." Bob wondered whether Jack had a wife or a friend with whom he might better share his secrets.

"I've seen you working. You love what you do and I like the way you do it." Returning to his theme he added, "I don't horde these things, you know. I will take this egg to Sotheby's, furnish them with provenance and ask them to respect my anonymity."

"You could be famous. These finds alone..."

"Fame is precisely what I don't want. I need to be..."

"Undercover."

"If you want to go all John le Carré about it. It is not just me. There are teams of investigators just as there are gangs of criminals. We probably all know one another, too," he smiled. "I try to keep a low profile. And I have a legitimate business to run."

"And a farm to re-wild!"

"With your help."

This brought them back to the project in hand. They agreed on dates and Bob went on his way. As he left Jack said,

"Next time I'll show you the other barn. That's where the real art is. But I'd rather you kept quiet about it. Low profile and all that."

Jack did seem to be a man of great enthusiasm for whatever he did. When he could he joined in the making of the crates the tree volunteers built to protect young trees from livestock. Bob suggested that as Jack had no livestock they might not be necessary on his farm but Jack said what about those longhorn cows and fell ponies. He had been down to Knepp Wildland in Sussex and found the work done by Isabella Tree inspiring.

"She has Tamworth pigs," said Bob.

"So she does. You have been there, then?"

102

"Not yet but I have read her book."

"You can meet her here. She has agreed to come up and advise me of the possibilities for doing something similar on Fowler's Farm and a large parcel of adjoining land that I have acquired. After which," he teased, "we might need even more trees."

Bob was impressed. "I'd love to join in," he said, "but shouldn't we just let them regenerate?"

"I'm sure we can give nature a helping hand. Just give me time."

Bob was not then to know that Jack had very little time left.

Some weeks later Jack took Bob into the second barn. It was quite different inside, an architectural equivalent of a Russian doll, for it contained a series of sealed air-conditioned and temperature-controlled units. The lighting was subdued. On one side was a row of tall, steel cabinets with sliding compartments such as museums and galleries have in their basements to store archives and paintings.

Jack opened one panel, removed a painting and turned it towards Bob, whose eyes widened in disbelief.

"Is that original?"

"Of course. I am not into fakes or copies."

The painting was unmistakeably by Vermeer. The lighting alone told Bob so as did the black and white tile floor. In the picture a woman in a long dress sat at some kind of keyboard instrument. Another stood in the foreground singing. More strikingly, though Bob knew this painting.

"That was stolen from a museum in Boston."

"You do know your art." Jack replaced it and came out with another, older canvass by Van Eyck that also rang a bell. It featured a man on a white horse behind which were ranged some solemn men.

"Are they..."

"Go on."

"Are they the Just Judges? Where on earth did you..?"

"I recovered these paintings."

He showed Bob more missing works. There was a Picasso, "Pigeon aux Petits Pois" and an even more recent portrait of Francis Bacon by Lucien Freud that had been stolen in Berlin. Bob gazed in amazement and admiration at these pictures. There was no gallery in the world where he could have handled such famous masterpieces nor have examined them so closely. He was awestruck.

"How long have you had these paintings?"

"Some longer than others."

"Does anyone know they are here?"

"I hope not." The barn was filled with other works legitimately for sale, Bob supposed. He did not know what to say.

"I know what you are thinking," smiled Jack.

"Well I don't. Tell me."

"You think I am the thief. That these stolen works are now my stolen works."

"Please tell me they are not."

"Not exactly. I have retrieved them as part of my dealings and my investigations. Let's just say that Art Loss International does not perhaps know the full extent of my success. Yet."

"So you will return them?"

He smiled again, replaced his treasures carefully and locked everything up. "Have you time for a coffee?" he asked Bob.

Bob did not quite know what he was letting himself in for. He led a simple, satisfying life and was loath to get involved in anything even slightly shady. However he was mesmerised by the energy and the magnetism of this man. Jack led the way over to the house and asked Deirdre whether there had been any calls before they went in to his study. This time someone from what Bob took to be a back office came in with the coffee. Jack thanked him, asked a few questions about a recent sale and when the man had left said, "Jeff, my accountant. He helps out in all kinds of ways. A Mr Fixit."

"How many staff are there?"

"Well, you have met his wife Deirdre at reception. She arranges my diary and my travel, not to mention running the house."

"Mr and Mrs Fixit, then."

"You could say so," he laughed, "then there are packers and drivers who come when needed."

"No family?"

"Not here," he said in a tone that clearly meant this subject was taboo. He then softened his tone and said, "That's why I wanted to talk to you. Someone I can confide in and trust."

"I..."

"You have your suspicions, I can sense that. You are wondering if I am a thief, a kind of Arsène Lupin. It is simpler than that and not so romantic. But I do have a bit of a worry."

In the conversation that ensued Jack gave nothing away about his sleuthing methods, his contacts or the logistics behind his astounding finds. He clearly wanted to get this worry off his chest by telling Bob of his obsession, an obsession that he feared had become an addiction that he was finding harder and harder to break.

It had begun as he had earlier intimated, from his pleasure in hanging on to his acquisitions for a while and enjoying them as though they were his. He would sneak into the barn at all hours and sit with them. There had been no one other than Bob he had been able to share this pleasure with. His own staff was not aware of all that he had done. The Fixits were more occupied with the running of the business. They knew he had found and returned much art, particularly pieces stolen from religious buildings wrecked by terrorists or ransacked during civil wars. That was routine stuff. Jack had no one with whom to share his big secrets. He was finding it increasingly difficult to part with his fine art masterpieces.

"What I fear most," he confessed, "is that I am becoming a collector. I have acquired these pieces, often at great risk to them and to myself but always with good intentions. I know I should hand them over. But I say to myself, it won't hurt after all this time if I keep them one more week, one more month. The danger is that inevitably there are a few people, not all of them the most savoury of characters, who know I am hanging on to them. This is dangerous. I could eliminate the danger by handing them over rapidly to their legitimate owners. Or where there are no owners, I could sell them as I sometimes have to. I know this. But you have to admit, some of these paintings are very special. I think you felt what it was like to cradle these babies in your arms."

As the summer approached they planted fewer trees. Eventually there were just a dozen wild cherries to put in the ground. They worked together, Jack and Bob and the former talked about how his plans for the farm were progressing. Bob was about to pop the last sapling in its hole when Jack stopped him.

"I want you to see this." He took a packet from his pocket. Bob recognized the satin it was wrapped in.

"The Fabergé egg?"

"Yes." From a shoulder bag that he had hung on the gatepost Jack removed a leather box. He dropped the egg into the box still wrapped and placed it in the hole beneath the roots of the cherry sapling. He took the spade from Bob, filled the hole and straightening up said, "Now count how many trees we are from the gate."

"Seven."

"Remember that, Bob. That's my insurance policy."

"Insurance for what?"

"Who knows. Perhaps for you."

They had finished their task and walked back down to the farmyard together. Before they left Jack delivered one more surprise. He passed Bob a letter, asked him to keep it in a safe place and open it only if he disappeared or had an accident."

"That sounds melodramatic," Bob observed.

"It is a matter of life or death."

What with his remarks about insurance and now this letter Bob was beginning to think Jack was losing his marbles and not the Elgin ones. To humour his host Bob accepted the letter. When he got home he filed it with his own legal papers, cars, divorce, mortgage and yes, insurance. Bob never saw Jack again.

A few weeks later Bob went away on holiday to walk the GR20, the famous trail in Corsica. He did not therefore read or hear about the fire in Cumbria. Fowler's Farmhouse and one of the barns had burnt to the ground following an explosion. The barn left standing was the one that housed the vehicles, furniture and larger architectural pieces, none of which were damaged.

Opposite a skeleton of steel frames stood among the rubble and masonry, their contents ashes. None of the paintings had survived. No one seemed to know that there had been any particularly valuable paintings in them. The inventory of all the works had been destroyed when the office burnt down.

The house had been empty at the time except for the couple who lived in, the married fixers. Their bodies were almost totally consumed and their identities had yet to be confirmed. There was no trace of any other body.

The police tried to contact Jack Denton without success. Local people knew him to talk to but no one knew whether he had any living relatives. They all said he was very friendly but that he was not gregarious. The police contacted the art museums and galleries he did business with as well as antique shops and dealerships. Everybody knew him as an affable, likeable man, easy to do business with. None of them knew anything about him outside his work. The only address anyone had for him was Fowler's Farm. His mobile telephone number was no longer functioning.

The obvious lead was Art Loss International but the authorities there were less than forthcoming. Yes, he had helped in some investigations but apart from his name and address they had very little on him as a private individual. They did say that he had achieved excellent results for them.

Asked whether he was working on any case at present they thought not. No one at the organisation had seen him for a year or more.

When Bob returned from his holiday the police questioned him, too. He told them about the tree planting and Jack's wilding plans but like the others he had no contact for him other than the phone numbers already given; and he knew nothing about his private life. Bob remembered his letter, of course. Before he handed it over he opened and read it myself. It was hand written in ink with a fountain pen.

To Whom It May Concern

If you are reading this it is because I am missing or dead. If anything has happened to me it is no accident. I have been threatened for some time by those whom I list below. They belong to certain elements with whom I have failed to come to terms.

Art Loss International will confirm that over the years I have performed some useful services for them. Not all is on record. Unfortunately these investigations have made me enemies.

Jack went on to list criminal gangs in the art world and named a couple of individuals who wished him ill. Interpol would know of these figures, he claimed but the Russians would be more difficult to pin down because he felt the Russian State itself was implicated.

Bob handed the letter over the next day and apologised for not remembering it straight away. He said he hoped the letter would now help them with their inquiries.

The police did not take the letter seriously. They did interview Bob once more. They even asked for a sample of his handwriting, suspecting him of writing the letter himself. He explained in more detail how he had come to know Jack and the circumstances under which he had been given the letter. Feeling increasingly under pressure he told them about the masterpieces Jack had shown him. This convinced the police even more that Bob was a fantasist and a time waster. He was greatly offended and told them to check his story with Art Loss International. They did go back to the organisation but the officials there were no more forthcoming than before. They refused to divulge what operations Jack had been involved with. While reluctant to deny or confirm their own role in these operations, they were adamant that Jack could not single-handedly have solved historical thefts. They concluded that Bob's assertions were too far-fetched to be taken seriously and in any case there was no evidence that any of these art works had ever been retrieved.

Bob insisted to the police that he had seen the paintings with his own eyes but could provide no evidence. Everything in that barn had been destroyed, unless, Bob wondered, some of them had been removed before the fire. The police by now clearly thought Bob was an attention seeker and they were just trying to humour him.

"What about the Texas cannons?" he asked. "They were in the other barn. They must still be there."

At this they laughed in his face and told him again to stop wasting police time. He could not even persuade them to bring in an expert to verify his claim. Bob considered telling his story to the press but contrary to what the police thought he was not an attention seeker. Indeed, he was nervous that such publicity might expose him to the same dangers that Jack must have faced. So long as the criminals knew nothing about the letter, or more to the point, about Bob, he felt safe. For all he knew the cannons were now just another garden feature in some wealthy man's property.

Jack was listed officially as a missing person. He was not proved dead. Bob remained convinced that Jack's tales were true and that the masterpieces he had revealed to him were genuine. Bob knew he could prove the veracity of one of his finds. He had withheld one vital piece of evidence. For had not Jack and he together "planted" the Fabergé egg? His insurance or Bob's? Bob decided to let it lie another year or two. He was in no hurry to vindicate himself.

Because of his familiarity with the grounds, Bob was asked to keep an eye on the farm. It was left to itself so he was content to watch it slowly re-wild on its own. He liked this quiet contemplation. Jack had disappeared without trace. Bob was not sure he was dead. He waited still to see whether one of these days his friend, as he now thought of him, would wish to claim his insurance.

Saint Bernard

If anyone had asked him what she looked like David would have been unable to say. Was she young, old, severe or pleasant looking? He had not really noticed her, not at first, other than that she appeared tiny beside her dog. And it was the dog that had caught his attention, a dog as big as the sheep it obediently ignored. Its thick fur was quite as dense in its wiry tangle as the sheep's woollen coats. It was a Saint Bernard.

He had noticed it a week ago being walked around the village on a lead twice a day. He had watched the dog's unhurried gait and wondered where it and its owner came from. They were new to the village.

David liked to sit out in his garden and look down over the river and across the green. A footpath ran between his garden and the river bank. Part of it was concealed behind his dry stone wall and lilac trees.

From behind this cover he heard a shrill female voice shout, "Hubert! No, Hubert!" Hubert was evidently not paying much attention for David heard her call again, "Hubert, come here. Come here at once."

Then he saw the Saint Bernard, a truly great bear of a dog, lumber past his garden wall and walk to the river's edge. There it examined more closely a pair of mallards swimming against the current. The dog, heedless of its owner, was curious only. It did not seem to want to hunt the ducks and it had no intention of going for a swim like a common Labrador.

Now the little woman came into sight still shouting angrily, "Hubert, will you come here."

David thought her voice very loud for such a small being. Her size apart he paid little attention to her appearance. Besides, she had her back to him now. The Saint Bernard turned and slowly walked towards his mistress. Together they crossed the footbridge. They had not seen the man observing them from his garden.

When they met a few days later it was by accident though, familiar with her routine, David might well have contrived their encounter. He stepped out of his garden gate to walk towards the bus shelter a few hundred yards upstream. He reached the footbridge at the same time as the petite woman with the large dog and paused to let them cross first.

"He won't hurt you," she said, forcing a smile.

Now he could see her face, he supposed she was in her thirties. She might have been almost pretty were she not wearing such a troubled frown. Her straw-coloured hair was crammed into a green knitted woollen hat. She had on an old Barbour jacket, faded brown corduroys and sensible walking shoes. From her left hand dangled a dog's lead and, poking out of one of her pockets, a black poo bag.

"Oh, I did not think he would," he replied. "I like dogs."

Hubert led the way over the narrow footbridge as if by right. The three of them crossed the river in single file, rather more slowly than David usually walked. Seeing they were headed the same way along the bank he fell into step with them.

"Mind if I accompany you as far as the bus shelter?"

"Please yourself," she scowled. "Sorry if that sounded rude." She attempted a conciliatory smile.

"Not at all. I have been wanting to meet Hubert, actually," he said.

She looked at him suspiciously with probing green eyes. "How did you know his name?"

He explained that he lived just across the river in the house behind the lilac trees and that he had heard her calling her dog.

"Yes, he likes to paddle," she volunteered, "but if his paws get too muddy he makes such a mess in the house."

"I can imagine. He must be quite a handful." He thought it would be a bit forward to ask precisely which house she meant. It would be easy enough to watch her if he really wanted to know where she lived. Stick to the dog, he thought. "How old is Hubert?"

"Seven. He is getting on."

"I suppose that is a good age for a large dog."

She nodded. They walked on in silence, Hubert ignoring both of them. David guessed everyone must ask her how much her dog ate or make some tired joke about where she kept his brandy. His own experience of dogs had been of smaller, livelier breeds. Only recently he had been staying with a friend who owned a spoiled terrier. His first morning the dog had burst into his room and leapt into bed with him, greeting him like an old friend. This prompted him now to say to the woman,

"At least I do not suppose he sleeps with you in your bed."

They were walking alongside one another looking at the dog. Had he observed her face he would have seen a deep blush animate her features. He did not even realise, from her lack of a reply that he might have offended, even shamed her. She swung the lead round, called Hubert to her and without having to bend down very far, attached him to it, for they were nearing the bus shelter.

"Well, I must leave you here," he said. "Have a nice walk."

She hurried on without looking at him.

"By the way," he called after her, "any time you are passing my house you are welcome, both of you, to drop in for a tea or coffee."

She did not turn. She simply raised her free hand to acknowledge his invitation and carried on up the road, a childlike figure walking beside her stolid companion. The man watched the couple and thought, "and I never did get to talk to Hubert."

Bottle

A young woman climbed over a stile into the first patch of sunlight of the morning. Her tracky bottoms were wet to the thighs from wading through the rain sodden grass and nettles, but she was warm from the exertion and had rolled up the sleeves of her cotton shirt. Her fleece jacket was tied tightly around her waist by its sleeves. The pleasure of striking the lane where she had intended enhanced her warm physical glow. She sat on the top bar of the stile to check her Ordnance Survey map.

A man's face appeared behind her. It was pale, fleshy and beaded with sweat. "Lost, are we?" His breathlessness detracted from the intended accusation tone.

"Of course not," she said, trying to make light of the affront. She jumped off the stile as lightly as a cat and pointed down the road. "The entrance is about half a mile down this lane, beyond the bridge." She did not point out what the contours of the map had already made clear to her. There was a steep descent to the bridge and a stiff climb up.

"At least it's a proper road," conceded her partner. Alison knew she should give him a hug, a kiss for this concession; she should reward him, but she could not bring herself to do it. Something, the overcast weather, his constant carping, or perhaps her own disappointment in him, had spoiled the atmosphere.

Alison knew she should make the effort. After all, Podge had agreed for once to do something she wanted, to accompany her on a week's walking holiday rather than buy an off-the-shelf package to some sun and concrete resort on a polluted foreign shore. She had planned to break him in gently, starting here in the gentle Eden valley and ending perhaps with some fell walking in the Lake District. The weather, however, had put a dampener on any less black magic Mother Nature might have been brewing.

"Mud, blisters and wet clothes," was Podge's summary of the adventure so far.

The sun did remain out as they walked along the lane, Podge in his brand new hiking gear, stiff new Berghaus walking boots that once worn in would have done him proud on Everest, waterproof Goretex trousers and jacket. Everything Podge wore was bright and brand new. Clipped into the laces of his new boots were a pair of gaiters a salesman in the Outdoor Shop in London had convinced him were indispensable. Over a designer sweat shirt he wore a bright red and yellow Helly Hansen hooded cagoule. On his back he displayed a Karrimor rucksack. It was capable of carrying 20 kilos, though Alison knew that it contained, apart from a few of his survival toys, among which were a compass he had no idea how to use, a Maglite torch, matches that could be struck under water and mosquito repellent, Band-Aids, only the picnic lunch she had prepared. As well as the flask of coffee, she had packed some cans of lager for Podge and a plastic bottle of homemade lemonade for herself. What for Alison was an undemanding round tour of four or five hours, was for her town-bred partner an alarming expedition.

Beside her heavily armoured knight Alison skipped lightly along in her comfortable boots and faded clothing that complemented the colours of the countryside. While Podge in shining armour was pale and strained, she danced along pink-cheeked, her skin almost translucent, her red hair burning in this welcome burst of sunlight.

They strode side by side. Eventually Podge broke the silence. "We'll lunch at Monk's walk, then."

"It's still rather early."

"Well, I suppose when we find your grand canyon we've still got to trudge miles along it."

Alison ground her teeth. They had planned this outing together. She had shown him on the map the little-known beauty spot, a heavily wooded gorge cut deep between sandstone rocks. Several waterfalls were marked.

"There should be some perfect picnic spots," she had said, to lure him. "Secluded, too."

As she had expected, the road dipped abruptly to a bridge. They leant over the low wall and watched the fierce river assault the stone arches.

"I wouldn't like to fall into that," said Podge, awe-struck for once.

"That's the same beck that flows through the gorge," Alison pointed out. "It's going to be spectacular."

"Every cloud has a silver lining, then," said Podge with a sudden smile, referring to the heavy overnight rain. He gave Alison a squeeze and swung round. His rucksack nearly toppled her off her feet. "Come on! Race you to the top."

Alison should have been glad that Podge had rallied. He was at last making an effort. Instead she fumed at his carelessness. He might have knocked her over the parapet. Her irritation with him that had been simmering all morning boiled up within her. With dread she recognised the onset of one of her sullen moods. It spilled through her, as unstoppable as an incoming tide, soaking her spirit. She was not to know that that brief squeeze was to be the last touch of affection, however one-sided, between them. A token of what had been.

A faded wooden finger post marked the entry to the walk. Crossing an expanse of uncut lawn behind the monastery ruins they passed through a collapsing lych gate into a meadow. The path ran through an avenue of ancient trees planted along the contour of the hill before it plunged sharply down through the woods that concealed the hidden ravine.

Steps had been cut in the rock by the monks who had given their name to this walk. They had also hewn paths alongside the torrent and carved a passage through the sides of the great boulders that would otherwise have obstructed the way. This first descent was the most precipitous, the moss covered steps, slippery from days of heavy rain. At one hairpin bend within sound if not yet sight of a pounding waterfall, an iron railing was intended to prevent people from falling straight over. However, the rusting metal was as brittle as a ginger snap. The corroded uprights had broken away from the rock bases. Someone in the more recent past had tried to patch it up. In the way a child makes sand pies with a plastic bucket on a beach, little heaps of moulded concrete had been set around the foot of the iron posts in the feeble hope that it would fix them down to the rock. The concrete was now crumbling and much of the fence dangled in the void, ready to fly down with the first person foolish or unobservant enough to lean on it.

A railing like that, thought Alison, would not be believable in a murder film. As she contemplated it, a frisson of horror fingered her spine.

Their first glimpse of the higher fall tugged both Podge and Alison out of themselves. The rock reverberated from the pounding, vapour from the crashing water screened the full view, a deep cauldron of a pool heaved and thundered at the foot of the fall before the mass of crushed river raced on over further cataracts. Around this scene of raging animation moist lichen clung to the rock, ferns dripped on the ledges and from beyond this frame encroached a fascinated forest.

Podge and Alison stood enthralled at the power and the contrast of these elements, though Alison was still keeping her wary distance from the swing of Podge's rucksack.

The dilapidation of the footpath grew in proportion to the wild beauty of the scene. To follow the unruly river they had to cross a ledge sliced into the rock. Iron rings had been set into the inside edge and a length of handrail inserted. Just at the point where the path narrowed to a couple of hand breadths across a fissure, the flaking, orange rail had snapped completely, leaving the most dangerous ten metres with no support at all. Water, leaching out of the lichen made the smooth stone path wet and slippery.

"Delightful!" remarked Podge, confident now in the grip of his Berghaus walking boots.

Alison followed him, unafraid, but surprised there was no public warning about the state of this path, vaunted as a major attraction in leaflets she had found at the tourist information centre in Penrith.

By the time they had slithered deeper into the ravine it was close to lunchtime and Alison, who was now a few steps ahead turned and shouted, "Feeling hungry?"

Podge could not hear her above the thunder of the water. Alison mimed eating and Podge nodded vigorously. He wanted to sit on a ledge that bowed back into a bend. It was about ten metres above the troubled surface of the stream and overhung with dripping ferns. Alison objected that it was too damp and gloomy.

"It's out of the rain. Great view, too," argued Podge, easing the rucksack from his shoulders.

"Let's just look round the corner. If the sun does come out, we can take our time, relax..."

"I'm staying here," said Podge, dropping the rucksack at his feet. "I doubt if the sun will come out again."

As if affronted, the sun suddenly blazed into the dark valley, the slit in the earth through which they had been scrambling was flooded in colour. The sombre mass of the foliage crystallised into individual formations of green and yellow, and black where the shadows fell. The spray sparkled and the reeds and rushes and ferns were bejewelled with light. The tumbling torrent was transformed from opaque mud to a translucent river of cream and chocolate.

The couple laughed in delight and astonishment. Podge picked up the rucksack. "Okay. Let's find somewhere to bask."

He led the way round the corner, a bare rock that protruded twenty foot above the water. The remains of a rackety iron fence dared the walker to touch it. Gingerly the couple felt their way over the slithery surface and found themselves on a rock path that sloped down to the beck's edge. In places it was submerged by the high level of the flood water. Rising on their right was a grassy bank in the full sun. What made it perfect was that it commanded a view downstream of a whole cascade of waterfalls. A hundred metres or so further down the stream plunged out of sight between sheer walls. From that point Alison could see that the path diverged from the watercourse and rose again through the woods to the top of the gorge.

After a cursory glance Podge began systematically to open the various compartments of his rucksack. From underneath he drew out and unfolded a thin groundsheet which he spread on the grass. He sat on it and, gathering the backpack between his knees, took out the plastic containers holding their picnic from the inside and the drinks from the outside pockets. Alison watched his slow, precise movements puzzling why everything he did exasperated her so. A few months ago she would have smiled, would have warmed to him and his fussy little ways.

Before they had peeled their hard-boiled eggs and unwrapped their sandwiches the sun was blown away. A fine drizzle curtained off the scene and dampened their meal.

"Might just have well stayed under the rock," complained Podge, pulling his hood over his head.

"It could be worse," said Alison, attempting a bright edge to the remark.

"Probably will be soon."

The veil of rain dissipated as quickly as it had come. In the fleeting moments of sun, their tempers mellowed by the food, and in Podge's case by two cans of lager, the couple did relax, lying back, not touching, each on their own side of the groundsheet. Their exertions, the impressions of the falls and the unspoken hostility between them had tired them both. They slipped into a light doze.

Alison woke first, cramped and cold, after a quarter of an hour. Podge was still fast asleep. Let sleeping dogs lie, she thought. She poured herself the last of the coffee from the small flask and contemplated the flow of the stream. It was strange to think that all that water, all that energy, would in half an hour or so form part of the River Eden, itself fast flowing and youthful this far up the Vale. Yet the stream she watched, like the river it fed, was a constant, was always there, never static, continually renewed. If she shut her eyes for a minute and opened them again she would be looking at the same stream and yet at a completely different one.

She picked up the lemonade bottle she had emptied earlier and turned it in her hands in despair. Why, amid all this beauty in the very heart of the countryside she loved, did she feel this aching loneliness? She looked again at her partner. She could share nothing of this with him. She had the idea of writing a message, of sealing it in the bottle and letting the waters carry it where they would.

She would need something to write on and to write with. She stretched out for the rucksack. There were some paper napkins that might serve and there was a fair chance Podge had packed a pencil or a pen in one of the zip up compartments.

116

Dragging the bag towards her, she jarred the sleeping man's foot. He stirred suddenly, kicking the bottle from the tuft of grass where Alison had laid it. It rolled down the bank lodging itself in some rushes that shuddered at the edge of the pulsing stream.

"What the hell are you up to?" he growled.

Was Alison's reply a premeditated lie or simply a statement of intent?

"Writing a message," she said.

"Saying what?"

Alison was silent. She wanted to explain, *it was a scream for help. A cry for someone to rescue us.* All she said was, "oh, nothing."

"Well, you can't leave the bottle there, littering the countryside."

"As if you cared," she muttered.

"Of course I care," he said. "I can't stand untidiness."

Alison found herself apologising. "But I can't climb down there. It's too risky. I'd slip." She threw a stone to dislodge the bottle. The stone missed.

"Wait," ordered Podge. "What have you written?"

"Nothing. There's nothing in it."

"I want to see."

"There's nothing, I tell you."

Podge, stiff from his snooze on the hard ground, got up too suddenly, and began to slide down the bank. Struggling for balance, he stumbled and was pitched head first into the water. The splash swallowed up the bottle. The stream was deep and swift and alive with whirlpools caused by the throbbing falls. Podge disappeared completely. What seemed like minutes later Alison saw a body swept over the rocks into a series of pools lower down. She ran after it along the rocky path, shouting his name. She reached the point where path and stream went their separate ways. Sheer walls of pink sandstone rising straight from the flood blocked her way. Any track beside the water was submerged thigh deep beneath the boisterous current.

Alison turned to make her way back the way she had come. Facing her, a collapsed sign read, *Danger. Monk's Walk closed for restoration.*

"Bloody silly place to put it," she sobbed. There had been no warning at the monastery entrance, though the state of the ropes and rails was evidence enough of the run-down condition of this wilderness walk. Her first instinct was to collect the rucksack, but immediately she lifted it she realised her folly. She dropped the bag down amid the ungathered picnic debris and ran back to the top of the cascade.

There being no mobile phone signal in this area, she needed to return to the road, maybe stop a motorist or reach a house with a landline and the possibility of rescue. She knew there was no time to waste but in her heart, recognised the ambiguity of that phrase. There was no time to waste because their time had run out. She felt certain it was too late to save Podge. She pressed on nevertheless, she did all the right things, she manifested the right emotions, controlled panic, despair, grief, but inside her, displacing all the anger, all the sullen resentment of the last few days, rose a sense of relief, of happiness.

She was all in when she reached a farmhouse. When the police arrived the crew found a sobbing, laughing, hysterical woman. After the questions she calmed down and the kindly farmer's wife took her in and gave her a cup of tea while they waited.

Four hours later a body was found snagged on a rock in the River Eden. An hour after that Alison identified the body.

Some days later two boys fishing downstream near Wetheral Abbey noticed a bottle bobbing towards them. As if to attract their attention it entered an eddy and circled back against the main current. One boy waded out towards it.

"What you doin'? You'll scare the fish," said his friend.

"Might be something in it," he shouted back.

"Oh, yeah. A message, like. You daft or what!"

Unabashed the boy now thigh deep in the clear, cold water, reached out and grabbed the bottle. He unscrewed the top. Peeping in he recognised the smell of homemade lemonade and transferred the neck to his nostrils for a luxurious sniff.

"Watch it," sneered the other boy from the shore, "the genie might bite your nose off."

"Aw, shut up," said the first boy and held the bottle up to the light.

"What's in it then?"

"Nothing," he replied and threw the bottle back out into the mainstream. They both slung a few stones after it before the bottle disappeared from view.

From a Summer Garden

When we are in our twenties or thirties, even our forties, we may think some earth-shattering experience is the high point or the low point of our lives; that never again will we experience such ecstasy or suffer such grief. These moments, we feel at the time, will define our story. Indeed, they may well do, but we do not all throw ourselves under a train, take poison and die in the arms of our lover or get sent to rot in prison. Most of us, however damaged, will live on, some to experience more intense moments, a second 'love of our life', a further tragedy, shameful act of cowardice or bold stand of bravery; and these life events may mark us as strongly as the initial bliss or blow that once so disoriented us.

The people that David fell in with in quick succession that summer were themselves survivors. They were well into their seventies. With one exception all had survived love and loss, trauma and tragedy; some had settled into a more or less contented old age, others were gritting their teeth while they waited for the end to come. While these encounters all happened over a short few weeks their stories covered a life time, theirs and David's. The first came as more of a shock to him than it did to Amadeep.

Let us remember that David lived in a small Cumbrian village with a river tumbling through it. He was approaching one of the footbridges that crossed this beck and he paused to give way to a family group crossing towards him. A gaggle of brown-skinned children were running ahead of an elderly Indian man whom he took to be their grandfather. The man was dressed in casual clothes and sturdy boots fitting for a country stroll, but he wore a turban. There was something familiar about his bearing and the careful way he stepped out. The kids all ran past David but when the old man was half way across the bridge David recognised him. He was about to walk past, looking up only to thank him for waiting, when he, too, recognised the Englishman.

"David."

"Amadeep. What brings you here?"

"I might ask you the same," he countered guardedly. He spoke with an Indian accent whereas the children seemed to be fully integrated British.

"I live here," David told him. "That is my house." He indicated his riverside cottage behind the dry stone wall facing them.

They hesitated. Neither of them knew what to say next. It had been forty years or more since they had spoken. That last time, David remembered, he had behaved badly. It was too late now to make up for it. Amadeep had every right to bear a grudge. He could obviously see what was going through David's mind, but all he could think of saying was, "Very nice. Well, I must…"

"Wait. Would you like to come in? Come for tea? I can offer your grandchildren ice cream if they would like it."

There was a trace of bitterness in his laugh. "They are not my grandchildren. I was not blessed with…"

He could have run David through with a knife. Of course, when David had known Amadeep and especially his wife Jasminder they were young, and still childless. In those days before smart phones and social media David never knew what had become of them. He had not tried to find out. He felt too ashamed and guilty.

"Well, bring them in anyway."

It was a warm day. David led his old friend and the children into his garden and out on to the raised patio that overlooked the river. In fine weather he would sit and watch the goings-on in the village. Often people walking along the footpath beneath the low garden wall would linger in conversation.

David introduced himself to the children who turned out to belong to Amadeep's nephews. He invited them to make themselves at home while he went inside to brew tea and take the ice cream out of the freezer. He suggested to Amadeep that if the children preferred to play in the river or to venture over to the swings on the green they would still be able to keep an eye on them from where they sat.

"See if you can help Uncle first," Amadeep told the older boy, settling himself into a chair, evidently pleased to take the weight off his feet.

David led the boy into the kitchen, gave him the large carton of ice cream and told him to take it out and place it on the wall in the sun. "You'll find games in the garden shed," he added.

As soon as the children had eaten their ices they scampered off down the river, still within earshot of their anxious guardian.

"They'll be fine," said David.

"I don't know if I can trust you, David,"

"I promise," he said. "This time."

For what had remained unspoken between them, not just that afternoon but for forty-five years was what had happened in Delhi on the night of the riots. When her Sikh bodyguard had assassinated Mrs Gandhi, the prime minister, sectarian violence had erupted in the city and elsewhere. Sikhs in the capital were attacked, their houses and businesses set on fire. David had been a close neighbour of Amadeep and Jasminder. They were often in one another's houses. Jasminder and David had secretly become even closer.

On the worst night of the riots Amadeep and his wife had returned home to find a mob outside the house. They did not show their faces but ordered the taxi to drive on and to drop them off outside their friend's house a little further down the street. Some in the mob chased after the taxi. The couple leapt out and banged on David's door.

Many non-Sikhs, braver than him, gave shelter to their neighbours, but David had already barricaded his doors and ordered his bearer to let nobody in. He had always maintained that he did not hear Amadeep's frantic cries for help, Jasminder's screams. He did not open the door to his friends. He did not open the door for his lover. He assumed they had fled before the rioters reached his house. It did not help him. The house was attacked anyway. He escaped out the back and fled down a quieter road, eventually reaching the safety of the Park Hotel.

Having lost all his clothes and possessions in the fire he was evacuated by the British High Commission. The following weeks, still in shock, he was preoccupied settling in back home and getting to grips with his new job in the civil service. He never returned to India, neither did he find out what had happened to his friends, to his lover. He felt too ashamed that he had not opened the door to them. Not that it would have helped but that evening he learned an awful truth about himself: that he was a coward.

Over tea on his Cumbrian patio he finally broached the subject.

"Amadeep, I am so sorry."

"What for?"

"I have often wondered what happened to you and Jasminder."

"You had a narrow escape yourself," he said coldly. "You were lucky to get away."

"I was. I did not know whether you had. More tea?"

"No thank you."

"You haven't forgiven me, have you?"

"For what?"

"For betraying you."

"Turning us away, you mean? Or for sleeping with my wife?"

David replaced the teapot. He did not know what to say. He had imagined his affair with Jasminder had remained a secret.

"Is Jasminder still with you? What happened to her that night?"

"Now you ask."

"I was evacuated in the chaos. I wrote."

"I know you wrote to her. I did not reply. We were caught by the mob. I fought my way free but I let her down, too. Cowardice or vengeance. She was manhandled, stripped and beaten. She died in hospital.

It was only a few weeks later that his past came back to haunt David again. He had always been haunted by the loss, or death as he now knew it, of Jasminder, his first forbidden love. He was again sitting out on his ocularium on another sunny morning, drinking coffee and watching the regular dog walkers on the green. He still did not know what to make of his meeting with Amadeep. Neither of them had inquired about the other. No small talk about family, about how each had survived, enjoyed perhaps the interceding years. All David had learned was that Amadeep was still alive and that Jasminder, his first, perhaps his only, wife was dead. All Amadeep knew about David was that he had turned his back on them in their hour of need. What David remembered first and foremost was that he thought he had been in love with the other man's wife.

Lost in these thoughts he did not at first pay any attention to the woman crossing the footbridge. Then he noticed she had spotted him and was waving with her white, floppy hat.

He raised a hand idly to acknowledge her greeting and she called out, "David Lenham?"

From his seat on the ocularium, as the crow flies, the bridge is fifty metres upstream and within earshot, but not close enough for a conversation.

"Yes," he shouted back.

She replaced her hat on her head and came over to his garden wall. She was a tall, elegant woman of about fifty, wearing a straw-coloured summer dress that reached down almost to her white tennis shoes. She had loosely tied a light woollen cardigan around her neck. Beneath that floppy hat she wore sunglasses which she removed to address David.

"You don't know me," she said, looking up, "but we have mutual friends."

He invited her to follow the wall and come in through the garden gate which she did. He went to meet her. She was one of those smiley, open women, self-confident but intent on pleasing.

As was his wont with visitors in fine weather David settled her on the ocularium and went into the kitchen to pour two glasses of elderflower cordial.

"Wonderful," said his guest, sipping her drink. "Did you make it yourself?"

"I am afraid so."

"But it is delicious. Very refreshing."

She was rather delicious herself, he thought, though these days such adjectives cannot be spoken aloud. His guest was certainly out of the ordinary. The villagers were no slouches themselves but more often than not were attired in hiking or gardening clothes. But this woman was much more elegant in dress and bearing than most at the best of times, women included. She seemed to have dressed for a special occasion and perhaps this was it.

"Glad you like it," David said. "Tell me, who are these mutual friends?"

"That's why I wanted to meet you. I am Catherine by the way and you are David." There was a trace of interrogation in her voice even though he had already confirmed his identity.

She told him she was staying with the Flemings who were indeed well known to him, but it was not them she wished to talk about. "Lovely people though they are," she smiled.

The previous evening she had mentioned in conversation the name of Hugo Clarke. The Flemings remembered he had once spoken to them about Hugo. David had said that of all his former colleagues, Hugo had been the one he had considered to be a real friend. They remembered that he had alluded to some mystery or other concerning his death in France. Catherine's ears had pricked up and she asked the Flemings where David lived. And here she was, sitting opposite him in the sunshine sipping his elderflower nectar.

"Tell me about Hugo. About you and Hugo," she said. "I only knew him at the end, you see, though I feel I know a lot about him. But first your story."

She was pleasantly insistent. Since it was quite a long story David suggested they might make a light lunch and bring it out into the garden.

She went with him into the kitchen, looked around with interest and asked if he had any eggs.

"Straight from the hens," he replied.

She offered to make omelettes. To protect her frock, David gave her his late wife's apron that still hung on the back of the kitchen door. While Catherine busied herself he set about making a salad with the cucumbers, tomatoes, chives and lettuce from the garden. He bunged in a few olives for good measure. He felt blessed with the continuing warm spell and the presence of a delightful companion.

"This is almost Mediterranean," he said as they carried their plates and glasses outside.

"Yes, you must treasure days like this in Cumbria."

"Where do you live?"

"Oh, in St Vérand, Isère."

"That's Hugo's village."

"Exactly. But you promised your story first."

Much of what David told Catherine she must have heard from the horse's mouth, but perhaps he was able to put it all in perspective. Here is what he told her:

"Hugo and I were colleagues in Brussels in the 1980s, working at the European Commission. While I had chosen to transfer from a safe but dull civil service job in Britain to further my career as a eurocrat, Hugo had been parachuted in as a high flier to work in the cabinet of the British Commissioner. I had recently married Sylvie, an interpreter. She took generous maternity leave and we were enjoying a quiet home life. Hugo was flamboyantly single and a bon viveur. He craved the company of others and was the life and soul of any gathering. He enjoyed wine and most of all women. Nevertheless there were moments when he liked to retreat from it all, come to our apartment and sit quietly to talk and drink. It was as though he needed our calm and domesticity in between his bouts of a more riotous life style. We enjoyed the company of the more reflective, sober Hugo whom both Sylvie and I came to regard as a good friend.

Everything seemed to come easily to Hugo. He was gifted in languages and not only could he prattle away to our French, German and Italian colleagues but he was quite able to draft weighty projects and reports in the appropriate language. He also liked to have linguistic jousts with Sylvie in hers.

124

We were not his only friends. He knew people in high places and was never short of lovers. Sometimes Sylvie and I thought he only came to us to boast of his conquests – only he charmed us, too. He was never patronising or superior. As our babies became toddlers Uncle Hugo even charmed them.

He had no family of his own, no near relatives. When we tentatively invited him to spend Christmas Day, a very quiet one I warned him, with us he was delighted. "Just what I need," he proclaimed and turned up with armfuls of presents.

I know now in hindsight that behind the bluster he was a sensitive, lonely man. We never lived so intensely together again. He was eventually posted to the delegation in Bonn, then the German capital. Not so far away but in those days computers, smart phones and social media were but a glimmer in the Devil's eye.

We did visit him once in Germany and to our surprise found that he had fallen in love. The real thing, he assured us. Our visit was brief and we never did meet Gertrude. When they had been together for a year, a record for Hugo, he asked her to marry him. She would have done so on one condition and it was one that Hugo, the parent-less, self-made man could not contemplate. Gertrude wanted children, a family. Hugo was not prepared for such a commitment. There was no doubt that he loved Gertrude, a love that was more than simple possession. He realised however that they had no future as a childless couple. He persuaded Gertrude, against her will at first, to seek out and marry someone else. He would always be there for her, stand by her, but he could not give her children.

Sylvie and I were a little cynical when Hugo talked about this, but to our surprise, within a year Gertrude had found a man. To our astonishment Hugo continued a ménage à trois with Gertrude and her fiancé until the marriage, after which he resigned his job and returned to Brussels staying briefly with us.

He told us with tears in his eyes of their parting: "It was the most difficult thing I have ever done. On her wedding morning we clung for the last time, kissing, sobbing, squeezing the life out of one another. Then I whispered that she had better wash her face and put some make-up on. We did not know whether to laugh or cry. Anton, her future husband was there, too. He was also crying but waited patiently for their new life to begin."

"Anton must be a remarkable man," said Catherine.

"He is," said David. "Also a good friend. As I recount this, I can only hope that Gertrude and Anton lived happily ever after. Hugo retired from the Commission altogether and embarked on a new career. He disappeared from our lives, too, for a decade or more. Sylvie and I moved back to England for reasons beyond the scope of this narrative. The children began school; I commuted to work. All we knew about Hugo was that he had bought a house in France and that he worked as a tour guide. He accompanied coach loads of tourists around Europe. He reverted to his old self, revelling in being the centre of attention, drinking in the evening and, he told us, seducing the attractive women. We took it all with a pinch of salt, but we saw very little of him in person.

This was partly our fault, or rather down to circumstances. Hugo several times invited us to stay with him. He lived in a converted mill, he told us, a water mill in a village in Isère that had made oil from the almonds that grew in the area. He would love to see us and show us around. "Only," he advised, "give me plenty of notice. I am very popular and get a lot of visitors here."

We did not know quite how to take this and planning anything far in advance was difficult. Not only were our holidays restricted to school timetables but I had become a full time carer for my elderly parents. As a result Sylvie had taken a position as a language teacher in a sixth form college. We never did get to see Hugo again.

I did however have one long telephone conversation with him. We were sitting down to supper when the phone rang. It was unusual for him to call. I should have said we were eating and that I would call him back.

"Oh, I just wanted to ask when you were coming to see me," he said.

"Well, we've not thought about it really."

"You are always welcome, you know that."

I sensed almost a pleading note, a sense of desperation in his voice.

"You said you were overwhelmed with visitors," I said.

"Oh, those times are in the past."

"Are you all right, Hugo, you sound…"

Sylvie was signalling me to come and sit down but I mouthed, "It's Hugo."

"Can't you call him back?"

Hugo must have picked this up. "Sorry," he said. "Is this a bad time?" I hesitated and he said "I wanted to give you my news. Bad, I am afraid."

"Bad?"

"Bad for me."

Hugo had been diagnosed with cancer. There was a chance that a course of chemotherapy might help. This news had made him review his priorities. Things like catching up on old friends.

"Of course," I said, not quite grasping the urgency, "we'd love to see you. Maybe we could come over in the school holidays, if I can get a full-time carer for my parents."

"Forgive me," he replied in a more subdued voice, "I should not be disturbing you with my worries. Oh God, you are probably in the middle of a meal right now, aren't you?"

"Hugo, I'll have a chat with Sylvie and get right back."

He rang off. I did not get back to him. I got a second call that evening. My mother had died. It was weeks before we could think about Hugo again. We decided I should go over for a long weekend, see how he was and have that chat he needed. Perhaps we could plan a family holiday when the schools broke up. It was a while since Sylvie had been back to France herself. We started to make plans.

Probably months later I made several attempts to call Hugo but received no reply. At last a stranger took the phone. She told me Hugo had died."

Catherine had remained almost silent during David's monologue but now said quietly, "That stranger was me."

"Of course it was. How stupid of me. I should have recognised your voice."

"I hardly spoke. I did not explain his death. It was a long time ago now."

"Yes. Sylvie, my wife, has been dead for five years."

"I'm sorry."

David went in to make some coffee. When he settled down again he asked Catherine to explain what had really happened. She said she had moved into the village in France a year previously and had heard about a reclusive Englishman who lived in the mill. Rumour had it that he drank heavily. He appeared to have made no friends in the village.

Catherine called on him out of curiosity. Perhaps because he heard her speaking English, he invited her in. He seemed respectably dressed, sober enough but morose. Gradually she got to know him a little better. He even accepted her invitation to a meal at her house. She had to help him home afterwards because he had drunk rather too much wine.

Catherine and Hugo saw one another on and off. During one conversation he spoke about a woman he had known in Bonn.

"So you are that Hugo. I thought the name sounded familiar," Catherine had said to him.

"We haven't met before, have we? Sorry if that sounds like a cliché," replied Hugo. "Before France I mean."

"No, no, but it is Gertrude you are talking about. I met her at a spa a few years back and she told me a little about herself."

"Did it work out for her?"

"She seemed happy. She was having a break from her two children. The spa weekend was a birthday gift from her husband."

Hugo seemed moved but did not press for more information other than to ask, "Did she say how old the children were?"

"No. Hugo, don't go there!"

Catherine did not see Hugo for a while after that because she had to go away. On her return home to the village she went round to look Hugo up. See how he was getting on. No one answered the door. She returned later with the same result. She asked in the village whether anyone had seen Hugo recently but no one had missed him. She had the bright idea of asking the doctor who suggested Hugo might be in hospital.

"Why, is he unwell?"

She worried the truth out of the doctor who confessed that he did not know whether Hugo had followed the chemotherapy treatment. Concerned, they both went to the mill, forced an entry and found Hugo dead at the foot of the steep stairs. He had evidently fallen down and smashed his head on the flagstones. He had probably been dead for days. A post mortem revealed that he had been drinking heavily and that he had not attended his chemotherapy.

Catherine had searched for an address book so that she could inform any relatives or friends of his death. There was nothing. She got into his computer but his email record and contacts list had been wiped clean.

David listened to Catherine in disbelief. She and he might have been talking about a different person. David remembered the extrovert, the party goer and yes, the womaniser. He had been such a vigorous man. Catherine had briefly known a sad recluse, but even she had not foreseen this end.

"I wonder if it would have made any difference if I had not cut him off during our last telephone conversation."

"Who knows?" she answered truthfully. "The cancer would have got him in the end anyway."

"People are cured."

"I think Hugo was incurable in many ways."

128

"He was a good man."

"Who met a bad end."

David accompanied Catherine back to their mutual friends. They invited him in and Julia Fleming asked him, "Did you have a nice chat?"

"It was very revealing."

"For both of us, I think," said Catherine.

The following day she returned to her home in France.

David had failed two friends but he had little time to brood before yet another encounter occurred that extraordinary summer fortnight. Another story about what some people will do for love. It made him think that some of us lead as rich a life in our imaginations as we do in our daily lives. Call it delusion or wishful thinking, but it is as real as the quotidian.

Everyone was beginning to take the run of sunshine for granted. For David it was becoming almost a habit to pull on only shorts and shirt when he got up in the morning and sandals when he walked up the river bank to fetch his newspaper from the bus shelter.

One day, returning with his paper he saw an elderly woman sitting on the bench by the weir, a favourite spot in the centre of the green. He had noticed her earlier because she was quaint, and behaving a little strangely. She had reminded him of Miss Marple from the Agatha Christie novels. Good, he thought, he would be able to walk past and get a closer look. However when he did get closer he sensed something was wrong. The old woman was crying.

"Are you all right?" he asked

Startled, she blinked away her tears and said, "Yes, thank you."

"You seem upset."

"I am fine," she retorted sharply. "I have come to a decision."

"It must have been a difficult one." He tried to make his comment sound sympathetic, but in truth he was intrigued.

"It was indeed," she admitted and buried her head in her hands.

David would normally have hesitated so directly to strike up an intimate conversation with a stranger but this bewitching summer had emboldened him. He sat down beside her on the bench.

"Do you want to talk about it?" he asked. "Not here. Look, I live in that house just across the river. We can sit in my garden."

"I'm sure you would rather read your paper," she observed, but she accepted his invitation.

Beatrice had loved a man and he had loved her. It had been an intense relationship over a brief period before each went on their way. Both were attending a six-week summer school at the University of Oslo, studying Norwegian language and literature. Their motivation was different. Dom, already making a name for himself as a poet, wanted to study and translate contemporary Norwegian poets such as Rolf Jackson, Olav Hauge and Gunvor Hofmo. Beatrice worked on the cruise ships that plied the long and beautiful Norwegian coastline and took tourists north to see the midnight sun or the aurora borealis depending on the season. The course would deepen her knowledge of the country and its traditions. It was the poetry however that drew them together.

"He asked me," said Beatrice, her old woman's voice quavering, "what my favourite poem was. I was a little in awe of this man who struck me as more intellectual than sentimental. I thought he might scorn me but I quoted a romantic poem that I loved:

> [1]Por una mirada, un mundo
> Por una sonrisa, un cielo
> Por un beso. Yo no sé
> Qué te diera por un beso!"

"Lovely," he said. "You need give me nothing." And he kissed me. I pushed him off, laughing.

"Well, you asked for it. Or the poem did."

"You speak Spanish?"

"A little. I recognize the poems of Becquer at least."

Their time together was all too short. For some it would have been a summer affair, a happy memory; for Beatrice Dom remained the love of her life. Like most of us, she had moved on, had other relationships, another life, but as she was to reveal there was rather a special element to her devotion.

Dom became a well known voice, one of the few who made his living as a poet. Those who enjoy poetry would buy his collections at regular intervals or read single poems in various publications. He was not however a public figure. Few knew what he looked like. He thrived before the fashion for performance poetry and he rarely attended literary events or appeared on television. He was content to live simply in the country,

---

[1] *For a look, a world, for a smile a heaven, for a kiss. I don't know what I would give you for a kiss*

writing and translating. Just occasionally he would give a guest lecture at a university.

By the time Beatrice was telling David this Dom had retired, if poets ever do. He did not know Dom's poetry but the name still resonated.

"Then one day not so long ago," Beatrice told him, "Everything changed."

She had switched on Radio 3 one Sunday before lunch and heard Michael Berkely's programme, Private Passions in which well-known guests talk about their favourite classical music and extracts are played.

"Well blow me down. That week's guest was none other than Dom Scott, the poet. I went weak at the knees. Naturally I listened in fascination, fearful of what he might reveal. But he remained true to character. He explained beautifully why certain pieces of music appealed to him, he deftly batted away any questions that probed his private life. Until the end. It was how he finished his programme that sent a tsunami through my veins, through my heart." Beatrice fell silent. Again those tears of emotion.

"Beatrice," prompted David. "I know this is painful, but you can't leave me in suspense now."

"It is not painful," she resumed. "It was beautiful. You see, before introducing his final selection he said he had a confession to make. 'I have a secret love,' he said. 'I am happily married and so is she. She knows who she is.' Then he spoke to me over the radio without naming me, of course. 'If you are listening, this is for you,' And do you know what, the music that played out the programme was the Shepherd's Song from Bailero by Canteloube. Our song. We had heard it sung live together. A song of such peace."

"That's amazing," said David, "but surely his confession would have sparked a media frenzy, journalists would have been searching for the mystery woman."

"That is what I feared but apart from the radio critic in the Oldie Magazine wondering whether this secret love was his muse there was very little interest. Radio 3, serious poetry, even classical music are a minority taste.

"But were you his muse? Your name is appropriate."

"No," she said, "not in his published work at least. That was more pastoral than personal."

"What do you mean 'at least'?

"Well," she said, her eyes now twinkling like Miss Marple's, "I, too, have a secret. We never met again but we exchanged Christmas cards for a few years and he would send me poems from time to time. Love poems, of course, and always a Valentine poem. They were quite unlike his published verse."

"So he is your Dante. Did he never publish these poems himself?"

"Of course not. They were private and personal. Some have titles such as

Just Between You and Me
This is No Betrayal
Our Secret

Quite clear, no?"

David stared at Beatrice who was smiling now. She had indeed kept the poems secret throughout her life, her career, her marriage. There were, she told him, more than a hundred poems. Through them she had lived an alternative life.

"Presumably," David said, "he did too. Otherwise he would not have kept composing them."

"Perhaps because I was his ideal love, almost an imaginary lover."

"No, I don't believe that. It was an unusual arrangement but it sounds real to me. You cannot deny that you are his muse."

"Was," she said. "I have not finished my story."

She told David that presently she was alone again. Free. When she heard Dom on the radio she thought there was no longer any reason to conceal their love and to live apart. Or that at least she might spend a little time with him in the flesh. But had he not said on the radio that he was happily married? Beatrice had no wish to burst in and destroy the happiness that Dom and his wife enjoyed.

"I decided to stalk him. In the nicest way. I remained invisible."

This explained why David had noticed her in the village. He realised, too, who this Dom was. He had occasionally seen an elderly couple walking along the riverside hand in hand. They never came to the coffee mornings or joined in village activity. David had not even recognised him as the famous poet. Like many people he did not know what Dom Scott even he looked like. If anyone in the village had known they would have pestered him for a talk or a reading. David had simply assumed that the couple had their own circle and they went elsewhere to shop or perhaps had home deliveries. These were the questions Beatrice had also been asking. What she had not known was that shortly after Dom's broadcast he had had a stroke. He was back home again now but in a wheelchair. Worse, he had suffered vascular dementia.

Beatrice watched the house, saw Dom in his wheelchair and saw how his wife, a woman as neatly dressed and of the same age as herself tended her husband. A carer came to help with lifting and other tasks but his wife devoted all the time remaining to them to her husband. On fine days such as we had been experiencing, she would take him out in his wheelchair. It was quite a struggle for an elderly woman.

Eventually Beatrice got her chance. In order to let a tractor past, Dom's wife had pushed the chair on to the soft verge. It had sunk in and the wheels stuck. Beatrice made out she was just passing by and offered to help. Together the two women heaved the poet back on to the road. Dom had hardly reacted. His attention seemed to focus on a black admiral butterfly that was sipping nectar from some honeysuckle in the hedge. On an impulse Beatrice went round in front of him, put her face close and said, "Hello Dom." He did not recognise her and by way of explanation to his wife for her bizarre behaviour she said, "Sorry. I used to know him. He is the poet, isn't he?"

"I'm afraid his writing days are over now."

Beatrice asked Mrs Scott if she needed help getting him home but she said she would manage now. She thanked Beatrice for her help, took her husband's hand and said, "At least I think he still knows me."

Beatrice thought Dom smiled at the sound of his wife's voice. She walked back into the village alone. When I had found her weeping on the bench by the weir it had been the next day. She had made her decision.

"I should never have come." She felt she should not have intruded. Dom was being cared for by a faithful and loving wife. They were a couple with their own story.

The secret love story between Dom and Beatrice, as much in the imagination as in their day-to-day living, could wait. Wait until after Dom's death, after Beatrice's when perhaps the poems might be published at last.

"Unless of course I destroy them," said Beatrice. "I doubt Dom kept copies."

"I don't think you should, Beatrice," mused David. "I think you will go down in literary history as the English Beatrice, Dom Scott's true muse. You will live on in a way. Your love will live on."

"I think you are being ridiculously romantic and soppy," she said disapprovingly. She rose from the seat and smoothing herself down she added. "In any case, neither of us is dead yet."

"Indeed not," agreed David and that was the last he saw of Beatrice.

Thinking over these stories David is struck again that all these encounters occurred within the space of a few weeks of summer; more unusual perhaps for Cumbria, that the warm spell lasted even that long.

He sits now alone on his ocularium with its view over the river and the green. The water chuckles by, birdsong fills the air. A silent heron stands on a stone. He thinks of his own wife, his own love, his own loss. Despite these stories that people were kind enough to share, he feels more bereft than ever.

A Personal Alarm

It had been a dark, wet winter's day.

"No one's going to call round now," thought Trevor to himself and although it was still quite early he decided to light the fire and make himself comfortable. He slipped into his pyjamas and dressing gown and settled down in front of the wood burning stove ready for a cosy evening. He was wondering whether to read a book or watch whatever rubbish was on the TV when the door bell rang.

Trevor started in alarm. He was expecting no deliveries and any caller was unlikely unless someone was in trouble, or it was the police to tell him something dreadful had happened. He rose from his chair, took a moment to steady himself and went to open the front door. Immediately he unlatched it, two figures forced it further open, barged into the porch and grabbed hold of the old man. They spun him round and marched him into the sitting room.

"Steady on," he said breathlessly, shaking himself free. "On a night like this I would have invited you to step inside anyway. You are welcome."

The men were soaking wet. The older man wore a black oilskin coat with the collar turned up. It only reached mid-thigh and where the rain had run off it had saturated his cotton trousers. His bobble hat had acted like a sponge and was releasing a stream of water over his fat, unshaven jowls. He reminded Trevor of a wet sea lion.

The other man, though younger, seemed to be the leader. His peaked cap had kept his face dry and his cagoule was dripping water on to the carpet. Beneath it he was wearing a black T-shirt over damp jeans. His splattered white trainers trod mud into the carpet. For a few seconds the old man and the intruders stared at one another. Some instinct told Trevor he had to keep the initiative.

"You two look frozen," he said, "Can I get you a coffee? A cup of tea?"

Slightly dazed by the sudden warmth in the sitting room the men remained speechless, bobble-hat looking to his young comrade for a lead.

"Well, let's shut the door at least. There's a terrible draught," continued Trevor moving towards the porch.

"Leave it," ordered the younger man, pulling Trevor back. "Shut it," he nodded to his mate. To Trevor again he demanded, "Where is it?"

"Where's what?"

"Your money."

"Money? You're joking, young man. Who has money these days?"

The man raised his fist. Trevor stared down at the white trainers and went on, "Look, I'd very much appreciate it if you and your friend removed your shoes and hung up your wet jackets. I'll go and put the kettle on. Did you say tea or coffee?" He spoke with authority and a hint of kindness. The other man answered, "tea for me, milk, free sugars." He knelt to remove his bovver boots.

"What the fuck you fink you're doin', Len?"

"Takin' me boots off. Got to humour 'im, know what I mean. Find out where 'e 'ides 'is cash, like."

"There are quicker ways," said the younger man but Trevor sensed that even this young lout found the comfort of the wood burning stove a strong temptation.

"Make yourselves comfortable and we will talk about money. Right?"

"Forget the tea. I'm not lettin' you out of my sight," said his captor, but to Trevor's relief he removed his cagoule and cap revealing a close shaven head and tattooed arms. "Just sit down and tell me where you keep your money."

"It's not under my mattress if that's what you think. My small savings are in the bank."

"Oh yeah?"

"Go on then. Go and look. If Rory will let you."

"Rory?"

"My dog. He's probably asleep on my bed."

The youth eyed him sceptically. "I don't 'ear no barking."

"You're welcome to go and look," said Trevor, sitting down. The intruders seemed temporarily at a loss. Trevor pressed home his advantage. "Look, there's no need to threaten me. I'm on your side. We can help one another, can't we, Len?"

"How do you know my name?" said the sea lion, looking worried.

"Your friend just said it. I'm Trevor by the way, and you are?"

"He's Darren," said Len mutinously.

"Shut up."

136

Addressing both of them Trevor hurried on, "Anyway, there's no money in the house. But there's something else. Something a lot more valuable."

Len sat down. His woollen socks had holes through which his toes poked out.

"What's that then?"

"Have a look in there. Both of you." He pointed to a door to a room on the opposite side of the porch through which they had trampled in. "It's not a trick." Trevor rose. "Come and see."

They came suspiciously towards the door to Trevor's study. Trevor opened up and turned on the light. Standing aside he said, "What do you see?"

"Phwoah!" blew the sea lion.

"What?" said his mate, pushing him aside. From behind them Trevor said, "Phwoah is the word for it, isn't it?"

The two men faced the painting of a languid woman in a silky, orange dress reclining on a couch. Her shapely right thigh was in the foreground. The other leg drawn up behind it. Her sleepy face, slightly flushed with heat and drowsiness was framed between her bare arms while her thick, chestnut hair fell along the top of the divan.

"Do you like her?"

"Sexy all right," said the younger man.

"Sexy, but not in a pornographic way. Sensual, wouldn't you agree? But do you think it is a good painting?"

"'appy to have it on my wall," said Len.

"You ain't got no wall. Not of your own though," sneered his mate.

"It's called Flaming June," interrupted Trevor. "By Leighton. Look at her thigh. Closely. The silk dress is so thin it scarcely conceals the flesh. That's skill, don't you think?"

"We ain't at school, Grandpa. What you playing at?" said the suspicious younger man.

"I'm not playing at anything. I want to help you choose." Trevor was getting anxious himself. He would not be able to string them along for ever. His relaxed, cordial manner did not betray these nerves. "Let's go back into the warmth and I'll explain. As I told you I am on your side. You need money, right?"

"You'd better not be taking the piss."

They followed him back and the three of them sat down round the fire, the younger man very much on edge. Trevor had not won him over.

"I have no money in the house. Nor on me obviously," he smiled looking down at his pyjamas. "Nothing of value at all. Except my art. I am a collector of fine art." He waved an arm around the room and the men noticed for the first time that the walls were covered in a variety of pictures. "If you are intent on burgling me you need to choose the best. You couldn't carry all the paintings I have unless you've got a van waiting outside." Judging how wet they were when they burst in Trevor felt he could risk this assumption that they hadn't. "You know what that picture is worth? Flaming June?"

"Nah."

"If it was the real thing, several tens of thousands. Unfortunately it is a reproduction. But you liked it. You especially, Len. You have an eye."

"I used to paint meself."

"There you go then." Trevor's mind was racing. He had hoped the Leighton painting would distract them but he had to keep this up. "Now in this room alone I have a couple worth a lot more. Take your time. Look around."

There was a water colour, a study in blue of a lake, the water's edge in the foreground with dragonflies in the reeds; there was another rural scene and a couple of smaller paintings featuring fishing boats. On the wall on either side of the stove hung Indian miniatures. Len glanced at them all briefly until he hit upon a picture of a street scene. A large crowd bunched round the doorway to a pale building that announced itself in bold letters as a fish and chip shop. The street surfaces were all white, unpainted but peopled with stick like figures. A woman was pushing a pram, a man was walking a skinny black dog on a lead. All the men wore hats and the only blobs of colour lay in the clothes of some of the women. Darren came to look, too, not without interest.

"What do you make of that?" asked Trevor.

"Reckon I could paint better than that," said the young man.

"If so you would be wealthy. That's by a man who lived not far away. Manchester in fact. He was called Lowry."

"Oh yeah, that's right," said Darren to Trevor's surprise. "He done that crowd going to a football match, didn't he."

"Quite right. Now here's the crunch. His original paintings on canvass are worth a fortune nowadays. Sadly this is a print."

"What's that mean?"

"He was – still is – very popular, so prints were made in large numbers. They have some value if they are a limited edition of say a hundred copies. Look closer in the left-hand corner and you can see his signature in pencil and the number 37. That is proof that it is genuine but it is not worth a huge amount. Easy enough to sell on, though."

"Yeah, but what about the valuable ones. How would we pass them off then if they was famous like? People would know they was nicked."

"Not mine. Not if I did not tell the police. I have receipts from the galleries, I can prove where they came from."

"So?"

"We'd be in this together. I can help you."

"What's in it for you?"

Trevor was thinking much the same thing. His mind was racing. He did not know how much longer he could keep bluffing, or where it would end.

"Well," he admitted, firstly to save my own skin. I hate violence and as I have told you there is nothing else of value in the house."

"And second?" asked the younger man, revealing at least some interest.

"I was in insurance," he lied, "I have nothing to lose."

"Other than your pictures themselves," said Len, who seemed only dimly to grasp the situation. He'd come along to grab a few quid, to back up his mate. A simple robbery, he had been told.

Trevor remembered a conversation of a few weeks back with his daughter. She had visited him one afternoon with an unwanted gift.

"Here," she had said, passing him a plastic object the size of a matchbox with some kind of strap attached.

"What's this, love? I've got a watch."

"It's not really a watch. Anyway you never wear yours."

"What is it then?"

"It's an alarm."

"I don't want to alarm anyone." Then the penny had dropped and Trevor felt more hurt than outraged. Was this really how other people now viewed him? As a decrepit old man. He did not feel old either mentally or physically. He had not had a stroke, was not disabled in any way. "Oh no! I'm not wearing that, Patricia. I'm not senile you know. I'd still be flying if they didn't have their stupid rules."

"Dad, you had to stop flying because you had high blood pressure and that was years ago."

"It'll get higher still if you make me wear that contraption."

"You live on your own. You might have a fall."

"Stop treating me like an old woman. I mowed the lawn last week. I began cutting the front hedge this morning. Up a ladder!"

"So if you had fallen off the ladder you could have called for help with this."

"Doesn't look like a telephone."

His daughter had explained to Trevor that all he had to do was to press the button and those nominated would be alerted. They would call back and if he was unable to reply someone would come to his assistance. She realised she had wounded his pride and confessed that she had acted for her own peace of mind as much as for his safety. Furthermore that she had already programmed her own name and that of a closer neighbour into the apparatus. This had annoyed Trevor all the more.

"You did all this behind my back? Is everyone conspiring against me? Do I look like an invalid? Don't I have a say?"

"Calm down Dad. It's just a precaution. If I had told you in advance you would have refused."

In the end Trevor had relented. He was not going to wear it round his neck or on his wrist and certainly not in the shower which was the only place he had had a recent stumble. He reluctantly accepted the gift and put it in his pocket. When a few days later he had found it still in his jacket he removed it and chucked it in the drawer in the hallway where he kept his car keys, address books and useful bits and pieces.

Trevor felt someone shake his shoulder. Darren, the younger man, was insisting, "I asked you what else is in it for you, then?"

"You need my guidance. As I said, you need only to take the most valuable paintings, don't you?"

"So?"

"Look, Darren, please be patient. Let's get that cup of tea unless you'd like something stronger."

"I'll put the kettle on," volunteered his ever-hopeful mate. "Where is it?"

"Wait," Darren ordered him and to Trevor, "How many you really got? Valuable ones?"

"At least half a dozen worth over a grand. There's one more Lowry in here, actually. Can you spot it?"

The men looked around again but saw nothing.

"You stringing us along, or what?"

"I'll give you a clue. Lowry did another painting almost as famous as the football one that you mentioned. It's a busy beach scene, very crowded with colourful sailing boats on the sea in the background."

"You ain't got that 'ere."

"No, but look over there, beside the paintings of fishing boats."

"What, that titchy one? Kids building a sandcastle, innit?"

"Right again, Len. I can see you would make a good partner." The big man smirked as Trevor had intended him to do. "Yes, it's small but it is an original. Unusual, too, focussing on just these kids and their sandcastle."

"And another skinny dog," added Darren. "Useless."

"That's as maybe," said Trevor, "but it's worth a lot of money. It's barely known. I got it from a client of mine in Salford. He gave it to me. He had known Lowry and had bought it before the artist was famous."

"So how do we sell it? How do we explain how we come by an unknown masterpiece?"

This question, shrewd though it was, gave Trevor the chance he wanted.

"Provenance is all. Where it came from, in other words, and I have all the papers," he said, getting up. Before they could stop him he went into the hall where he opened the drawer containing his alarm. Just push the button his daughter had said. He had no idea if it was still charged. If it even worked, but he rattled all the keys and loose Biros that lay in the drawer while he fingered the alarm and pressed what he hoped was the button. Then he withdrew a notebook and went back to the men. They watched him flick through the book. "Oh no, I think I must have stuck it to the back of the picture."

"What you playing at?"

"You'll see if you remove that picture from the wall."

Len went over to it, removed it clumsily, nearly pulling out the picture hook, and passed it to Trevor who turned it over.

"There," he said, "that's the note signed by Lowry himself, 'to my friend Arnold Carpenter' from JS Lowry."

"That don't prove nuffink!"

"It proves the painting is by Lowry for a start."

"So how do I sell it?"

Trevor was encouraged by the fact that he had started a serious dialogue. He just had to sustain it. He knew from his experience, once during an attempted hijacking of the airliner he had been flying, that it was important to keep the perpetrator talking. He had been praised for his sang froid on that occasion. Here in his house he was on his own. Alone in a rural house in the dark. He tried to assess the educational level of the two intruders. The big man, Len, seemed simple and under the thumb of Darren, who it seemed knew very little but was sharper and more aggressive, more uptight.

"You would have to explain how you came by the picture, that's all. The evidence is all there."

"I ain't going to say some old git give it me, am I?"

"Why not? An uncle or someone. You found it in his loft when you were clearing out; or say you got it in a job lot in a boot sale and wondered if it was worth anything."

"It would have to be a story that could be checked out."

"We'll work on it. Now Darren, I don't want to try your patience but there are a couple more paintings I'd really like to show you both."

"Where are they?"

"Upstairs in my bedroom."

"Guarded by Rory!" said Len with a sarcastic smile. Perhaps he was not as daft as he seemed.

Trevor looked him in the eye, held his gaze and replied, "in a way, yes. Come and see." He stepped out again. The men did not try to stop him but made to follow. As they passed through the hallway to the stairs something happened that Trevor half expected and fully dreaded. The house telephone rang. It was time for quick thinking. He could just let it ring but that might be risky. Fortunately he was close to the phone and picked it up before either of them could prevent him. "Hello. Pizza? Oh, is it Wednesday already? No, not for me today, thank you. Either of you guys want a pizza?" he brazenly asked his intruders.

Darren grabbed his shoulder with a menace and Trevor hurriedly said, "No, not today but thanks for ringing." He hoped the men had not recognized his fairly obvious coded message. He explained to them, "I often get a pizza on Wednesdays." More casually than he felt he said, "Come and see Rory."

Darren released his grip and Trevor climbed the stairs. There were several paintings on the walls of the landing but he walked past those, opened his bedroom door and switched on the light.

"See! I wasn't making it up." For there over the bed was a life size painting of a dog.

"Now that's what I call art," said Darren.

"Yes, I am fond of it. I had Rory for fourteen years."

"I had a lurcher, too," said Darren showing a more human side "Faster than a greyhound he was."

"Yeah, took him hare coursing, didn't you? I remember."

"Shut up, Len."

Trevor pretended not to have heard and said, "A friend painted that for me. No commercial value of course." He knew that all he had to do now was to kill time before the men killed him, or at least did him some harm. He said what he really wanted to show them was the painting on the opposite wall.

"What do you think is going on here?" he prompted. The picture was well hung and Trevor had installed a spotlight above it. It depicted a sunlit evening on a fjord. Mountains rose steeply on both sides and in the background, their peaks were capped with brilliant snow. Near the water the shore was green and wooded. From a distant church perched on a rock over the fjord a line of large rowing boats headed towards the viewer. They had the high prows of Viking ships and each one was crowded with people in national dress. Even the oarsmen wore their costumes. In the foreground the leading boat took up most of the space. A fiddler leant back against the bow playing to the passengers astern.

"Looks like a party," said Len.

"Quite right. It's a wedding party. They are coming from that church back there and heading, probably, to some barn or farmstead. It's painted by a Norwegian artist called Hans Gude. This one is very rare because it was his first attempt. Later he collaborated with a German friend to put the final touches to the version that hangs in the National Gallery in Oslo."

"How come you've got it?" challenged Darren.

"That's another story we shall have to invent," said Trevor with a wink, hoping to make the young man compliant.

"Nah, I can't do this stuff. I don't know enough about it."

"I can train you up, Darren, don't you see? Len as well, since he seems to have an artistic streak himself."

The sea lion gave an imbecilic grin but Darren said, "I like Banksy best."

Trevor agreed that Banksy was very skilled but said there was just one more valuable painting he wanted to show them. For the moment the pair appeared content to follow him, acknowledging him as their master. He felt rotten, knowing all this was just a ploy, that in the end he was going to betray them, to break any trust that he might have created; any interest in art as well. If he could continue just a little longer to outsmart them, that was. A big if.

He showed them back to the landing and turned the lights full on. A bold, incident-filled painting stood out. It was mainly in red, brown and black but nevertheless very bright and powerful. It was a striking scene, the aftermath of a bull fight pictured somewhere off the main arena. Thin and exhausted horses, some gored and injured, one dead, surrounded the corpse of a bull hauled up by his haunches to be butchered by a man with an axe, another with a knife. Other men in soiled black and red uniforms were cleaning up tack and washing off blood and dust with buckets of water.

Len and Darren stood taking all this in.

"That's disgusting," said Len.

"It's the end of a bull fight," said Trevor. "Sometimes you can admire a painting even if you dislike the subject.

"Yeah, it tells you somefink about bullfighting," agreed Darren. "Stands out, like."

"That's why I bought it. It's by a Spanish artist called Solana. Believe it or not he loved bullfighting. He was a matador himself in his youth."

"Don't look like he enjoyed it," said Len.

"Well, it will add to your collection," said Trevor. "It's worth a lot of money nowadays."

The three of them stood on the landing, Trevor with his back to the banisters. Len was still examining the painting but Darren was silent and reflective.

"You keep on about money, Grandpa. Don't tell me there ain't no cash in the house. Where do you keep it?"

"All my wealth is in my paintings."

"That's not what I asked. We need some dosh now, me and my mate. Now where do you keep it?"

"Honestly, I don't." Then sensing a rising menace in Darren's attitude, he said, "Well, petty cash, I suppose like most people, just a few quid. In the biscuit tin in the kitchen, you know, for emergencies."

"How much exactly?"

"Ten, twenty pounds at a guess. Lots of pound coins and other loose change."

"Check it out," Darren ordered Len.

Trevor tried to maintain a cheerful attitude. "Put the kettle on as well. We can all return to the fire and work out a plan."

144

"You know what I fink?" said Darren as though he had woken up from a trance, come to a decision. "I reckon you're taking us for a ride. We ain't stupid."

"I know you are not stupid. That's why I am offering you a partnership."

"Sure, old man, but you need capital to be that kind of criminal. And we ain't got none."

"From where he stood, Trevor could see out of the landing window along the road that led out of the village. The sight that met his eye filled him with both horror and relief. A flashing blue light was approaching. Bloody fool police, he thought, talk about announcing your arrival. Fortunately there were no sirens. He answered Darren with assurance.

"Well, you'd need ambition as well. As for the capital, we would build it up. Sell one painting at a time at first."

"Take too long. We ain't got time, Grandpa. We gotta eat."

"Let's talk about it at least. Len, lift that painting off the wall. We'll take it downstairs. I'll do the kettle."

Attack was the best method of defence and somehow Trevor asserted his authority again. He almost hustled them. Darren went ahead, Len struggled with the heavy painting, lifted it off the hook and held it in front of him as he felt for the first step of the stairs. Both men had their backs to the landing window through which Trevor saw the police car enter the village.

"I'm sorry," he breathed and gave Len a terrific shove in the back. This sent him toppling blindly forward, painting and all and crashing into Darren a few steps below. Trevor did not wait to see what happened next. He had his own safety to think of. He turned, hurried into the bathroom and locked the door. He barricaded himself in with the sturdy, wicker seated chair he used to put his clothes on when he took a shower. And he waited.

He heard shouts and groans firstly from the intruders who must have been picking themselves up. Then came a crash as the police, who could have entered through the unlocked front door but had chosen to smash down the back door in dramatic fashion. There was a lot more shouting followed by silence. Trevor thought he would wait a little longer, make sure the coast was clear, as he had done years earlier, locked in his cockpit during the hijack attempt.

When he judged it safe, he removed the chair from under the latch, unlocked the door and peered out. He heard his daughter's voice call up the stairs, "Dad, Dad, you all right?"

"Of course I am darling," but he was shaking like a poplar in a breeze.

A policeman came up behind her. "I'm sorry, sir, but we shall have to ask you a few questions."

"Give us a minute, please," said Patricia. "I'll bring him down shortly." She ushered her shaken father into his room and they sat on the bed. "Are you sure you are okay?"

"Seems you gave them quite a beating," she laughed, "and that ghastly Spanish painting has taken a bashing, too."

"Oh, that's not worth anything. Just a reproduction I bought in the gallery as a souvenir. I feel sorry about the villains, though."

"Not surprised. The little one seems to have broken his leg when his mate fell on him."

"Oh, that's not what I meant. I mean I am sorry I led them such a dance. I feel in a way I have betrayed them."

"Hmm! Good thing you had that alarm on you though, wasn't it?"

Trevor did not admit to his daughter that it had been in the drawer where he had flung it weeks ago. "Yes, he agreed, but I did not use it in quite the circumstances you had envisaged."

"No, well we had better go and face the coppers. I hope you have got your story worked out."

"Nothing they will believe," he said. "Come on, then."

Under the Carpet

What Sandra told David astonished him. Now in her eighties, she was the older sister of his best friend. All three had known one another since childhood. Sandra still treated David the way a big sister treats younger brothers, but on this occasion, their talk turned to serious matters.

They had the time. They had always got on well, even though through their separate careers and marriages their paths had crossed less often. Sandra was now staying with David in Cumbria on her way up from London to visit a grandson in Northern Scotland. She still drove but welcomed a break half way and David was delighted to put her up.

They were lucky. Cumbria could be cold, wet and windy at any time of the year, but Sandra had struck a rare spell of warm summer sunshine. They sat out on David's ocularium, a raised patio that over a low stone wall had a view across the river towards the village green. It was a still and perfect evening, silent except for the tumbling stream, birdsong and the occasional bleating of grown lambs calling the ewes for reassurance.

Sandra poured herself another glass of wine and said, "this is a lovely spot."

"Yes," agreed David, "I had to move up from the south. Too crowded, and what they did to the farm was the last straw."

"I don't go back either. Falconfield is no longer a village. It's a treeless sprawl. I feel more comfortable in London now."

"Not really London, though, is it? Hampstead."

"Can't complain. I swim in the ladies' pond on the edge of the Heath most mornings."

David looked at the trim little woman. She had always been wiry and lively. Regularly beat him at tennis when she was a girl. As a teenager she and her brother George helped run the family farm and kept it going for a while, too, after their parents died. David sometimes helped as well during his university vacations. For all of them it was a happy time. They enjoyed a carefree rural upbringing before entering the cruel world of work and other people.

As Sandra and David sat on the ocularium they recalled their friends, certain parties, car accidents, deaths and Christmases. They'd had none of today's hang-ups about the countryside in those days. No blinkered urban attitudes. David and George shot squirrels for the two-shilling bounty on their tails, pigeons and rabbits for the pot in those times of rationing; they killed rooks because they damaged the crops. They caught fish for their mothers to cook.

Sandra had particularly fond memories of the meets of the Romney Marsh Hunt in their farmyard. All kinds of horses and riders assembled, from fine hunters mounted by men in their pinks and equally well turned out women to the modest ponies carrying sometimes quite small children. Most of the villagers came to admire those horses and the hounds. Sandra, George and David did not participate on horseback but like so many others followed the hunt on foot or cycled along the village lanes closest to the action. There was no resentment, no protest, no class envy. The hunt was part of country life and they participated joyfully in the ritual. There was no sentimentality about the appalling suffering of the foxes. They were, supposed David in retrospect, country folk at heart.

"I can still smell the flanks of those hunters," said Sandra.

"The riders or the horses?"

She ignored David's remark and added, "and the sound of the horn and the baying of the hounds."

Conversation soon turned to what-happened-to-so-and-so. All their parents' generation were now dead as were many of their contemporaries, yet in their minds' eye at that moment they came vividly back to life again, as young and active as ever. Time was so short, they agreed, yet it all seemed so long ago nonetheless. It was a contradiction.

Despite these childhood ties and what David still thought of as an idyllic period they all eventually moved away. George and Sandra sold the farm. George trained as a pilot and went to live and work in the USA. Sandra went to university where as a more mature student she studied psychiatry and met and married a law postgraduate student. She eventually became a family psychotherapist.

The weather continued warm and sunny, the village was at its best, the grass was green, the trees heavily in leaf, and the river tinkled cheerfully past the garden. Sandra decided to stay another day during which time the pair lazed on the ocularium and took most of their meals al fresco. This far north in midsummer, it is light on cloudless days until long after 10pm. Even then the darkness is transparent, if not translucent. They donned cardigans and sat late chatting spasmodically and watching the bats come out. Touching on their previous careers, David asked Sandra, "Didn't you find it depressing day after day to listen to so many horror stories in your work? Talking to all those traumatised people?"

"But I was helping them, too, I hope," she said, while admitting that some sessions had been profoundly disturbing. Nevertheless, she told him, when she went home to her husband and children and later, grandchildren she was able to switch off and immerse herself in her domestic duties. "It was so much easier then to compartmentalise. There were no smart phones, no email or social media to trouble you. There was work and there was home."

Between their long, contented silences one of them would remember something else and their thoughts would return to people they had known in their youth. Sandra was older than George and David and had gone to a girls' grammar school whereas they had attended the boys' school. Nevertheless they all knew a few of one another's friends and of course most of the children of their own age in the village and their parents.

"Do you remember Mickey Watts?" David asked with a laugh.

"Yes. Only child. Attention seeker. Always playing the fool." This was the family therapist speaking.

"He was all right on his own. A pity he did not play the piano more. He was quite musical but would not practise. Then he failed the 11 plus and went to the secondary modern school. We lost touch after that."

David did not notice Sandra's cautious silence as he continued to dredge his memory. "Actually, I did see him again. He had left school early to do an apprenticeship He was the first of us to get a job and to get married. Married a very strange girl."

It all came flooding back to David. He had accompanied a mutual acquaintance to Mickey's house at the latter's insistence. Mickey and David vaguely remembered one another. David even thought he had seen Eleanor, his wife, somewhere before but could not remember where. Later in the evening he had a strange conversation with her. Those were the days of the hippies and unconventional behaviour was not unusual so he was not unduly surprised when Eleanor confided that she and Mickey did not have a bed. There were no beds in the house at all and very little other furniture.

"Where do you sleep?" he asked.

"When we are tired we lie down and sleep wherever we happen to be."

Mickey overheard and said, "That's not quite true, Darling, is it?" To David he explained that Eleanor did not like sleeping in the house. She had a horror of bedrooms so she slept in a caravan at the bottom of the garden."

"I am frightened of spiders," she said, as if that explained anything.

"Aren't there more spiders in the garden?" wondered David.

"Not in my caravan."

Now, years later and sitting on his ocularium, David repeated this anecdote to Sandra. That is when she broke her silence.

"You know who his wife was?"

"She seemed familiar. A bit like a ghost in the memory even then. I could not place her."

"You remember Robert Glover the auctioneer?"

"Going Going Glover. Of course I do. Everyone did. He was a great friend of my father as a matter of fact. They would go sailing together. And Mother and Father and Robert and his wife would attend parties and dances together. I think they played tennis, too. I am not sure Mother was quite as close to his wife, a shy but pretty woman as far as I remember. Very much under her husband's thumb I should think."

"You and George used to cycle to farm and house auctions, didn't you?"

"Yes, we had a craze for it and on viewing days we would wander around big empty houses and derelict farms looking at what was for sale. Mr Glover never objected. He was very friendly in fact." Suddenly David remembered something else. "And of course, there was that tragedy about his death. I had left home by then, I think, but I heard about it. He was found dead in his boat in Rye Harbour. But why are we talking about Robert Glover?"

"Eleanor was his daughter."

"Daughter? I didn't know he had a daughter."

"There were two. One committed suicide in her teens."

"I never knew that."

"It was hushed up. I didn't know the daughters either. Not then. A lot goes on in village life that is brushed under the carpet."

Although Sandra did not voice the thought, David wondered if, and how much, his own parents had known.

"Tell me more," he asked and she did. A lot more.

It was many years after leaving Falconfield that Sandra in her professional capacity received a patient whom she quickly recognised as the Eleanor from their childhood. Eleanor had not known Sandra so her therapist did not let on for several sessions that she came from the same village and knew of her family. She simply let Eleanor talk, gradually eliciting the woman's story.

It emerged that she and her sister had been sexually abused throughout their childhood by their father. Her mother had been too frightened to stop the abuse; even to accept that is was happening. Eleanor's sister, having no one to turn to, had been driven to self harm and eventually to suicide. This did not put a stop to her father's unwanted attentions towards his surviving daughter and in the village the outwardly so congenial and popular man received only sympathy for his loss.

David was aghast at Sandra's revelation. Although all this had happened sixty years ago and he had not known the girls himself he found it hard to believe that Robert Glover had been such a monster and that his own parents had not suspected it either. Mr Glover's abuse of his daughters was bad enough but for David the real shock was that this man whom everyone had liked had been capable of such depravity. He did remember his mother once remarking that she would not like to be alone in a boat with Robert, but then she hated sailing anyway. That was his father's hobby. Once or twice he had sailed over from Rye to Calais with Robert in his thirty foot folkboat.

Sandra understood David's reaction, but there was more to come: having started she had no qualms about telling David the sequel.

"But," he was to ask, "are you not obliged to inform the police if you uncover criminal activity?"

"Well, I'm not a catholic priest. There is no secret of the confessional, but I have always used my own discretion," she concluded, for there was even more.

In this case it had to do with Eleanor's behaviour as much as that of her father. After her sister's death her mother became distant and remote and shrank from her husband's demands. This made him force himself all the more frequently upon his daughter. The crunch came when he took her down to Rye Harbour to his boat. He had promised her a day's sailing, but on arrival he said they could not set off straight away: they had to wait for the tide. He started to drink and after a while Eleanor realised he had no intention of going to sea where she reckoned she would have been safer. Someone, after all, had to keep a hand on the tiller. When Robert tried to drag her below she gave the drunken man a violent push, he fell backwards into the cabin and broke his neck. Eleanor ran to the harbour master's office and said, "Daddy's fallen down the hatch and he isn't moving." Accidental death was recorded but Eleanor confessed to Sandra, "but I killed him. I meant to kill him."

Sandra turned to David as they sat together that summer's evening over half a century later.

"I think I helped her," she said, obliquely answering David's earlier question. "I couldn't heal her and I certainly was not going to condemn her. But I hope I helped."

"Is she still alive?"

"I doubt it. Mickey divorced her after a few years. I don't know whether she ever remarried. Perhaps she lived happily ever after. We shall never know. I am not going to write my memoirs and you, young man," she said, adopting her big sister tone, "are the only person I have ever told this to. If you were to tell anyone else," she added mischievously, "I would deny it. I would say it was just another one of those stories you dream up sitting on your ocularium."

Planting

Two men in their late sixties walked side by side up a farm track. They knew one another only by sight, both being volunteers in the same group. By the end of that morning they were to know one another rather better.

Robert led the way, holding a hand-drawn map of the farm in one hand. He was a gaunt, wiry man dressed in Rohan mountain trousers and a windproof Nordic jacket. Ian, the taller of the two, though a little stooped wore old corduroy trousers and an ancient wax jacket. Both men were shod in solid boots: they were prepared for a morning of tree planting.

"This must be our gate," said Robert, opening it.

"Yes, then I think Danny said we cross two fields."

Robert studied the map and nodded his agreement.

A dozen volunteers had met in the farmyard, split into pairs and were despatched to different areas where saplings, stakes and wire surrounds had been left for them. Spades, hammers, crowbars and staples were also ready for use.

"At least we have nothing to carry," said Ian for the sake of something to say to his taciturn partner.

"No, Danny and some of the others drove everything up in the quad bike."

"They must have made several trips, then. We are spread over a sizeable area."

The grassy fields rose steeply. They paused at the top to regain their breath and to enjoy the view. To the east the morning sun lit the Pennines and breaking the horizon to the west rose the mountains of the Lake District.

"Can't imagine a better place to be," said Ian. "When it's not blowing or raining at least."

"Grand," agreed his partner, "as they say up here," and Ian realised that like him Robert was a southerner though both of them were now settled here in Cumbria. "Better press on," added Robert.

"I think I can see our pile over there by the stone wall. Just to the right of that rowan tree. "

Sure enough they found a spade each and crowbar, the saplings and everything else they needed all stacked neatly together. Consulting his plan Robert suggested that each of them dig a few holes for starters then they could come back together again to stake, plant and protect the trees, which was a two-man job. They set to and found they worked well together. They shared the crowbar when needed, to loosen the larger stones in the rocky ground. When they had dug a dozen holes between them they paused.

"Well, that's a start," said Robert, straightening his back.

"Yes, warms you up, doesn't it, Robert? Or should I call you Bob?"

"Oh, Robert, please." He picked up a stake and a club hammer. "You're fairly new here, aren't you?" he asked unexpectedly, but in a friendly manner.

"I've been here a couple of years. We'd been here on holiday before, though, many times."

"Me too. I started with a holiday home but when I more or less retired I moved in for good."

"No regrets?"

"No, we love it here." He handed Ian the stake. "It's easier to do all the stakes first then come back for the trees and do the surrounds."

"All right. Get the hard work over with," said Ian.

"You hold the post, then. I'll bang it in."

"Hope I can trust you."

In fact they took it in turns and had to use the crowbar frequently to deepen the holes for the stakes. They worked slowly and methodically and there was time for conversation.

"What did you do before you retired?" asked Ian.

Robert told him he had had his own electrical business, manufacturing components for the defence industry amongst others. Eventually he had sold his business and moved up to Cumbria where, comparatively late in life, he met his wife.

"And you?" he inquired.

"Nothing so exciting. I was a civil servant. I commuted to London."

As they worked on and began planting the trees, Robert prompted Ian further. "Civil servant, you said. Which branch?"

"Treasury. Actually it is not quite so boring as it sounds. I did get to travel and was involved in negotiations with development banks and such. Had a stint in Russia, too."

"How come?"

154

"Well, I had studied languages and I spoke Russian. The Embassy thought they could use me on a contract to do with oil and gas. Of course I knew Pushkin and Tolstoy backwards but had none of the vocabulary appropriate to that industry at first." Then, picking up another sapling and placing it carefully in the hole, he added, "but I blotted my copy book in another way."

"How so?" asked Robert, pushing earth around the sapling.

"I met a Russian girl. She was a local staff member in the British Council. She wanted to perfect her English and I wanted to practise my Russian as much as possible. Besides she was very beautiful and I have always thought the best way to learn a language was in bed."

Robert laughed. "How many languages have you learned like that?"

"This was the best. And I married her, too."

"Nothing wrong with that, was there?"

"We didn't think so. It was all very sudden. Then there was the terrible hassle getting her into the UK, even though in those days spouses could claim British nationality."

"Impossible now, I should think."

"Yes."

They finished all the trees and next came the fiddly part. Unwinding the wire surrounds, encircling the trees and stapling this protective mesh to the stakes they had driven in required concentration. Both were quite deft at knocking in the staples with the smaller hammer, but there was the odd banged finger. After a while Robert prompted Ian to continue his story.

"Well, Roza and I got back and I continued to work at the Treasury, but I no longer found it so interesting. I grew tired of the commuting, and no overseas trips seemed to be in the offing any more. Roza, or Rosalind as she began to call herself to her English friends, urged me to stick it out. She enjoyed her own trips to London."

"Shopping, I suppose."

"That, and she would spend whole days in galleries and museums and visit other exhibitions. Sometimes she returned home after me. We did sometimes meet after my work in London and go to the theatre, too. She revelled in it. The commuting tired me, though and after a few more years I took advantage of a generous redundancy scheme to set up my own consultancy in conflict resolution. Freelance but more enjoyable and it paid the bills."

"And your wife Roza, Rosalind?"

"She got freelance work too. In the Foreign Office actually, escorting, or should I say meeting and greeting foreign dignitaries. Taking them to their appointments and so on. It was on account of me she got the job I suppose. I was trustworthy, whatever else they thought of me."

"I wonder whether she ever took anyone to the Ministry of Defence. I had a lot of contacts there through my work."

"I don't know. We were both so busy that we agreed never to discuss our work when we were home together."

The men worked on, lost in concentration and in their own thoughts. There were still several more trees to plant in another position, beyond the stone wall. They carried the saplings and stakes they needed across the field and returned for the tools and the wire mesh.

"This is hard work," panted Ian.

"Yes, but we have plenty of time yet."

They dumped all they needed at the selected site and paused for breath.

"Where did you commute from? I mean where did you live?"

"Oh, you wouldn't know it. A small commuter town called Wadhurst on the Hastings to Charing Cross line."

"Wadhurst. Yes I do know it. At least I used to know someone who lived there. Love of my life actually. Well for a few months. Then she dumped me. Disappeared. A year later I met my wife."

"No regrets then. When was this?"

"Ten, fifteen years ago. I don't suppose you knew her."

"It's a large commuter town. And you know, Southerners don't speak to one another, especially not on trains. What was her name?"

"Lynne."

"Doesn't ring a bell. Where did she live?"

"She wouldn't say. I went there once. We met in a hotel. I think it was just across the road from the station."

"Yes, converted to housing now I believe."

"I never went into the town proper, come to think of it. Caught the first train back to London in the morning. Perhaps you were on it, too."

"That we'll never know. Paths cross in curious ways."

The men's attention was concentrated for a while on their new task. New holes, new stakes to strike in, trees to plant and protect. They now worked as an efficient team, each knowing what to do, where to place the staples, where to twist the wire. But Robert's memory had been stirred and he told Ian how he had first met Lynne at an arms fair where he had been exhibiting. He had gone to a cafe in the same hall for a break and

156

was sitting at the last free table when an attractive woman, holding her own coffee asked if she might join him.

"I remember it as though it were yesterday. She had penetrating green eyes, short black hair and a big smile. She was very assertive," he recalled. "Even if I had said no I am sure she would have occupied the spare chair regardless. Of course I said yes. I was enchanted from the start. She asked about my work and I must have gone on a bit, staring into her watchful, cat-like eyes. She seemed interested, though, seemed to have a good understanding of what I was trying to explain. Either that or else she was a good actress. I came to my senses, realised I must have been boring her but on an impulse I invited her to join me for dinner. She said she had to get home but we agreed to meet in town for lunch the following week. That's how it began. I was infatuated."

"How long did you say it lasted?" asked Ian cautiously.

"A few weeks. Months possibly. Seems like a dream now. Unreal, but it was most intense period of my life. As I said I even went down to Wadhurst to see her but she did not want to take me home. We talked until late and I spent the night in that hotel we mentioned. I do not know how or indeed whether I offended her but she went home. I never saw her again. Or heard from her."

When they had firmed in the last tree the two men piled the spades, hammers and remaining staples in a corner by the wall and set off back across the fields to the farmhouse to catch up with the other volunteers who would be gathering in the courtyard. On the way Robert suddenly returned to the present reality and said, "Oh my God, what was I thinking? I must have sounded like a sentimental old bore."

"No, I am touched that you should have confided in me."

"What about you though? Does your wife like it here?"

"My wife died."

"Oh, I'm sorry."

"It was a long time ago."

"Was she ill for long?"

It was Ian's turn to reveal a little of his personal history. "No, she was poisoned in London. Died within days."

"What, food poisoning?"

"That's what I was told to say. It was hushed up." He changed the subject. "I had left the Treasury for good by then but Roza still had contacts as did I through my consultancy work, some of it still for the government. Conflict resolution. I think I told you. It was building up nicely and that's what kept me going really. Much later I moved up here to make a fresh start."

As they approached the yard they found that the other volunteers were already waiting.

"At last," said Danny their genial leader, "thought we would have to send out a search party."

"We planted the lot," said Robert. "Sorry if it took too long."

"Saw you chatting like old women," said one of the volunteers.

Robert gave him a cold look and said, "We found we had a lot in common."

"Indeed," added Ian. "Turns out Robert knew my wife."

Coffee Morning

"You coming to the coffee morning, David?"

David paused his dead heading of the red rose that climbed the white wall beside his front door. He turned to face the dog walker who had shouted to him across the stone garden wall.

"Oh, hi Bob. What did you say?"

"Coffee morning. You coming?" There was a splashing as his black Labrador waded into the river. The two men ignored it.

"Is it the first Monday already? Yes, I suppose so."

"See you there, then," and to his dog Bob said, "come on Smokey. Leave the ducks alone." The dog came out of the beck, shook the water off itself and on to its master and the pair of them resumed their morning walk around the village.

To visitors and delivery folk, this seemed an idyllic village; to those who lived there, lured initially by its charm, it grew on them even more. It was a welcoming place, as evidenced by the monthly coffee morning held in the village hall. This took place on the first Monday of the month and only those free were able to attend. They were mainly retired people but there were also a good few who worked from home and liked to pop out for a break and a chat.

David went indoors to change his trousers and spruce himself up a little. When he stepped out of his front door and through the garden gate he was wearing clean, though old, chinos and a clean sweater. He crossed the footbridge, inevitably disturbing the heron that flapped slowly up the river and over the giant sycamore trees. David followed the opposite bank. The river ran through the village green. Very little water was flowing over the weir but there was enough to cascade brightly down the salmon steps. Reaching the road bridge he climbed the short distance up the hill towards the village hall. There were about a dozen cars parked outside, among them a police car.

He went inside, ignoring the sign to remove his boots. It was a dry day, he was wearing sandals. The sign was intended for the muddy winter months. He made straight for the hatch that divided the kitchen from the seating area where the tables were set out. He dropped some coins into the saucer, greeted the two elderly women who regularly volunteered to make the coffee and asked for a white one with no sugar. He also took a small plate and from the display of homemade cakes he chose a slice of carrot cake.

"Good choice," said Brenda, one of the volunteers, "Pamela made it only this morning." David looked around. Pamela, wife of the postman and active in village life was, to his relief, not there yet. He could do without her badgering him into this or that useful function. Although he always tried to attend the coffee mornings and to keep in touch, David was not naturally sociable. He invariably felt awkward to start with, deciding which table to join or whether to take his cup and plate to an empty table where others might join him. He preferred to sit with people he did not know, partly because he could meet his friends any time and partly to get to know other acquaintances better; or in the case of newcomers and passers-by, to make them feel at home.

Today he spotted Beth, the policewoman who was sitting on her own in a table in the corner, pretending to be busy on her phone. She was a community policewoman. She had a car and covered a beat comprising several villages, her job being to get to know as many people as possible and to provide a presence. Attending coffee mornings and other village activities were ways of doing this. She often waited to be approached in case someone had something to tell her, some concern to express.

"May I join you?" asked David.

"Of course," smiled Beth.

David sat down opposite the uniformed woman feeling a little as though he were about to be interrogated. They had spoken before but he doubted that she remembered him. Someone had to speak first.

"Nice cakes," he said.

"Yes, I had a fruity flapjack. What's yours?"

"Carrot," he said, "recommended by Barbara." He nodded in the direction of the counter.

"Of course." She seemed as ill at ease as David in making small talk. Strange, he thought, since networking was part of her job description. He was about to make a stupid remark like, 'caught any criminals lately,' when they were both spared by the irruption of a flustered elderly woman crashing through the door. She spotted the policewoman with relief and went straight over to their table, barely acknowledging David except for a quick, "Hello, David," before blurting out to the policewoman. "I must speak to you. I think I have been robbed."

160

David stood up, offering his chair to the woman whom he introduced. "Beth, this is Joan. She lives just up the hill."

"Yes, we know each other," she said, her voice and manner more confident. She was now in police mode. "No need to go away, er…"

"David. Thanks." He took the empty chair beside Beth and facing Joan. It made him feel now that he was interrogating the newcomer. Good cop, bad cop. Which one was he? Then he stood up again.

"What am I thinking? Just let me get Joan a coffee. Another one for you Beth?"

"Milk no sugar," she ordered fully back in command. "Thanks. And no more cake."

Joan ignored all these niceties and continued, "I think I have been robbed and I think I know who did it."

"You *think* you have been robbed?" Beth took a notebook from the breast pocket of her tunic.

"Yes."

"Have you reported it?"

Joan was calmer now. She had been a headmistress, and spoke to the policewoman as though she were addressing a slightly dumb pupil. "I am," she carefully enunciated, "reporting it now."

When David returned with the coffees and cakes both women cleared space for them and he sat down again to listen.

"What does this man look like?"

"That," replied Joan, confidently back in her teacher mode, "is a much more difficult question than it might seem."

"His age, his height perhaps?" prompted Beth.

"You see," explained Joan in full didactic flow and taking in David with her glance, "most people are neither strikingly good looking nor particularly ugly. Most people make no impression at all. Visually unmemorable. If you tried to describe them the next day you would fail; if you passed them in the street you probably would not recognise them. We all look the same. Like sheep."

"I wouldn't say that," said David glancing around the room.

"What was he wearing?" persisted the police woman.

"Wearing? Nothing startling. Ordinary work clothes. I think he put on a dark anorak when he left. And he was carrying a toolbox."

"So he had a car?"

A van, I think. I did not look."

Little by little and with prompting by the policewoman the story came out. Other villagers came and went but David sat on, listening. Joan, she told them, had been having trouble with her kitchen cupboards. Some would not remain properly shut and some of the drawers were sticking. She knew there was an on-line group where people could post their skills and services either for money or to swap. There she had found Len who described himself as an odd job man "Nothing I can't fix," he boasted. Joan contacted him, described her problems and they made an appointment.

"He seemed such a nice man. Well spoken, and he removed his shoes at the door," Joan told Beth.

"Roughly what age?" she asked again.

"53."

"That's very precise for a man you can't describe."

"Well, he told me that. He told me he had been a banker but had taken early retirement to pursue his hobby."

"Sorry," said the policewoman, "but you think this hobby handyman robbed you?"

"If so," ventured David, "he should not be hard to find." Pamela gave him a frown as if to say that this was her investigation now and he should keep out of it.

Undeterred by either of them Joan was determined to continue her narrative as it had unfolded.

Len, for she remembered his name now as well as his age, had not taken long to sort out the kitchen though he scattered various tools all over the place. He also pointed out that one wall unit was rather insecure and that if she would empty it of the cups and saucers and glasses he would make it safe. She did so and left him to it. When he had finished she offered him a coffee.

He accepted and they sat at the kitchen table. From his well informed remarks she wondered whether he had been a politician or a councillor. That's when he confessed to having worked in the City. They also shared literary interests. He claimed to know MW Craven, the famous crime writer whose stories were all set in Cumbria. Joan would have liked to chat further but she realised Len must have other clients to get to.

"I mustn't keep you," she said.

He said he was in no hurry: the highlight of his job was meeting people and talking to them. He loved fixing things but he also enjoyed getting to know his clients a little.

"But you like to get paid, I presume?"

"Afraid so, but I only charge for the time I spend working. The talk is free!"

Then he explained that he had a handicapped daughter, a little girl of five, who required full time care. He and his wife took it in turns to stay at home with her. To spend this valuable time with his daughter was another reason why he had given up commuting to the city and moved up here. Also of course to relieve his wife who was trying to work from home. Between them they managed but at the moment his daughter was increasingly unwell.

"In fact," he told Joan, looking at his watch, "I ought to be getting along. Maggie my wife has a client to meet in person this afternoon."

Joan paid him in cash from the wallet that she kept on a shelf between some cookery books and a shopping list. He gathered his tools still scattered about the kitchen and put them in his tool box.

"Have you got a dust pan and brush," he asked. "I cannot leave you in this mess."

She went out to her utility room and returned with a long handled broom, a dustpan and a small brush. He took them from her and in no time made the kitchen spick and span.

"If there is anything else I can do for you, give me a call."

"I will, thank you. And I hope your daughter gets better soon."

It was only when Joan was getting ready to come to the coffee morning some days later that she needed her wallet again. It was not in its customary place among the recipe books and she could not find it anywhere else.

"So what made you think it was stolen?" asked Beth, not unreasonably, "and in particular by this Len fellow?"

Joan explained that she had not been out of the house since his visit and no one else had visited either. Moreover, before coming to the coffee morning she had rung Len's number and there was no reply, no voice mail facility.

"What were you going to say to him if he had answered?" asked David. "Sorry!" he said to Beth. "Just curious. I will leave the questions to you."

"I don't know. Ask him if he had seen my wallet. Stupid. Of course he had seen me pay him and replace the wallet."

Beth said she would attempt to trace him if he was still listed on the website, but she had to have a reason for confronting him. She could hardly search his house for the wallet which, if he had stolen it, he would have disposed of by now anyway. She promised however to follow this up.

The room was emptying as the coffee morning drew to a close. David offered to walk Joan home, suggesting they could have another look for the wallet in her house just in case it had fallen down behind something. The trio stood up to leave. Joan went to the rest room to 'freshen up'. Beth asked David if he thought the old woman knew what she was talking about.

"Yes, she is no scatter brain. Excellent at quiz nights for example. She is an ex-headmistress and normally quite reserved and self-confident. Today I think she is just flustered as anyone would be at the loss of their wallet."

Beth nodded. She confirmed she would do a search of the job pages. Len would most likely have worked for others in her patch, some of whom might have left comments. She would try to find out discreetly whether anyone else had lost anything subsequently. She said goodbye with an understanding smile and drove off in her police car.

When Joan emerged visibly smarter from the toilet, David as promised walked up to her house with her. They searched this very tidy and orderly home again and did not find the wallet. David told Joan that the policewoman was going to investigate other customers of Len.

"Why didn't I think of that?" said Joan.

"Well, you only discovered your loss just before coming out, didn't you?"

"I would know anyone else better than that woman," said Joan. "I could give them a call."

"Best to leave it to her," advised David.

"I'll just take a quick look." She opened the laptop and went to the website. David was curious and lingered. Oddly there was no trace of Len or of any other handyman for that matter.

No reports either, but fashionable though appraisals had become, there was no obligation on customers to rate a piece of work.

"He doesn't exist. It's all bullshit!" David laughed, wondering how Joan had picked up this vulgar Americanism. "He made it all up. His love of handicrafts, his sob story. Yet he seemed such a pleasant man. He certainly took me in."

"Yet he did a good job, you say."

"In more ways than one apparently."

They decided not to report this research to the policewoman. Beth would no doubt come to the same conclusion herself.

"I don't suppose he told you where he lived."

"Of course not."

164

Before leaving David asked whether Joan needed any shopping done until she was able to replace her debit card but she told him she was well stocked up.

"Well, if you want a chat, you know where I live. Drop in for tea or coffee any time."

It was several weeks before David saw or heard from Joan again. One late sunny morning he was sitting on his ocularium overlooking the river; he was wearing shorts and a loose T-shirt. He noticed an over-dressed figure striding along the river bank towards the footbridge a hundred yards from his vantage point. Half way across she spotted him and shouted, "David, I was coming to see you."

"What?"

"Good news." The noise of the river over the stones drowned her words.

"Can't hear you."

She hurried over, entered through his garden gate, breathless and perspiring in her thick stockings, tweed skirt and brogues; she even wore a 'sensible' jacket over her cotton blouse. She was excited, rather than flustered as she had been when she entered the village hall, and very determined. David could see she was bursting with news. He led her first to his ocularium, told her to take off her jacket and sit down, while he went indoors to get them both a cold drink.

"Make mine champagne," she said, wiping her brow.

"Will a rosé wine do?"

"At a pinch."

He returned with two glasses, a bottle cool with condensation and a bowl of peanuts.

"Now then, Madam, what is it?"

"I saw him again. And do you know what?? I did not recognise him."

"Saw him where?"

"I can't explain it. When I was a teacher I knew the faces and names of all the pupils in my school. Now I failed to recognise the man I could not describe in the first place. Some people must be born to look anonymous."

"I take it you are speaking of your thief. Alleged thief," he corrected himself.

"You are right there. Alleged. He had not stolen my wallet at all."

"Joan, calm down. Firstly, is it the same man we are talking about? The one who fixed your kitchen?"

"Yes. He had to remind me who he was."

"You have spoken to him?"

"That's what I am trying to tell you if only you will pay attention." She raised her bony bottom, smoothed down her skirt and said, "He came to my door."

It was beginning to make sense now. Len had returned to the house. Joan had not at first realised who it was, until he held out her wallet.

Gradually Joan got her thoughts in order and became more lucid. Len had found her wallet in his toolbox. He must have gathered it up, he thought, when collecting his tools from around the kitchen. Since then he had not opened his toolbox because on returning from Joan's house he had found that his daughter had taken a turn for the worse. He and his wife went with her in the ambulance and for the next few nights remained with the child in the hospital. During the vigil Len cancelled his entry on the website and turned off the phone to concentrate fully on his sick daughter; he and his wife willing her to recover. After some days the little girl was well enough to go home but her parents still needed to keep a close watch on her.

Len only opened his toolbox again to fix a leaking gutter in his own home. He was surprised to find the wallet which looked like the one from which his last client had paid him. He verified this from Joan's name on the credit card inside.

"He came straight round with it," said Joan. "He said to me, I hope you didn't think I had stolen it."

"Of course not, I said. I invited him in for a cup of tea and I think he was relieved to have someone to pour out his troubles to."

"I suppose you informed the police that you have found the wallet," said David.

"Yes, I phoned that nice Beth. Told her a white lie, actually. I said I had found it in the inside of my gardening jacket, my old Barbour. She will either do me for wasting police time or put me down as a dithering old fool."

"When all you are really doing is misleading the police!" laughed David, topping up her glass. "Though," he added noting her disapproval, "you were ninety per cent right all along in fact. He had taken it, if only by mistake. It is odd, though, that there were no other clients in the village."

"He explained that. They had only recently moved here. I was one of the first in this area. As a matter of fact I have asked him to come back and look at my boiler when he is in action again."

"How is his daughter?"

"Much better, but it was a scare. A scare for me too when I lost my wallet."

David remembered the state of her when she had irrupted into the village hall for the coffee morning and agreed,

"I know it was." Then he exclaimed, "Damn! You know what day it is today?"

"Monday."

"Yes, but what Monday?"

"The first in the month again. Coffee morning."

"Too late. I think we have missed it now."

"Just as well," said Joan. "That policewoman might have been there again. I should not like to have embarrassed her so soon."

"Her!" exclaimed David.

Joan returned a conspiratorial glance and drained her glass.

The Summer That Never Was

The first time David met the child was on the village green.

The small boy ran up to him and in French told him, "Aujourd'hui c'est mon anniversaire." *(It's my birthday today.)*

David replied in the same language, "Félicitations! Tu as quel âge?" *(Congratulations. How old are you?")*

"J'ai cinq ans." *(I am five).* David was still wondering what to say when the child asked boldly, and still in French, "How old are you?"

"I am seventy-seven."

The child stared incredulously at the old man for a few seconds and asked, "Why aren't you dead?"

"Should I be?" laughed David, though he had asked himself the same question more than once.

The pair was interrupted by a breathless young woman who had hurried over from Cuthbert's Cottages. She reprimanded her son for going out alone and apologized to David in heavily accented English. "I 'ave told 'im not to spick to strangers."

"I am not a stranger," said David. "I live here."

"You speak French?"

"A little. You must be Lucy Martin's daughter-in-law." Lucy had often spoken to David about her son and his wife who lived in France.

"Yes, Marianne."

"Enchanté. I am David." They shook hands and the boy told his mother that David was seventy-seven.

"Manu!" exclaimed his mother. And to David, "I am so sorry."

"Il n'y a pas de quoi," *(Nothing to worry about)*, said David. "Manu. Is that short for Emanuel?"

The precocious child agreed, "I am Manu. What is your name?"

"Methusela," replied David, suddenly inspired, "but you can call me Methu. Uncle Methu."

It was another year before David next encountered Manu. The child was playing in the river by himself.

"Hello, Manu." At first the lad did not remember him, until David said, "I'm still alive."

Occasionally that year and the next Manu's grandma would invite David over for tea or coffee with her visiting family, and now Manu had a baby sister. He had also become bilingual but spoke English with a French accent. Whether it was this, his nature or the fact they never stayed long he remained quite a solitary child. He seemed content and very independent. The third year he built a den on the river bank. David lived within sight and lent Manu a piece of tarpaulin, a length of rope and a garden chair for his den, constructed mainly of branches and driftwood. David was pleased to see him one day chatting to some local children whom he had invited inside the den and a few days later they were helping him improve it further.

The year the summer never came saw Manu alone with his grandmother for almost the whole holiday. His parents and sister had to remain in France to sort out a family crisis and it was Manu who had asked if he could stay on with his grandma. He seemed pleased to be free of his sister for a while. The whole of that July and August the sun rarely shone. Cumbria was shrouded in murk. Manu kept himself occupied indoors, and it was partially due to the poor weather that he became a household name.

David, who really was beginning to feel like Methuselah, occasionally came across the child during breaks in the dreek drizzle. One afternoon he put on a warm fleece and took a cup of tea out on to his ocularium to peer out over the village green. It was more verdant than ever after so much summer rain. The newly shorn sheep looked whiter and cleaner than usual. Among them a boy with a backpack was strolling about depositing objects between tree roots, behind rocks and in gaps in the dry stone walls. Eventually he approached the footbridge over the beck and was thus in hailing distance.

"Hello, Manu," called David but his thin voice was carried away on the gusts of wind and the boy did not hear him. Instead he turned and made his way along the river bank, stooping every so often to conceal another object from his backpack.

Intrigued, David stepped down from his viewpoint, left his garden through the gate on to the bank and walked to the footbridge. He sought the cavity beneath it where he had observed Manu place something. He found a stone, but it was not any old stone. Manu had painted it, and presumably many others. That explained what the lad had been doing shut up in his gran's house all these weeks. He must have prepared dozens of stones.

Gradually people walking their dogs, children playing, tourists visiting came across these stones, all signed EM. By now Manu had made friends with several other village children, all bored by the long, dull holiday. He had instigated a kind of huge Easter egg hunt only it was not Easter and instead of chocolate eggs there were decorated stones. Within days he was showing other children and in some cases their parents how to paint patterns on the stones and persuading them to distribute them around the village.

"To be a nice surprise for someone," he said.

The craze grew and became a major pastime, so much so that the artistic decoration of each stone became more important than their concealment about the place. The artists, for so they had become, began to display their work openly on the steps up to the village hall, in the bus shelter, on the parapets of the road bridges. The village almost became an open air gallery and it being the silly season, a reporter from the local newspaper wrote a story about "The Mystery of the Painted Stones." Of course it was no mystery to those living in the village and Manu and in particular his grandma were not seeking publicity. Nevertheless the newspaper's social media account repeated the story with illustrations and, by playing up the 'mystery' they caused it to go viral. People started visiting Mary's Beck to view the stones. Most were colourful enough, but crude, the dabbling of children. But there was something about those signed EM that gave real joy, radiating warmth and light. Manu had a gift for simple design, pattern as well as colour. In the same way that a sculptor uncovers a form hidden inside a block of marble so Manu extricated something sensual from the stone, a vibrant, beating heart. It gave pleasure simply to hold one of his pieces, to roll the stone in the hand.

It was a while before visitors associated the better stones with any one child. At first no one in Mary's Beck minded people pocketing a stone that took their fancy. The children got pleasure in painting and displaying their work; their aim was to brighten this dismal summer. It changed when a journalist from a national daily reported on the phenomenon and likened the stones signed EM to the art work of Banksy. Everyone locally knew who EM was and no one hitherto had imagined that his or any other of the stones were great works of art. Painting and spotting them was for most of those involved just a bit of fun, something to absorb them indoors when it rained and during the odd break in the rain there was the recreation of setting the pieces out in the open.

As a result of the articles, however, strangers from even further afield came to the village to seek out the stones signed EM. The inevitable happened. Many of Manu's stones in particular disappeared, shortly afterwards to appear for sale on eBay and other sites. The prices asked were ridiculous and of course none of the money, if the stones did sell, came back to the artist, to Emanuel Martin.

Several responsible adults in Mary's Beck became aware of this and they called for a meeting in the village hall. David went along and sat by Manu and his grandma. There was general agreement that this exploitation should be stopped before it got out of hand. Some people thought they should call a halt altogether to the painting of the stones, or at least to displaying them publicly.

"It's been fun for everyone," said one parish councillor, "but it has gone a bit too far."

"For whom?" asked another. "It's put Mary's Beck on the map."

"We don't want to be on the map," retorted a a grumpy recluse. "That's just it. This is a peaceful village and that's the way I like it."

"I agree. It is not as though we had any shops or cafes that would benefit," pointed out Jackie, a retired teacher and energetic hill walker.

"And my B and B is booked years ahead already, as are most other second homes," said Doris, a single woman who supplemented her let by working in a supermarket in town off season.

The discussion grew heated and as at all meetings it ran off the tracks; some attacked the proliferation of second homes in this corner of the national park, others deplored the lack of amenities. David rose to his feet and spoke softly but firmly,

"The real issue is over the stones painted by young Emanuel Martin sitting here beside me. We have all come to realise that he is very gifted. Colourful as the stones decorated by the others may be, there is little interest in them as objets d'art. Now Manu has a suggestion."

With the help of Manu, prompted by his grandma a new strategy was proposed. Manu suggested he would stop signing his own stones but put his signature on some of those painted by his friends. It was a generous gesture but Manu thought it might be more fun. David added that it would test the ability of the so-called experts to identify the genuine article. Those present agreed to give it a go. No one, surprisingly enough, had yet thought to sell and market the stones either for the children themselves or to pay into the village hall restoration fund. Like all such meetings its original aim had been lost among the egos.

The dark, wet weather continued. Occasionally it was stormy, but by now several children had grown bored with the game while others joined for the first time. Manu signed only those he thought good and also put out a few of his own unsigned.

Treasure hunters continued to invade the village. Those who found the signed stones were disappointed and wondered what the fuss had been about; the more discerning searchers of the Holy Grail were not fooled. They only had to hold Manu's pieces in their hand for confirmation of their authenticity. David happened to pass a man literally weighing up one of these stones, handling it with obvious pleasure. He recognised the man as the owner of the famous Silver Moon Gallery in Rutland. He knew him as an honest and shrewd art collector.

"Yes," he said to him, "that's one of Manu's."

"You know the boy?"

"Have you time to drop in for a cup of tea? I could tell you the whole story." A sudden squall of rain caught the two men. "I live just over the footbridge. Let's hurry before this turns heavy." The gallery owner, named Paul Durand willingly followed David home.

David explained that Manu was a very young child and that he would soon be going back to France when the new school year began. Meanwhile his 'uncle' was keen to protect the child and his grandmother, who was not capable of fending off paparazzi if it came to it.

"We are trying our best to keep this low key," he concluded.

"Quite," agreed Paul Durand. "The child is gifted, but it is only early promise. He will probably go back to school and forget about his summer spent painting stones. Nevertheless I have a proposition that might suit us all."

Paul's idea was this: he would pay Manu or his parents directly for a dozen or so of his painted rocks to be completed before the boy returned to France. He was not proposing an exhibition, but he would put one or two on display for sale in his gallery. The rest he would keep as an investment.

"I think the boy probably has a future and will make a name for himself in some other field of art one day. Think then what value these stones, evidence of his earliest work, would have."

David respected Paul's judgement having himself purchased rare lithographs from him in the past. He agreed to discuss the idea with Manu and his grandma and said he would invite them over the next day if Paul Durand could wait that long.

Their plan was almost scuppered by a news splash in the Daily Star, a paper that usually reported kidnaps by aliens or made some other preposterous headline or other. For while David and the gallery owner had been talking the sky had cleared and several children had ventured out to conceal their latest production of stones around the village. A man who had been seen poking around earlier and who had learned who EM was began stalking the lad. As Manu was placing a stone in a hole in the wall the stalker called his name, Manu looked up and found himself facing a camera lens.

"Ta, Manu. Now you will be famous," said the reporter and hurried off.

A couple of days later the Star carried a full-page picture of Manu under one of its typical headlines: "Stone the Crows! Boy genius revealed."

This was no surprise, of course to the villagers though they scoffed at the brief and inaccurate write up of their children's summer activities. Manu himself thought all this attention was silly. He was more flattered by his commission for the Silver Moon Gallery and he concentrated on that. Because of the French connection however, the press across the Channel eventually got wind of the story which Manu's parents read in disbelief. It was nearly time for La Rentrée, the return to school and the parents hurried over to Cumbria to collect their son.

David was able to calm the parents' anxieties when he met them at the grandmother's house and the general situation was saved by the weather gods. A storm brought heavy rain causing the river to overflow and flood parts of the village. Any remaining stones were washed away and this put paid to further activity. In any case by now, everyone was thinking about the new school year.

When the storm subsided Manu and his parents left for the airport. Just before they drove off Manu popped over to David with a present. It was one of his finest stones.

"You must keep it as a souvenir."

"Thank you. I will. I hope you enjoyed yourself despite the English weather."

"Well, I tried to light up the summer a bit," the boy replied with the most self-deprecating of Gallic shrugs.

"Bonne route," said David "See you next summer."

As he ran off back to his parents Manu turned and with a cheeky grin shouted, "If, Uncle Methu, you are still alive next summer."

Disconnect

Part 1

It was such a quiet night that all David could hear was the faint passing of air through his nostrils as he breathed and for one brief moment a distant gurgle in his stomach. The air outside was still.

Downstairs he knew the fridge in the kitchen would be keeping up a persistent, low hum and in the sitting room the grandfather clock its reassuring tic and toc. These sounds did not reach his bedroom but he did hear the clock when it struck the hour.

Through his closed eyelids however, he sensed a light. Normally the village was as dark as it was silent at night. He opened his eyes and found his curtains backlit. Had they been drawn, the milk white moonlight would have flooded the room. For this light could only have come from a full moon.

David swung his feet out of bed, pushing aside his cosy, double duvet. He went to the window and stood there for several minutes transfixed. He could not see the moon because it was directly overhead, right above his roof, but its light was reflected off the frosted ground. The river that ran through the village green now lit like an iced cake, glittered with silver diamonds. David could make out every detail of the village, of the houses and of the sleeping sheep as though it were midday rather than well past midnight. The winter trees were silhouetted in black detail against the clear sky. Higher, the lustre of each star was lazer-bright and there were so many of them. Clear though it was, this was a black and white scene. The only colour was the pale yellow of the moon that he could now see if he craned his neck, and the more intense brilliance of the stars. There were shades of grey and black; shades of white and silver also.

It was too cold for any wild life or domestic cat on the prowl, yet suddenly David saw a movement. A figure dressed in dark clothes emerged from the blackest shadow behind a house further down the river. Odd that he had not switched off a light when leaving, but of course no light had been on. He did not need to carry a torch, either, for the moonlight was more than adequate. David could see that the figure was male and carrying a rucksack that he swung across his shoulders before pulling a bicycle from behind the wall that surrounded the house. The man adjusted his crash helmet, put on gloves, mounted the bike and without lights, cycled out of the village.

David had been standing long enough at his window. It was cold out of bed and he curled up again beneath his warm duvet. He was more in wonder at the beauty of the still and silent night than the appearance of the man on the bike. This whole episode had lasted no longer than ten minutes. He would no more remember it in the morning than he would a dream. As he dozed off again he was trying to think who lived in that house: probably now used as an airbnb.

Part 2

In December it did not get properly light much before eight, but this morning the green was still white and frozen, the sky clear and visibility good. The temperature remained well below freezing when David ventured out mid-morning to pick up his newspaper from the bus shelter. Only then did he recall getting up in the night and standing enthralled at the moonlit view of the village. Instead of following the riverside back to his house he walked along the road, making a slightly longer loop. He passed an Audi car that he had not noticed before, parked rather poorly in a lay-by a few metres short of the house, which he now recollected was indeed used as an airbnb residence. The car, David conjectured, must belong to the people renting the house. It was an expensive vehicle but not a recent model. A sticker in the rear window gave the name of a dealer in Sussex. The occupants must be late risers, he thought, as he left the road to cross the footbridge towards his own house, for there was no sign of life.

At midday a woman drove up and parked in the road right outside that same house. She lifted a hoover and cleaning materials out of the boot of her car and dumped them at the front door, returning to collect some clean sheets from the front seat. She took out her own key to open the door but found it had not been locked. Careless, she thought and stepped inside with the bedding. She was not expecting to find anyone still there.

Across the river in his warm kitchen, David continued to read his newspaper until he was distracted by the wailing of sirens. He stood up to see what was going on. An ambulance, soon followed by a police car, stopped outside the airbnb house, their blue lights still flashing. Ever curious, David went upstairs to his bedroom to get a better look. A vague sense of *déjà* vu crossed his mind as he peered out, but he dismissed it, as most mornings the first thing he did was to draw the curtains to see what the weather was up to. What he now saw was more unusual: Maggie, the cleaning lady, was talking to a police officer. She looked quite shaken, which was unlike the Maggie he knew. David hurried downstairs, pulled on his coat and crossed over to help her.

"You look as though you need a cup of tea, Maggie," said David before the policeman asked him to move away. "Drive round to mine and you can tell me what happened when you are free."

She was a tired looking woman in her sixties who must have been good looking before two husbands wore her down; she needed no further invitation to unburden herself. She soon recovered after a gulping down two cups of tea and then David could not stop her talking.

He learned that she had found a body at the bottom of the stairs. It was a youngish man she had let in the day before. He was now wearing what she took to be his night clothes. One of Maggie's 'mistakes' as she called her former husbands had been an alcoholic and had himself once or twice fallen down the stairs. Maggie's first reaction this morning therefore had been to kneel over the body in order to make him more comfortable but as soon as she touched him, she knew he was dead.

"Cold, stiff and very pale," she explained. She thought he had clearly fallen down the steep stairs and banged his head on the flagstone hall floor.

"Who was he?" asked David.

"I dunno. I told the policeman to get in touch with Mr Dart, who owns the house. I also told him I needed to clear up. Another tenant is arriving at 4pm, I said. Only the copper insisted it would not be possible today, and I told him to tell Mr Dart that an' all."

"I suppose they thought it might be a crime scene."

"Don't see why. He was there all on his own. I met him yesterday. He was just staying the one night on his way to Scotland."

"So you saw no sign of a struggle, then."

"Struggle? Who with? Anyway I was not allowed back in after I called the police."

This incident gave rise to a few weeks of lively gossip in the village and a brief report in the The Herald. The victim, it turned out, had eaten in the pub in the neighbouring village the previous evening. The pub had been exceptionally crowded due to a large party celebrating the fortieth birthday of one of their number. Those locals who had noticed the stranger did not think he had had a lot to drink.

"In any case," said Dougie from the farm, "it did not stop him driving off to his airbnb in Mary's Beck."

Danny, one of the tree planting fraternity who regularly drank in the pub, thought he had heard the man boasting about getting away with some insurance claim following a car accident, but he had paid no attention. He and his colleagues were more concerned about when they would find time to heel in some saplings for the winter, particularly as it had already turned cold.

The inquest recorded a verdict of accidental death and quite irrelevantly chided the owner of the house for not having installed a fire door on the landing.

The consensus was that the unfortunate young man must have got up in the night, perhaps for the toilet, and taken a wrong turning. Given the strength of the moon this seemed unlikely to David, but perhaps the brightness of the moon was a detail most of the witnesses had slept through.

Part 3

Matthew and his wife Agata were driving slowly along the seafront in Hastings with their toddler strapped in the back seat. An Audi car driven by a young man and full of his friends careered suddenly out of a steep side road without stopping and crashed into the rear door of the family's old car. The Audi driver reversed, leaving part of its front bumper in the road, turned and drove off at speed back up the way it had come. Matthew's car was at a standstill, badly dented, the rear door stove in. Bruno, the baby, was very quiet. Agata leapt out to release him from the child seat. He seemed more shocked than physically hurt. He did not seem to be aware of what had just happened. Agata insisted they take him to A&E to check him over.

The coast road was always busy and several people had witnessed the accident. One woman had taken a photo of the Audi. She did not get a picture of the passengers or the driver but at least she had caught the rear of their car and the number plate. Other people helped push Matthew's damaged car to the side of the road, to relieve the congestion.

"We must report this to the police. They will be able to trace that maniac," said Matthew.

"Yes, but first I want to get Bruno checked over," said Agata. "He seems a bit limp." She, too, was feeling shaky. She kissed her baby, that she was still holding in her arms and he smiled back at her.

The couple got back in their car, Agata with her toddler on her lap. They were still shaken but once their brain fog cleared they became calmer. Matthew found the car, though damaged, was still drivable if now unsafe. They agreed they would proceed slowly to the hospital and since the police station was on the way they would report the incident first. Little Bruno seemed to have got over his shock as well.

"Anyone hurt?" asked the distinctly unimpressed policeman at the desk.

They explained briefly what had happened and gave their address for follow-up, explaining they were in a hurry to get to A&E with their toddler. They also gave the police the car's registration number and a sketchy description of the driver and his passengers, gleaned mostly from others at the scene.

"I will need to identify the car and the driver for insurance purposes. And by the way, when you find the car, you will see that it is missing a front bumper."

"We will look into it, sir," said the policeman before he was distracted by a phone call. Matthew and Agata hurried off.

During the anxious wait in the hospital Matthew had ample time to contact his insurance company which as expected required the other driver's particulars. It was some relief a couple of hours later when a rather rushed nurse gave young Bruno a clean bill of health.

"Just give him plenty of rest," she smiled.

"I think we all need that," sighed his mother.

Their relief was short-lived. The accident had marked only the beginning of an unending nightmare. The trio did have an unusually uninterrupted night but in the morning baby Bruno had a fit. Agata travelled with him back to the hospital in the ambulance, leaving her husband to sort out the car and their lives.

This time a doctor suggested that the fit could be the result of delayed concussion following the crash, but that given a period of quiet the child should make a normal recovery. As regards the car, the garage told

Matthew that the chassis was so badly damaged and the car so old that it was really beyond repair. In insurance terms it was a write-off.

It was not only Bruno who was not his usual perky self. Agata at the best of times could lapse into anger or hysteria. Matthew put it down simply to her Polish temperament, but now she seemed consumed with anxiety. The couple was so tied up with Bruno, and adjusting to life without their car, that several days went by before Matthew chased up the police about the driver of the other vehicle.

The police had kept no record of the couple's initial report and had taken no action. Matthew had to go over the story once again. It was two more days before the police traced the driver who lived in nearby Eastbourne. When a policeman went to talk to him, the young driver denied knowledge of any accident. He showed the officer his car. There was not a scratch on it. The front bumper was intact. The policeman could only check that the car was taxed and insured and that he was indeed talking to the owner. He thanked the plausible young man for his time and drove off.

Matthew could not believe the police had been so lax. There had been witnesses, even a photo of the car, or at least of its rear number plate. Any investigation, he argued, might find traces of the Audi's paintwork on the damaged door of his own car; there must also have been CCTV footage of the car in Hastings on the day in question. The police's response was that since no one was seriously injured such a time-consuming forensic investigation would not be a priority, even if they had the manpower to conduct it. This was not a TV crime thriller. It was just everyday Hastings, where much worse things happened.

Over the following weeks Bruno remained poorly and Agata turned her distress on her husband for the lack of action by the police and by the insurance company. She even blamed Matthew for the fact that they no longer had their own transport. When she found her baby lifeless in the night, she was totally overcome. Both parents' grief was made worse when a post mortem revealed that the child had had an earlier blow to the head. The parents were suspected of maltreatment if not child abuse; they were visited by a social worker and subsequently interviewed by the police. Despite evidence to the contrary these authorities even suggested that the parents' account of the road traffic accident had been fabricated. Matthew was too dazed to think of involving the press about these injustices, in trying to track down witnesses to the original accident; neither did he fully understand the toll all this was taking on his hysterical wife until she took an overdose. He was alone at the double funeral and, returning to an empty house, he learned that he had also lost his job.

Part 4

A man dressed in dark blue Fjåll Raven hiking trousers, warm shirt and sweater, his all-weather cagoule hooked behind him on the chair, sat at a table for two in a very noisy, very busy pub. He was alone, finishing his meal. On the chair opposite he had placed his backpack and gloves. He was wondering what to do. Perhaps he had embarked on a foolhardy venture. A cycle tour of the Westmorland Dales National Park was fine in summer but he had left arrangements rather late even for winter. It was just more of his bad luck that this cold spell had come on so suddenly and so early. What's more he had not expected a small village pub to be so crowded. He had hoped to secure a room there for the night, but being on a bicycle in unfamiliar territory he had not tried to book in earlier as he did not quite know where he would get to, or when, by evening. When he did try to call he found that there was no phone signal, and now it happened this pub had no rooms anyway.

He ordered an espresso to finish his meal and told himself he should really be thinking about the positives of his expedition. He was well fed, warmly enough dressed for the cold, and the weather had been clear and bright. After nearly two years of grieving and despair, he had now almost completed this project, this escape. He had got right away. The first few days of his planned ten-day tour had been tiring but he had felt his health and strength build after a while, and his mood lift. In another day or two he would return home, if home it still was, restored and ready to start a new life. It would be difficult, he knew that, but he felt he was on the road to recovery from a dark period.

Musing thus, his attention was caught by a loud young man at the bar talking to another drinker. Initially it was the familiar southern accent that drew his attention but then he listened to what the man was saying.

"You can get away with murder these days," he was boasting to the other, older man. "The police, the income tax, the local authorities, car insurance companies, they are so stretched and understaffed they never follow anything up."

"Yes. Try to get planning permission up here," agreed his companion in gentle, Cumbrian tones.

"I'd ignore it," advised the younger man.

"You might get away with that in a town, but in a small village, and I live in one similar to this one I suspect, everyone knows what you are doing. Someone would report it. Wrong window, wrong colour door…"

"You may be right, mate, but I live in a town where everyone has to mind their own business if they know what's good for them." He then went on to tell his fellow drinker how he had avoided an insurance claim a while back. He had driven with his mates into a town on the south coast where he lived and had driven out on to a main road at the bottom of a steep hill. He had crashed into a passing car. "Just a small bump," he said, "but I didn't hang about. Mikey, one of me mates reckoned we should have stopped to make sure no one was hurt, like, exchange insurance details an' that. But I didn't want no 'assle. Anyway no 'arm was done. I drove off fast as I could."

When he got home, he told his listener, Mikey, who was a bit soft like, got out to inspect the car and told him half his front bumper was missing and the paintwork all scratched.

The man at the corner table who had been listening to this half rose in anger but something told him to bide his time. He sat down again, hardly able to believe what he was hearing.

"What's this got to do with your insurance scam?" probed the Cumbrian somewhat disapprovingly.

"Well, I got me car fixed pdq, just in case. Got another mate with an Audi franchise, you see. In fact I bought the car from the same place. Just as well I did. Quick thinking you see. A couple of days later a policeman come up me 'ouse, didn't he, and asked if I was the owner of an Audi car. I showed him the car, parked just outside. The copper looked at the tyres, asked me to turn on the lights and then inspected the front of the car. That's all. Never even asked me if I had been to Hastings. He checked my licence and insurance, all in order, thanked me for my cooperation and drove off. I never even asked him what he was looking for. Didn't have to. Case closed. Never knew how they had got on to me, mind."

The Cumbrian man might have had questions to ask, but he seemed relieved when his wife dragged him away. She berated him from straying away from the birthday party but told him she was ready to leave now as they had a long way to go.

The young man said he wanted an early night and would also be getting along. "Been good talking to you," he said.

The older man grunted and followed his wife out.

The cyclist rose quickly, put on his cagoule, shouldered his backpack and went up to the bar to pay his bill. Thoroughly disturbed and a little confused at what he had just heard, he followed the younger Southerner out, unsure of his own intentions. As he unlocked his bicycle from the fence post, matters played into his hands.

That Sussex voice said to him in friendly but self-satisfied tones, as he clicked his key to unlock his Audi, "Rather you than me, mate."

"Yes, well I was rather hoping to spend the night but they have no rooms."

"Bit bloody cold to sleep out, ain't it?"

"I'll think of something. Maybe go to Appleby. I might find somewhere there, and I am heading for the station tomorrow anyway."

"How far's Appleby, then?"

"No more than an hour I reckon."

Whatever brought on the Audi driver's invitation, generosity or just the need for company, he said, "I'm staying just over the hill in the next village for the night. Airbnb. I can put you up on the sofa bed if you like. Only I aim to leave early in the morning."

The cyclist thanked him, asked directions and said he would be there in fifteen minutes. "I appreciate it, mate," he said, affecting the manner of speech of his host.

As he cycled down the hill, the village was revealed before him in bright moonlight. He recognized the Audi parked a bit askew in a lay-by and found the house further on, a light shining in the porch. He dismounted, concealed his bicycle behind the wall, removed his helmet and rucksack and rang the doorbell. The door opened immediately.

"Hi mate. Sorry, didn't get your name. I'm Darren."

"Matt."

Rather incongruously, they shook hands and Darren invited Matt into a warm kitchen where a kettle was boiling.

"I always have a cuppa before bed. How about you?"

"Tea, then. Cheers." He did not know how to proceed. Neither man wanted to stay up. Both wanted an early start. "Last leg," explained Matthew. "Train across to Leeds then another down South."

"With your bike?"

"I hope so, yes." He told Darren about his cycle tour.

Darren remarked it was a bit late in the year.

"Yes, it took a bit longer to plan and even longer to motivate myself."

"Why'd you do it, then?"

"I'd been through a bad patch. Lost my wife and child a while back. It was time to pull myself together."

"Tough. Covid, was it?"

"No. Accident. I don't really want to talk about it."

"Well, get a good rest and let's hope you pull through."

Matthew looked Darren steadily in the eye and said calmly, "I think I will now." He rose and the two men prepared for bed. Matthew asked if he could use the bathroom. It was upstairs. When he emerged his host was on the landing in a T-shirt and what Matthew believed were called tracky bottoms. Matthew engaged him in one last conversation.

"Darren, that accident. It was caused by a hit and run driver."

"Shit."

"In Hastings."

Darren frowned but the penny had not yet dropped, "You don't want to be finkin' of that now, mate. Like I said, we both need to get some sleep."

"The car was an Audi. I got the number."

Darren was now paying more attention. He turned paler. "Told the police, then, did you?"

"Yes, but as you were saying in the pub, they never properly followed it up."

"Typical," Darren breathed, but he was a poor actor.

"Only now I know who the murderer was."

"You accusin' me?"

"You were driving that car."

"I dunno what you are talking about. I don't even live in Hastings."

"You were seen there."

"Now look 'ere. It was only a bump," he blustered. "Nobody could have been hurt."

"You killed my wife and son."

Darren resorted to the only defence he knew. Violence. "You've 'ad too much to drink. I fink you better get outta my 'ouse. Go on. Scarper." He attempted to push Matthew towards the stairs.

Matthew resisted, swung round and in so doing pulled Darren with him. Darren missed his footing and twisted his ankle on the edge of the top step. He crumpled and rolled head over heels down the flight. His head hit the stone floor first, and he was silent.

That was easy, thought Matthew in satisfaction. He went slowly down. Darren seemed lifeless, but Matthew was not going to take a

184

second look. Darren had fled the scene of one accident. Matthew certainly did not want to get involved in the investigation of another.

He turned off all the lights and lay down on the sofa bed to think. Whether it was the shock or the natural fatigue of a long day on the road, he fell asleep. He woke four hours later with the moon flooding into the room. He got up. Darren lay where he had fallen.

Matthew knew what he had to do. He put the sofa bed up and washed the tea cup he had used, all this by the light of the full moon. He unlocked the front door and stepped out, leaving the key where it was on the inside. He removed his bicycle from beside the wall, put on his crash helmet and gloves and cycled out of the village. He had a strange feeling that someone was watching him, but dismissed the thought. He had ample time to get to Appleby for the first train. The last day of a long tour, and already he felt better.

Keep on Planting

"Would you like to do something useful?" suggested Bernie to his bored nephew, Mark. "If Mum and Dad don't object, that is."

The idea that his parents might object pricked Mark's curiosity. Besides on top of the lockdown and his disappointing GCSE results he was not so much at a loose end as dangling from a noose.

"What?" he challenged.

Bernie was one of the founder members of the village tree planting group. They always welcomed new volunteers and Bernie explained the task he had in mind. "It's more demanding than you might think," he concluded.

"I'll come if I can bring Jenny. She's well into nature and the environment and that."

"Jenny, your girlfriend, right? Is she tough enough?"

"Jenny," Mark said proudly, "makes Greta Thunsberg look like an amateur. She is going to save the planet."

"Aren't we all? Well, all right, if no one objects."

Next morning found Bernie with his nephew and his girlfriend at the bottom of Wild Fell Farm. He had warned them that the going would be rough and noted with approval that both wore sturdy walking boots. Jenny's jeans already had holes torn into them. They would be more fashionable still when this stint was over, he thought. Both youngsters wore a kind of camouflage on top. Bernie sported his old wax jacket, cord cap and gaiters. The tall, coarse grass was wet from the rain and this field, like many of the others was thigh deep in docks, thistles and nettles. The old farmer, something of a recluse, had been too ill to tend to his fields and hedgerows for some time, but he had agreed to their survey of his trees. The volunteers had received a generous grant to plant more trees in and around the parish subject to a survey and to the agreement of the relevant landowners. Caleb, despite his age, was all in favour of new trees.

"I know I have explained it all to you once," said Bernie to the teenagers, "but before we start I am obliged to make the following spiel."

"I know," smiled Jenny, "like fasten your seat belts and in the event of an emergency adopt the brace position."

"That kind of thing, yes. We must not enter any fields where there is livestock, be sure to close all gates and in general to observe the country code. In return the landowner is to warn us of any dangerous animals or natural hazards."

"What's that mean? Like a tree falling on us or something?" said Mark dismissively.

"No. Well there are no livestock and I do not think old Caleb even keeps a dog. But there is one significant hazard. It's in the middle of one of the fields, so we shall not need to go near it."

"What is it, then?" asked Jenny, tossing her long black hair out of her eyes. A man trap?"

She looked rather like a man trap herself, thought Bernie. No wonder Mark was infatuated with her.

"Unexploded ordinance?" Mark hazarded.

"No, there is a deep sink hole. If you fell in you would not be able to climb out. Odd it is not marked on my map, but I think I know where it is. But as I say, we shall not go near it. The grass is so high we probably would not see it anyway."

"Until too late, you mean," said Mark.

"So we keep clear," he repeated. "Now then, let's make a start."

They had agreed that they would go round together at first until the youngsters got the hang of it. Their task was to record every single tree on the farm by species and by age. Bernie gave them a chart showing how to estimate the age of a tree: quite simple really, once they had identified the tree.

"No problem there," said Jenny. "I've got the Woodland Trust app on my phone."

"Jenny knows the name of every tree, flower and bird," said Mark with full confidence in his friend.

"Well, if there is a difficult one, take a photo and we can check it out later."

"Actually, Uncle, may I call you Uncle," she said looking at the chart, "I don't know how to age a tree."

Bernie pointed out that most common trees were listed on the chart. You measured the girth of your tree four feet up the trunk and read it off against its name in the chart. An adjacent column showed the age of a tree that size.

It was a difficult start. They made their way through a rickety wooden gate and strode through the overgrown grass and nettles to the farm boundary. There was a hedge so long abandoned that several of the shrubs and trees had grown tall.

"Normally," Bernie explained, "we could just mark the whole length off as a hedge: hazel, hawthorn or whatever. But this is a very old and neglected hedge and it is full of a variety of trees that must be recorded."

"Yes," said Mark, not wishing to be outdone, "already I can see wild cherry, alder, probably elm."

"Hang on," said Bernie, "let's just make sure they are all on this side of the fence."

Mark fought on ahead through the undergrowth and suddenly disappeared.

Jenny gasped, "not the sink hole!"

Mark reappeared swearing, "there's a bloody ditch there. Be careful."

They all fought their way up the perimeter bagging willow, crab apple and the trees Mark had spotted as well. Bernie was confident his helpers now knew what they were about. He gave them the tape to measure an old field maple and the elms. It took them half an hour to reach a magnificent oak in the corner. It required all three of them to measure it. The 175-inch tape did not even go half way round the trunk so their six hands and thirty fingers were put to use.

"It is over 200 years old," Bernie said.

"We could have guessed that," said Mark.

"What a wonderful tree," said Jenny, and indeed it held them spell-bound for several minutes as they gazed up through its universe of branches.

They had spent an hour in this first field before Bernie fished out a flask from his backpack and they all had a drink of coffee, passing round the small plastic cup. Studying the map of the farm they worked out who would do which fields. Woodland itself did not have to be counted and as Bernie had explained, obvious hedgerows could be recorded as such. In many places there were stone walls with just the odd tree alongside. This made the job a lot easier. The most common trees were ash, many suffering from die-back, which rather justified their work. In many places, because the land had not been mown or ploughed or even grazed for years, trees such as silver birch and alder had self-seeded and marched out into the fields. One or two large old shade trees of beech and oak, reminiscent of the livestock they had once sheltered, did still stand across the fields. As Mark had said, they could put them down as well over two hundred years old simply by looking at them.

Bernie reckoned they might finish by lunchtime and suggested they meet up at one pm in the farmyard, as he needed out of courtesy to drop in on the old farmer and tell him what they had been up to. So they went their different ways. This was something Bernie was forever to regret.

After a while Jenny and Mark, becoming rather warm and tired sat down for a rest. As was only natural the sitting down led to lying down and the lying down led to kissing. They lost track of time. Realising they were meant to meet Mark's uncle in the farmyard they took a short cut across an overgrown field and in their haste stumbled into the sink hole.

By the time Bernie had finished chatting to the reclusive farmer and emerged from his dark old house, stepping over a dozen cats, it was later than he had intended. Mark and Jenny were not in the yard as they had agreed. Bernie thought perhaps they had got tired of waiting for him and had gone back to the car parked at the top of the farm track. He walked up but they were not there either.

He had little desire to fight his way through the rewilded fields once again so he walked back down the track. If he waited in one place as agreed they would eventually find him, he reckoned. But as he passed the pond half way down the track he had a horrible premonition. He had told Jenny and Mark about the sink hole but not where it was. From the farmyard he set off across the fields to where they should have finished their surveying. In the second field he disturbed a deer. This indicated to him that no one had passed that way recently, so they could not have reached the farm yard at all. He tried to remember where the sink hole was supposed to be. There was a lot of gorse and a thicket of blackthorn to go round and the field, like all the others was dense with tall grasses. Progress through them was slow and laborious, like wading through deep water. In any case he was stepping gingerly, unsure exactly where and how wide the sink hole was. In his mind he envisaged a kind of hollow, but really he had no idea what he was facing.

Pausing to orientate himself and regain some strength he thought he heard a cry. He strained his ears but the only sound was a lark singing high overhead and the distant bleating of sheep on another hillside.

"Hello," he called. "Mark, Jenny, are you there?"

This time he was certain. A weak voice was crying for help. When he reached the hole he could see why it was so dangerous. The grass and the nettles went right up to the edge on his side. On the other docks and grasses were flattened as though someone had tramped through. They would not have seen the pit until it was too late. It was like a ragged tear in the ground, the opening as large as a gate laid flat but the edges were uneven and ragged.

"Hello. Are you there?" he called from a safe distance.

"Help! Help!"

He edged forward, choosing what seemed a reasonably solid surface. He peered over the edge. He saw them immediately. They were a long way down. There appeared to be a pool of water at the bottom but the sides were rougher than a well. Nevertheless it was too smooth and sheer to climb up or down without a rope.

"Mark, are you all right?"

"No," he groaned.

At least they could hear one another but Mark was inconsolable and in pain. Jenny lay crumpled, quiet and still.

There was no phone signal in that part of the world. In blinding panic Bernie struggled back to the farmhouse hoping there was a working phone. He searched the barn for a rope but had made no use of it before the fire brigade arrived followed by an ambulance and the police.

"I killed her," sobbed Bernie to the police. It was my fault." One of the ambulance workers tried to calm the distraught man, who had to be dragged right away from the scene.

The incident was reported in all the papers. Mark had broken his leg but recovered. Jenny had not been so lucky. At the inquest it was revealed how Bernie had instructed the couple to keep away from the danger. No one blamed him for the accident but he remained inconsolable.

The tree planting group rallied round, joined by many fresh volunteers. With the agreement of Caleb, the old farmer, they filled the sink hole and planted two hundred oak trees around it. When they had finished Bernie led a small ceremony attended by Jenny and Mark's parents and other well-wishers. In memory of the idealistic young woman, the plantation would be called Jenny's Wood, though few of those present would see it in their lifetimes. Bernie still blamed himself for killing Jenny. It was little consolation that she was probably spared inevitable disillusionment, her dreams of saving the natural world would in time have been shattered the way things were going. Unless, and this was their only hope, everyone kept on planting.

Last Thoughts from the Ocularium

David was sitting on his ocularium where for many years he had felt so much at peace as he looked out across the river and the Green and contemplated life. Everything had changed when the health and safety cult got out of control.

Ten years ago the village had been quiet and peaceful, dark and still at night and as close to nature as any human settlement could be. It was blessed with a great many old and beautiful trees. A row of copper beeches welcomed arrivals, tall sycamores in places shaded the river and large horse chestnuts stood alongside the roads and bridges, gifting conkers to the children in the autumn. There were several oaks and colourful rowan trees. Sheep wandered about with their lambs in spring, ewes and grown lambs sheltering beneath the trees in the summer. Trout swam up the river as did the occasional otter, at times of flood. Kingfishers and herons had their territories and the river was host to many other waterbirds.

The change occurred gradually at first. Little did David know when he spotted the man in a high visibility yellow jacket and hard hat, computer in one hand and a clipboard in the other going from tree to tree, that this was the very beginning of the end.

Deciding to stretch his legs David rose from his seat, crossed the footbridge over the river and in a friendly manner approached the man.

"Hello."

"You all right?" came the Cumbrian greeting.

"Fine thanks. Just curious. Are you measuring these trees?"

"That's right," replied the man nervously as though caught in a criminal act.

"What for, might I ask?"

"The Parish Council has asked me to survey them."

"Surely anyone can count them. Most of them have been here hundreds of years."

"That's the problem," replied the man in the yellow jacket. "I have been instructed to give them a health check."

David shuddered, remembering that not so long ago a team of tree surgeons had severely coppiced the oldest and finest of the horse chestnuts. It was now so disfigured that it had borne no conkers since. The reason given for this mutilation was that a branch might have fallen on someone.

"I hope you are not going to spoil any more trees."

"I'm just doing my job."

"Which is?"

"I told you. To assess the health of the trees."

"They look in fine shape to me,"

"The disease does not always show. Some are rotten within. I am afraid I shall have to condemn them."

David was indignant. "Given their age, that's like asking a toddler to euthanize his grandpa."

"I am just doing my job," apologised the man and David could see his heart was not in it.

"I'll leave you to it then," he said, disgruntled.

Soon after that encounter six great trees were felled. A team came at first light which in the summer was well before most people got up. They were woken by the sound of chain saws and shredding machines. The trunks were cut into lengths and left at the roadside. A notice appeared informing anyone interested to bid to further cut them into logs, remove and sell them. The money was to go to the Parish Council, but the successful bidder could keep the proceeds from subsequent sales. There was another cut, that which rewarded the bidders who had been forewarned of the impending sale. Quick disposal of the trees by all concerned covered up what an inspection of the trunks would have revealed: none of the trees was rotten. The fresh timber weeping on the grass had been healthy through and through. It had supported much other life to boot, insect and avian.

David was not the only one appalled by the slaughter of these giants. It was too late to slap a tree preservation order on them. In any case the tree officer whose job it would have been was the same individual who had called in the tree surgeons. Such an ironic name, thought David. In medical terms surgeons are there to heal, not to kill. When David protested to a friend who otherwise belonged to that band of egoists who formed the Parish Council, that worthy said to him, "David, what you do not realise is that we are obliged to take out insurance over the village green. We cannot do so when the trees are a risk to the public. We must observe health and safety."

"A tree is hardly dangerous. A challenge for children who like climbing them perhaps."

"We had the word of an expert that several trees posed a hazard. Suppose a branch had fallen on a child or an elderly person in a storm."

Why would they be out in a storm, wondered David. Though not an active anarchist he had a deep distrust of any kind of authority, religious or secular. In the same way that Prime Ministers and Presidents got too big for their boots after several terms in office, so he found that after a while the smaller fish in the puddles of committees, councils and local authorities seemed to surrender to their egos. The taste for power always took priority over what was just or right or just plain sensible. In the case of his village a collective insanity fell upon these officials like a virus; they were consumed by the cult of health and safety. Much of it was provoked by the false conclusions reached by artificial intelligence, resulting in inaccurate algorithms.

Thanks to such misinformation it was decided to cut down any remaining trees and once again the same individuals profited from the sale of the timber. It did not occur to the health and safety gurus that the highly priced logs would, when burned in wealthy people's stoves or fireplaces, pollute the very air they breathed, free of the branches that hitherto swayed and cleaned that self-same air.

No, because they had more urgent concerns now. The river that ran through the village was the next victim. Most of the year it was a gentle, tinkling beck that could be walked across quite easily. Most of the summer children played in the river, caught tiddlers in their nets and swam in the deeper places, pools that only came up to the waists of adults. Only after heavy rain did it become a torrent and that only for a few hours or a day or two at most.

The river was deemed a serious health hazard. Not only might it be polluted but people could drown in it. A heritage grant enabled a gang of men to funnel the whole river into a pipe that was buried underground. This was then concreted over, but with a nod to climate change a long strip of solar panels, funded by a Saudi backed company, was laid across the devastation. The compensation was that this would provide the local community with its own electricity. It did but, being a monopoly, the power was sold at a higher price than the national grid, the profits going to help a foreign nation oppress more of their women.

The Parish Council did profit in another way however. In the old days there were signs as you entered the village reading, "No vehicles, no caravans, no camping." Now that the trees had gone and the Green despoiled a caravan park was set up in the middle of it. A Chinese firm offered free internet and surveillance cameras from which they harvested the data of visitors. The green grass tended for decades by the grazing of sheep was turned into dry desert or mud depending on the weather. There was no longer anything that attracted visitors to the village itself any more but it became a convenient dormitory for tourists wishing to visit the Lake District and the North Yorkshire national parks. For the same reason disillusioned residents moved out and their houses were bought up to be used as airbnb lets. David for the moment held on but the view from his ocularium was no longer over the river, the Green and the trees. There was no longer any birdsong. No quiet either. All he could see were solar panels, and caravans with cars and mobile homes coming and going at all hours.

Another thing he had previously valued had been complete darkness at night except for when a full moon had silvered the river and spread across the Green like a snowy purification. And it had been still. Now for health and safety reasons street lights had been installed along the roads and on the caravan site while many owners of the private houses in the old days left unlocked at night had now felt the need to install security lighting.

David knew he would have to move away. The village had become an ugly suburban settlement, the village he had loved a lost dream, the ghost of a memory. Those few who like David still remained had given up the fight. Most of his friends had already sold up and left. He was particularly saddened when one long-standing acquaintance of his own age said, "I am going forest bathing in the woods over towards Penrith. I find it very calming. Would you like to come?"

He sighed. It was not so long ago, before terms such as wild swimming and forest bathing had caught on in the urban media, that he had done just that without a second thought and certainly ignorant of the vocabulary of what to him were just natural, every day activities. Not so long ago he had walked under the trees along the river daily to fetch his newspaper from the bus shelter. That shelter had now become a betting shop that also sold vapes to under-age kids from the caravan site, something the health and safety algorithm had missed entirely.

The crunch came when the whole country was shaken by the political crisis. After what came to be known as the ten-week civil war in the 2030s there had been a coup d'etat by the army. They installed a right-wing government without a vote and in an attempt to boost the economy all planning restrictions were revoked. As had happened with the oligarchs in

Russia many decades earlier, wealthy entrepreneurs took advantage of the situation. In the village the same company that had covered the river with solar panels now erected huge wind turbines, one at each end of the village. The noise from these bird slicers even in a gentle breeze drove the caravan dwellers away. It was impossible any longer to live in the ex-village. In a commercial sense David had left his own move too late. No one wanted to buy houses there anymore. His property was worthless. The caravan site was derelict, the weeds at least attracting a few seed eating birds. The ghost village of the past had become a ghost town of the present. Then the flood finished it for good.

Not since Storm Desmond of 2015 had it rained so steadily for so long. Water poured down the fells into the valley where the village lay. Since the river was no longer there and the pipe that had replaced it had insufficient capacity, the flood water swept through the village, the remaining static caravans were washed away, the houses submerged and toppled.

During the storm David sat on his ocularium in wonder watching the inland tsunami approach, waiting for the end. He who had always surrendered to nature now awaited her final embrace.

~ The End ~